"Let's get something on those scratches."

For the next five minutes, Alex sat in one of Taylor's kitchen chairs as she swabbed his cuts with antiseptic. His own mother hadn't fussed over him this gently when he'd skinned his knees as a boy.

What made Taylor's attentions seem so... different? Maybe the way her hands shook, ever so slightly, as she touched the swabs to his cuts. Maybe it was the way her voice trembled just a little when she asked, "Does that hurt?"

And maybe, just maybe, it was the look in her eyes that said even something as insignificant as cat scratches were important...because *he* was important.

If only—

Books by Loree Lough

Love Inspired

Suddenly Daddy #28
Suddenly Mommy #34
Suddenly Married #52
Suddenly Reunited #107
Suddenly Home #130

*Suddenly!

LOREE LOUGH

A full-time writer for more than a dozen years, Loree Lough has produced more than 2,000 published articles, dozens of short stories—appearing in magazines here and abroad—and novels for the young (and young at heart). The author of twenty-nine romances (including the award-winning *Pocketful of Love*, *Emma's Orphans* and bestsellers like *Reluctant Valentine*, *Miracle on Kismet Hill* and *Just One Christmas Wish*) Loree also writes as Cara McCormack and Aleesha Carter.

A comedic teacher and conference speaker, Loree loves sharing in classrooms what she's learned the hard way. She lives in Maryland with her husband of nearly (gasp, sputter, choke!) thirty years.

Suddenly Home
Loree Lough

Love Inspired®

Published by Steeple Hill Books™

STEEPLE HILL BOOKS

Steeple
Hill™

ISBN 0-373-87137-6

SUDDENLY HOME

Visit us at www.steeplehill.com

Printed in U.S.A.

Come home with me, and refresh thyself,
and I will give thee a reward.
                                    —*I Kings* 13:7

To Elice and Valerie, my daughters,
my friends...may the romance of true love
care for you all the days of your lives.

Prologue

Date: December 17
Time: 1600
Coordinates: 17° 22.3 minutes north
66° 45.6 minutes west
Altitude 500 feet

Like blue-green tentacles, lightning snaked along the F-16's wingtips, brightening the Puerto Rican sky and blacking out the entire control panel. Lieutenant Alex Van Buren had mere seconds to decide: Eject…

Or go down with the fighter.

He jerked back on the throttle, but it was no use. He couldn't bring the aircraft out of its nosedive. If he abandoned the plane, there'd be no time for his chute to open. Not while flying over the choppy waters at an altitude of five hundred feet.

He hoped for a miracle. There'd been times when, under similar conditions, other pilots' parachutes had released…right…?

Who was he kidding? He'd been a test pilot a long time.

More than long enough to know a guy didn't bullet through the sky at nearly six hundred miles an hour and survive a crash. But even if he didn't die, he'd be so broken and battered he'd be lucky to *see* a cockpit again, let alone manipulate its controls.

Death didn't scare him. Living—if it meant he couldn't fly—now, *that* terrified him. As a much younger man he'd entertained the idea of pastoring a little church in the boonies. But every Van Buren before him had been a naval officer. Who was he to break tradition, especially for something as meaningless as a boyhood dream?

So many thoughts, so many questions racing through his mind....

As the sparkling surface of the water hurtled closer, closer, Van Buren held his breath and closed his eyes, steeling himself for the rib-racking effects of ejection, and did something he hadn't done in ages.

He prayed.

Prayed he'd pass out, so he wouldn't hear his bones breaking, his muscles tearing. Prayed that God, in His infinite mercy and wisdom, would let him drown quickly in the warm island waters; better that than go home as something other than the man he'd worked so long and hard to become.

Van Buren felt his body catapult from the cockpit.

And as he became one with the sky, he wondered if he'd survive the impact.

Date: December 17
Time: 4:00 p.m.
Supra-Air Flight 550
In the skies above Puerto Rico

If she spoke, even to order coffee, she'd break down. And so when the flight attendant stopped the drink cart beside her seat, Taylor pretended to be asleep...

And remembered the last time she'd talked to her mother.

Back then, Taylor had been working at a small pub in Houston. As usual, her mom ended the telephone conversation with a warning about what becomes of folks who live in the fast lane. In her mother's opinion, Taylor—who'd traded her physical therapist smock for a microphone—had spent the past five years doing exactly that.

Taylor wasted no time pointing out that, in her opinion, it was the other way around. Because six months before, her mother had taken up with a has-been race-car driver who, frustrated by a dead-end career, had begun hurtling through life at maximum overdrive....

These past twelve hours had been a crazy, hazy blur: the phone call to her uncle Dave, then booking a last-minute flight from Puerto Rico to Baltimore, packing, hailing a taxi.... Through it all, Taylor fought tears, asking herself why she hadn't called her mom more often, why she hadn't visited home more frequently. Because if she'd *been there,* she could have steered her mother around the hazard signs in the road ahead.

It hardly seemed possible that just the night before, Taylor had been sitting on a tall padded stool at San Juan's Posada Felicidad, strumming her Yamaha and singing "In Your Arms" when her boss had waved an arm to get her attention, then pointed at the phone, letting Taylor know the call was for her.

A slight frown, a small head shake had made clear what she'd mouthed between verses: "Take a message."

Later, alone in her hotel room, Taylor had returned her uncle's call. "For a while there," he'd said, "your mama seemed to be holdin' her own. That's when she asked me to get hold of you." He went on to explain how, despite the best efforts of the emergency-room team, her mother had died of complications suffered in a fiery car crash.

Would there have been time for a final goodbye, one last "I love you" if Taylor had put down her guitar long enough to accept her uncle's call? She'd never know. Because now, every chance she had at being a better daughter was dead.

And so was her mother.

Looking out the airliner's thick window, she watched as lightning sliced through the Puerto Rican sky. Shielding her eyes with the palm of one hand, she steeled herself against the if onlys and what ifs, remembering one of her mother's favorite sayings: "The road to nowhere is paved with regrets."

Small comfort, but a comfort nonetheless.

In a few hours, when this overcrowded 747 landed at Baltimore-Washington International Airport, Taylor would head for the funeral home to view her mother's body.

Would she survive the impact of that?

Chapter One

Eighteen months later
BWI Airport
Baltimore, Maryland

From start to finish, the red-eye flight from Ireland had been a nightmare, complete with keep-your-seat-belts-fastened turbulence, crying babies and a grumpy crew. She'd barely cracked the spine of her novel when an overweight gent tromped on her foot climbing into his window seat. If Taylor had known his first words would be the kickoff to an eight-hour gabfest, she'd have kept reading the scene that began, "His dark-lashed eyes bored into hers with an alarming intensity...." Something told her she'd have to wait until she got home to find out how the heroine reacted to the hero's scrutiny.

And she'd been right.

Her seatmate, who'd hogged the armrest and spilled coffee on both of them, now left his boot print on her other white sneaker as he joined the mad race to be first off the plane.

After the aisle cleared, Taylor stood and, looking at the space he'd occupied, bit back a groan. She considered calling out to him, "You've forgotten something..." so he'd have to shoulder his way back through the crowd to retrieve the peanut packages, napkins and candy wrappers he'd left behind. The flight crew might appreciate her efforts, but all she really wanted was to pick up Barney at Pampered Pets Kennels, brew herself a soothing cup of tea and settle in at home. Stifling a yawn, she reached into the overhead bin for her carry-on...

And collided with the man across the aisle.

"Ooomph," he grunted.

A feeble "I'm sorry" sighed from her lips.

Shaking his head, he raised one dark eyebrow, reminding her of the passage from the novel she'd been reading. *His dark-lashed eyes bored into hers with an alarming intensity....*

"No problem," he said, his voice deep and gruff. Then he grabbed the straps of her bag and dragged it from the compartment. "This one yours?"

Nodding, Taylor clutched it to her. "Yes. Yes, it is. Thank you."

Turning, he slid his own bag from the bin above his seat and stepped back. With a grand sweep of his arm, he said, "After you."

She couldn't tell if the gesture was sincere or not. But Taylor thanked him, and headed down the aisle.

"Don't mention it," he growled. "My pleasure."

She hurried from the plane, and halfway through the tube connecting the jetliner to the terminal, he passed her, aiming a curt nod and a two-finger salute at her. Taylor couldn't help but notice his pronounced limp. During the flight, as he'd made his way to the lavatory, she'd blamed turbulence for his halting half step. Now she couldn't help but wonder if an accident or a birth defect had caused him to favor his left leg.

Accident, she decided, remembering his grumpy demeanor; if he'd been born with the limp, wouldn't he have adjusted to it by now?

He rounded the corner just as a terrible thought occurred to her—had *she* caused the injury when she'd backed into him? Had she stepped on his foot harder than she'd realized?

Well, surely she'd see him in baggage claim. And when she did, Taylor would apologize. And make it sound a little more sincere this time.

It shouldn't have been difficult to find him, tall as he was. But she didn't see him at the baggage claim. Or the taxi stand, either. Not even when she stood on tiptoe, searching the crowd. Taylor gave up looking for him when a cabbie said, "Where to, lady?"

"Ellicott City," she said as her driver tossed her suitcase into the trunk.

The taxi driver made small talk as he maneuvered through the traffic on I-95. But Taylor barely heard him, because she couldn't seem to shift her attention from the man with the limp.

She tried thinking about Barney, and how happy he'd be to see her after spending so many days at the kennel.

She tried thinking about all the gossip Mrs. Dansfield would share when she delivered the mail she'd been picking up for Taylor.

About getting back to work—a job far more satisfying than singing for her supper had ever been.

But it was no use. The image of his dark eyes seemed frozen in her mind. He looked familiar, and for the life of her, she didn't know why. Had they met? But where? And when?

His expression flashed in her memory again. Was he as

sad and forlorn as he seemed? Or had it been fear she'd
seen in his big brown orbs? Taylor's heart ached a bit on
his behalf, because she'd learned something about *that* in
the past eighteen months. She said a quick prayer, asking
God to help the poor guy cope with whatever had painted
such a doleful expression on his handsome face.

The familiar facade of her house came into view and
she smiled. Not the Victorian she'd always dreamed of,
but close enough for the time being.

She paid the taxi driver, shoved her suitcase through her
front door and headed straight for Pampered Pets Kennels.
Once she and the fat orange tabby were settled in, Taylor
would have a day and a half to recuperate from her trip to
Ireland. Thirty-six hours to readjust, pick up where she'd
left off.

Maneuvering her car through Ellicott City's side streets,
Taylor sighed. Because where had she left off? Better question, she wondered, *What did you leave behind?*

Other than Barney, regrets mostly. Regrets that she'd
spent those last precious months of her mother's life "find-
ing herself" instead of being the doting daughter her
mother had deserved. Regrets that she hadn't accepted the
phone call that night in Puerto Rico.

The big pink-and-white sign that said Pampered Pets
came into view and Taylor heaved a deep sigh. Parking in
front of the pink-trimmed brick building, she thought again
of her mother's favorite saying: "The road to nowhere is
paved with regrets."

Her mother, Amanda, also liked to say, "Life goes on!"

It had been eighteen months since the accident. And true
to her mother's witty wisdom, life had indeed gone on. A
year and a half had passed since Amanda's death. Eighteen
months without so much as a syllable of motherly advice.

Yet Taylor had gone to work, had attended various

church functions and social events, and had even gone out on a date or two.

Like it or not, her mother had been right.

Had he gone to Ireland simply to put an end to his mother's nagging?

Alex groaned inwardly, knowing even as the thought crossed his mind that it wasn't fair to call it "nagging." Badgering was more like it. But her insistence hadn't been the sole reason he'd taken the trip. He'd known better than anyone that a change of scenery had been in order, that doubt and self-pity had pretty much taken over his whole life since the crash, that if he didn't get a handle on it pretty quickly, there was no telling how he'd end up, or where.

The so-called "vacation" was his last-ditch effort to get back a semblance of the man he'd been before the accident. And to give his mother her due, the trip had worked. Something about the Emerald Isle touched a long-forgotten…something…inside him, and that *something* had awakened his desire to fully participate in life again.

Now Alex was glad that before departing for Ireland he'd set certain things in motion, because it meant there was no turning back.

Not without losing face.

Soon his life would be fine and dandy. Right as rain. Good as new…

Keep that up, he told himself, *you'll be eligible for the next Channel 13 TV Jingle King contest.*

All things considered, Alex believed he felt about as good as a man who'd survived a near-death experience could feel. He'd prove it when he woke up in his new apartment with its spanking new furniture, climbed into his shiny new car and headed for his brand-new job.

"Yippee," he grumbled under his breath.

The cabbie met his eyes in the rearview mirror. "What's that, sir?"

He frowned. "Nothing," Alex replied. "Just... nothing."

Alex had found that the best medicine for self-pity was thinking of something besides himself. This time, it surprised him when the new subject occupying his thoughts was the young woman who'd crashed into him on the plane. She was petite and pretty, and he'd been watching her from the corner of his eye during most of the flight.

Well, not *watching* her, exactly, but he'd noticed that when the man beside her spilled coffee on her jacket, she'd casually blotted up the mess with a paper napkin. "It's okay," she'd said, smiling. "Time to take this old thing to the cleaners, anyway." Amazing thing was, she seemed to mean it.

Her forgiving words seemed to invite her seatmate's jabbering, which didn't stop for the rest of the flight. What kept her from yawning from boredom as he droned on about his pedigreed Yorkshire terriers, his job as a tech systems analyst, his tomato garden, Alex didn't know.

He only knew that, from his side of the aisle, anyway, she appeared to be interested in everything the man had to say.

Before he'd crashed his fighter plane, if he'd met a woman like that under *any* circumstances, he'd be having lunch with her by now, flirting his socks off, working his way up to inviting her to dinner. Wasn't that what test pilots were expected to do, after all?

Why he felt he'd lost something meaningful when she disappeared from view, he didn't know. He only knew that she was gorgeous. Kind. Special in ways he'd probably never understand. That look she'd given him when he took her bag out of the overhead bin kept flashing in his memory, a look that said she'd survived some pretty tough stuff in her life, too.

But since he'd probably never see her again, he wasn't likely to find out *what*.

The cabbie stopped in front of Alex's town house, popped the trunk and tossed an already battered suitcase onto the sidewalk.

Alex peeled a twenty from his money clip. "Keep the change," he said, grabbing his bag.

The meter read $17.50, and even behind the iridescent wraparound sunglasses, the cabbie's indignant expression was obvious. Tucking the bill into his shirt pocket, he slid in behind the steering wheel. "Gee, thanks, Mr. Trump," he muttered as he slammed the door.

The sarcasm was lost on Alex, who stood at the end of his walk, staring at the black numbers above his front door. Shaking his head, he took out his new house key and jammed it into his new bolt, hoping the air conditioner was working, because it was uncharacteristically hot and humid for June in the Baltimore suburbs.

A note taped to the brass door knocker flapped in the sultry breeze. "Welcome home," said his mother's delicate script. "Remember: Life is what you make of it!"

Shoving open the front door, he stuffed the message into his jacket pocket. "Thanks, Mom," he grumbled. "Next time I meet a gorgeous li'l gal, maybe I'll remember your good advice."

Taylor dropped her purse on the floor and opened the cat carrier. "Good to be home, isn't it, Barn?" she asked, gathering him near. The gold-striped tabby nuzzled her cheek and *chirruped* happily, then leapt from her arms and headed straight for the long-fringed afghan at the foot of Taylor's bed. As she watched him stretch, sadness cloaked her. Because Barney had been her mother's cat, and wouldn't be here at all if...

She straightened her shoulders. No point in dwelling in the past. *What's done is done,* she told herself.

Taylor hurried into the kitchen and washed down two white pills with a glass of water. Prescription medication took care of Taylor's allergy to cats, but who would have taken care of Barney if Taylor hadn't adopted him? The better question was, who would have taken care of *her* if Barney hadn't *let* her adopt him? By now, the cat was far more than a beloved pet; he was Taylor's only living connection to her mother.

He rubbed her ankles as she filled his bowls with water and cat food. Once he'd finished nibbling at the kibbles, he headed for Taylor's bedroom. Taylor followed, and watched as he sashayed toward the down-stuffed pillows at the head of her bed and began batting at the fringed trim.

Barely six months old when he lost his former mistress, Barney had quickly adapted to his new life. Taylor, on the other hand, had struggled with the loss every day since the accident.

Sighing, she tried to focus on the cat's antics. Forcing a smile, she admitted that the pillows' plumpness did look inviting, particularly after the long flight home from Ireland.

Ireland...

If not for her mother, Taylor probably wouldn't have gone overseas at all.

After Taylor's father died, her mother began traveling...and pestering Taylor to get a passport and see the world with her. Amanda visited dozens of countries in the years after Jake's heart attack, but her favorite place in all the world had been Ireland. "If you go there," she'd said, "you'll find yourself drawn back, again and again."

And just as Amanda had predicted, Taylor had fallen in love with the land and its people. If her budget allowed it, Taylor would return *every* June to commemorate her mother's first trip there.

Shaking her head to clear the cobwebs, she decided Barney was right. Those pillows *did* look irresistible. And they'd look even better after a hot shower and a soothing cup of herbal tea.

Ten minutes later, wrapped in a white chenille robe, long brown hair tucked under a thick towel, she carried a steaming mug of Lemon Clouds into the living room. "Just look at this," she complained as Barney snuggled up close. "Do you have any idea how many trees had to die so this junk mail could be printed up?"

The cat gave the stack a slant-eyed stare and emitted an expansive yawn.

Grinning, she ruffled his fur. "Where would the rain forests be if everyone had your attitude?"

His response was a bigger, longer yawn.

Taylor smiled. Being needed, in Taylor's opinion, didn't get the notice it deserved. Having Barney to take care of, to look after, had made the difference between wallowing in grief and getting back to the business of living. She gave him a gentle pat. "Thanks, Barn."

He rolled onto his side, as if to say, "Don't mention it."

Which was what the stranger on the airplane had said when she thanked him for getting her bag from the overhead bin....

Taylor shook her head and stuffed the junk mail into the pantry's recycling bin, then gathered the important mail and headed for the home office she'd fashioned in a corner of her bedroom. Laying the envelopes on the desk, she faced her suitcase and groaned. The only thing she hated more than packing was *un*packing.

Barney slunk into the room, stopping to sniff the suitcase. Forepaws resting on the handle, he continued his investigation.

"Oh, don't be such a nag," she teased when he meowed at her. "I'll put things away tomor—"

Frowning, Taylor crossed the room. "Hey, where's my luggage tag?" she wondered aloud. "And my bungee cord?" Her uncle Dave—self-appointed protector and Taylor's only living relative—had insisted she secure the suitcase with a sturdy strap. "For extra protection," he'd said.

Why hadn't she noticed before that it was missing?

Jet lag, she thought, excusing the oversight.

On her knees now, she laid the suitcase on its side and pulled at the lock. It opened easily. Too easily. Ordinarily, it took several hard tugs to pop it. Unzipping the case, she threw back its lid and stifled a gasp.

Inside, where skirts and blouses should have been...

A jumble of rumpled blue jeans, wrinkled T-shirts and rag-knit socks. "Eee-yooo," she complained, "just look at this mess."

In her hurry to get home, she'd obviously grabbed the wrong suitcase. Had someone else picked up hers? Or was it still there, going round and round on the belt, waiting to be claimed?

Taylor glanced at the clock. Nearly six in the evening—far too late to call the airline now.

Attention on the suitcase again, she lifted one well-worn running shoe from the pile, held it at arm's length. "Look at the size of this thing, Barn. Who would have guessed that the Jolly Green Giant was a jogger?"

In response, Barney hopped into the suitcase, purring as his forepaws kneaded the messy clothes inside.

"Get out of there," she scolded, gently shooing him away, "before you snag something." Though she honestly didn't know how any of it could look any worse.

The cat gave an insulted meow and swaggered from the room, tail pointing indignantly toward the ceiling.

Taylor barely noticed. Pinkies raised and nose wrinkled, she searched for a business card, an address book, anything that would tell her the owner's name.

She felt like Little Jack Horner as she stuck her hand into a side pocket and pulled out a business card. "'Alex Van Buren,'" she read. "'2345 Lancaster Road. Ellicott City, Maryland.' Good. He's local."

A second glance at the clock told her it was early enough to call him.

Perched on the edge of the bed, she dialed Alex Van Buren's number, and counted the rings.

"Alex's answering machine is broken," said a deep male voice. "This is his refrigerator. Leave your name and number, and I'll put the message under one of the magnets he's got stuck all over me."

Giggling, Taylor rolled her eyes and waited for the beep. "Mr. Van Buren? My name is Taylor Griffith. It seems there was a mix-up at the airport, and I picked up your suitcase by mistake. Hopefully, you have mine, which, co-incidentally, looks an awful lot like yours...."

She cleared her throat. Why was she rattling on this way?

"Would you give me a call, please, and let me know when it's convenient for us to get together and, um, make the trade? If you have my suitcase, that is. If not, we can arrange a good time for you to pick up your suitcase." She recited her phone number and hung up.

Then, stretching, she slid under the covers, remembering his voice. Wholly, soothingly male, it reminded her of someone. Someone she knew.

But *who?*

The voice continued to echo in her mind until she drifted off to sleep.

* * *

"Mr. Van Buren? My name is Taylor Griffith."

Alex lifted the corners of his pillow and pressed them against his ears. But it was no use. He could still hear her. "I picked up your suitcase by mistake...."

He'd locked up tight and closed the blinds before climbing into bed, intent upon making up for the many nights of sleep he'd lost while in Ireland.

If only he'd remembered to turn off the answering machine.

Groaning, he levered himself up on one elbow and flicked on the light. Eyes shaded by one hand, he squinted across the room. Well, the bag he'd brought home certainly *looked* like his....

"Would you give me a call, please, and let me know when it's convenient for us to get together and, um, make the trade?"

Alex turned the volume on the answering machine down, clicked off the light and flopped back onto his pillow. Rolling onto his side, he took a deep breath, hoping to pick up where he'd left off when Taylor Griffith had interrupted his dream.

He'd been strolling along Ireland's Dingle Coast, staring out at the great expanse of churning gray sea, when a lovely blue-eyed lass had stepped up beside him and offered to share her home-baked brown bread. But it was no use. Instead of accepting a slice, his thoughts returned to the Griffith woman's message.

Knuckling his eyes, Alex decided the suitcase news wasn't nearly as interesting as his dream. Punching his pillow, he tried again to return to Ireland and the lovely blue-eyed lass.

But a question popped into his head, disrupting the dream yet again. Its answer was obvious—this Taylor person had gotten his name and number from his luggage tag.

Jaw set with determination, he forced himself to remember Galway Bay. Bunglass Point. The thatched cottage on The Burren where he'd spent his first night abroad, listening to the gentle lowing of Black Angus cows.

But he couldn't concentrate on Ireland or anything related to it, thanks to one Taylor Griffith.

Alex sat up, threw his bare legs over the edge of the bed and growled under his breath. There seemed to be a conspiracy these past few days to keep him from getting any shut-eye at all.

At a bed-and-breakfast in Ballydehob, the owner's short-legged dog—named Bruce, of all things—barked the whole night away. In a small hotel in Killorglin, trains that ran like clockwork woke him every hour on the hour. Last night, the darlin' woman who owned the house near Shannon Airport couldn't seem to comfort her colicky baby. And now some girl seemed to think she had his suitcase, and he had hers.

He wouldn't get any sleep until he got to the root of this, so why try?

Heaving a deep sigh, Alex hit the answering machine's play button and turned the sound up. As the tape rewound, he opened the nightstand drawer, poked around until he found a pen buried under paperback novels and soda straws. Dig as he might, he couldn't find anything to write *on.*

He listened to the first part of her message, and when she began reciting her number, Alex scribbled it on the palm of his hand. He'd call Ms. Griffith first thing in the morning, see about straightening out this mix-up she'd referred to.

After tossing the ballpoint back into the drawer, he turned the answering machine's sound down. For the last time tonight, he hoped.

Then the red, white and blue ID tag on his bag caught

his eye. Why hadn't he noticed it before? He'd lost the original luggage tag soon after buying the suitcase, and had been making do with the paper ones provided by the airlines ever since.

Alex hobbled toward it, rubbing his bad leg and doing his best not to think about how he'd earned the limp. Try as he might, the crash was something he'd never forget, or live down. And why should he be allowed to do either? It wasn't every day that a test pilot lost a multimillion-dollar aircraft in the middle of the Caribbean.

He grabbed the luggage tag. "Taylor Griffith," precise black letters spelled out, "142 Old Belle Way, Ellicott City." Grinning, he thought, *She sure didn't sound like an old belle....*

He unfastened the stretchy red-and-yellow band wrapped around the suitcase, then unzipped it. Inside, in neatly folded stacks, lay delicate, feminine articles of clothing in every shade of the rainbow. A tiny, pointy-toed black shoe poked out of a side pocket, and he held it by its long, slender heel. Chuckling, Alex said under his breath, "I guess not all elves live in hollow trees." Turning it this way and that, he added, "Some of 'em live at 142 Old Belle Way."

He put the shoe back where he'd found it. At least, he hoped he had. The idea of disturbing the perfection inside bothered him, and he chalked it up to years of rigorous military training.

Training. One more thing to remind him of the man he used to be. It hadn't been hard, turning deliberately back into the not-so-tidy guy he'd been before enlisting....

Padding barefoot across uncarpeted hardwood, he picked up the telephone receiver. Tucking it between ear and shoulder, Alex punched in the number printed on his palm. Two rings, three, then a melodious "Hello?"

Nope, doesn't sound a bit like an old belle, he thought again, grinning.

"Hello?" she repeated.

There was something about that melodic voice. Something rich, something vibrant. Where had he heard it before? Clearing his throat, Alex said, "Miss Griffith?"

There was a considerable pause before a soft "Yes?" sighed into his ear.

"This is Alex Van Buren." She hadn't corrected his "Miss" to "Mrs.," and for a reason he couldn't explain, Alex was relieved. "I, ah, I understand you have my suitcase?"

"Oh, yes, of *course.* Mr. Van *Buren.* I'm so sorry for the inconvenience. I don't know what possessed me to grab your bag without checking first to make sure it was *mine.* If you'll just tell me where you'd like it delivered, I'll be happy to—"

He had a feeling she was ending every sentence by accenting the last word out of nervousness, or worse, fear. "Hey," Alex interrupted, giving in to a need to soothe her, "there's no way of knowing which of us got to baggage claim first. Maybe it was *me* who picked up the wrong bag."

He listened to the silence that prefaced her quiet sigh.

"Oh, thank *goodness!* You *do* have my bag. I was beginning to worry I'd have a long uphill battle with the officials at the airline...."

"It's here," he assured her, "safe and sound." Then, remembering that he'd promised to drive his mom to a church brunch the next day, he said, "Tell you what. I'll be in your neck of the woods tomorrow." He knew exactly where her street was, and could easily stop by her place on the way to his mother's. "How 'bout we make the switch then?"

He remembered the delicate perfume that had wafted

from her clothing, the soft fabrics, the feminine colors. He very much wanted to meet the woman with feet half the size of his, who packed with such precision, who had the voice of an angel...and the strength to haul his big, heavy suitcase home.

The instant he realized he'd been daydreaming, Alex coughed. Twice. "Well. Now, then. So tell me, Miss Griffith, are you an early riser?"

"An early riser? Well, I—I, um..."

Easy, he warned himself, because if the rest of her was as small as her shoe, she was probably just a little bit of a thing, and easily frightened.

"Do you need directions?" she asked.

Chuckling, he said, "Nah. Ellicott City is my hometown. I used to drive a delivery truck during my college years. I bet if I put my mind to it, I could draw a map of the place."

Alex shook his head, more confused by his odd behavior than he'd been by anything in quite some time. It wasn't like him to make small talk, particularly of the humorous kind. At least, he *hoped* she'd heard the nonsense he'd been spouting as humorous....

"Well, all right," she said hesitantly. "I'll see you around ten, then?"

"Right-o. Ten, then."

Right-o? Where had *that* come from? Was it her voice or her attitude—or both—that had rattled him so? Alex wouldn't have been able to explain why if his life had depended on it, but he didn't want to say goodbye.

"Thank you, Mr. Van Buren, for going to so much trouble."

"No thanks necessary, Miss Griffith. Like I said, it's no trouble. No trouble at all."

When she hung up, Alex felt disconnected from more than her lovely voice. Smiling, he climbed back into bed and snapped off the light. Fingers clasped under his head, he stared at the darkened ceiling. "If she looks even half as good as she sounds," he said to himself, "you're in for a real sweet treat, Alex, m'boy."

But that was the flyboy in him talking, and he knew it. A test pilot was expected to behave like Romeo and Casanova and Valentino rolled into one. Alex had spent his share of compliments on the opposite sex, but unlike his contemporaries, for whom flirtation seemed second nature, he'd had to work hard at it. If flattery didn't get him a date with a beautiful woman, the flight suit was sure to have a positive effect. If he'd been in civilian clothes, talking plain talk, would the ladies have paid him a moment's attention?

Alex didn't think so. And the dishonesty of it all had always bothered him.

Talking with Taylor Griffith hadn't been like that. Instead, the conversation had been smooth and easy. Maybe for no other reason than the honesty that had prompted her phone call, and his.

He closed his eyes and rolled onto his side, remembering that sweet, lyrical voice.

It didn't surprise him when he had no desire to conjure up the image of his pretty Irish lass.

The minute she was dressed and ready, Taylor called her uncle. "Ready for the ladies' auxiliary brunch?" she teased.

"Don't rub it in," he complained. "If it wasn't for the fact that the money they'll raise is for a good cause—"

"Oh, Unc, you know you enjoy these functions."

He chuckled. "Says you."

"Says anybody who sees you." She giggled. "You certainly *look* like you're enjoying yourself, surrounded by ladies all the time."

"Yeah, well, I'd have a lot *better* time if they didn't all have blue hair," he added, laughing.

"Well, at least you can always depend on great food." Taylor heard him smack his lips. "That's true," he agreed.

"I'll be there by noon. That'll give us plenty of time to get a good seat."

"Okay. See you then, kid—"

The doorbell rang, interrupting his farewell. "Who's that so early on a Sunday morning?" he demanded.

"It's five of ten," she pointed out. "Hardly *early*."

"Well, don't open that door till you've checked first to see who it is. *Through the peephole,* mind you. We're not living in the world *I* grew up in," he warned.

"I'll be careful," she said as the bell rang a second time. "See you at noon."

After hanging up, she half ran to the foyer, and stood on tiptoe to peer through the peephole.

A man, hands in his pockets, stood on the porch, staring across the street. Taylor opened the door as far as the chain lock would allow and spoke through the crack. "Yes?"

When he turned, the sight of his wide, friendly smile made her wonder if it was possible for a human heart to burst through its rib cage.

Because it was *him*, the man she'd nearly mowed over in the aisle of the plane.

"Hi," he said, removing his sunglasses. "Alex Van Buren." He used the glasses to point at the porch floor. "I've got your suitcase?"

"Oh. Yes. Of course." She closed the door to unlatch the chain, then opened it again, wider this time. "Won't you come in?"

It was fairly obvious that he hadn't gotten a clear view of her while the chain lock had been in place. But now, eyes wide and brows high on his forehead, he said, "No way."

She couldn't help but smile at the coincidence. Couldn't help but remember that he'd occupied most of her dreams last night, either.

He lifted the bag as if it weighed no more than a gallon of milk. Taylor had packed the thing. She *knew* how heavy it was. Well, she told herself, he was tall and good-looking and strong. She grinned inwardly. But what were the chances he was single...*and a Christian?*

Putting the bag at the bottom of the stairs, he noticed Barney. "Hey, there," he said, crouching and extending his hand. "What's the matter, cat got your tongue?"

She was about to warn him that Barney did not take well to strangers when the cat rubbed its face against the man's hand. A tremor of envy coursed through her. It had taken months before she'd earned that kind of affection from the cat.

Blushing, Van Buren stood, pocketed his hands again. "Kids and animals..." he said haltingly, and shrugged. "What can I say?"

Taylor surely didn't know what to say, and so she said nothing.

She caught him staring, and followed his gaze to see what had so thoroughly captured his attention. On the foyer table lay the church bulletin, where she'd circled the ladies' auxiliary brunch in red. But why would he be interested in *that?*

"Is that my suitcase?" he asked, nodding at the bag near the door.

"Oh. Yes." She clasped her hands in front of her. "I'm afraid I, ah, sort of messed things up inside, looking for some, um, identification. I hope you won't mind that things aren't quite as you left them." Fact of the matter was, the muddled mess had driven her to distraction, and she'd dumped the whole thing out and repacked it, *her* way.

He shot her a sideways glance, narrowed one brown eye. "You didn't do my crossword puzzle, did you?"

She grinned. "No. But only because I couldn't find a red pen to match the one you'd been using."

"That's too bad," he said, winking, "'cause I can't figure twenty-seven across to save my soul."

Taylor laughed. She was strangely drawn to this man, and didn't quite know what to make of it. She glanced nervously at the face of the grandfather clock that stood beside the front door. She'd promised to pick up her uncle at noon. But first she needed to shower and—

"Nice place," he said, nodding approvingly. "Very homey."

"Homey" had been precisely the look she'd been going for when Taylor had begun decorating her house. Funny that no one before him had noticed.

"I, ah, have an appointment this morning, or I'd invite you to stay for coffee, to thank you for coming all the way over here."

He unpocketed his hands, drove the right one through his hair, leaving wide finger tracks in the dark waves. "Oh. Sorry," he muttered, grabbing his suitcase with one hand and the doorknob with the other. "Nothin' worse than a guy who overstays his welcome." He shrugged. "I'll just be on my way."

In the doorway, he turned slightly and smiled. "Nice meeting you." He hesitated, as if he wanted to say more. "Well, guess I'll hit the road, then."

"Drive safely. You know how those Sunday-morning drivers can be."

Chuckling, he nodded. "Yeah. Crazy." He clumped down the porch steps and across the flagstone path, then dumped the suitcase unceremoniously into the back of his minipickup. Snapping off a smart salute, he slid in behind the wheel. "See you," he said, slamming the driver's door.

"See you," she returned, waving. But her words were drowned out by the growl of his engine.

Taylor's professional side kicked in, and again she wondered what might have caused his limp. He'd done quite a job trying to hide it, but it was there, nonetheless. Was he getting regular physical therapy treatments? Or was he beyond that sort of help?

Barney jumped onto the window ledge to watch him back down the drive, continued staring until the pickup was completely out of sight. Then he aimed a golden-eyed stare at Taylor.

"Don't look at me like that. It isn't my fault your new best friend is gone, is it?"

He leapt to the floor and pranced off, as if to say, "It most certainly *is* your fault."

The phone rang, and Taylor picked it up. "It's just me," her uncle said, "calling to—"

"To make sure whoever was at the door hasn't chopped me into little pieces and stuffed me into the garbage disposal?"

"Miss Rosie's posies, Taylor. What a thing to say!"

"Sorry, Unc." And she meant it.

"You can never be too sure these days, y'know."

"I know." She'd been hearing the "be careful" lecture since her mother's death.

"What say we get to the brunch early, put in an appearance, fill our bellies and hotfoot it outta there?"

Laughing, Taylor said, "You're one of a kind. I just have to shower and dress. See you in about an hour."

"Remember…Sunday drivers…"

"Yeah. Crazy."

From nowhere, a picture of Alex Van Buren flashed in her mind. Taylor swallowed a lump of regret. Why hadn't she invited him to the church social? He'd certainly seemed interested enough when he noticed the bulletin....

"I'll be careful," she told her uncle, "so don't worry."

"I always worry," he said.

And she knew it was true.

She hit every green light and didn't get behind a single slowpoke. Her uncle was sure to think she'd been speeding. Rather than go through the rigmarole of explaining how she'd made the trip in record time, Taylor drove around his block a few times. It was a lovely sunny day, and she took advantage of the extra moments by taking in the summer foliage glowing on both sides of the street.

"Well, let's get this nonsense over with," Uncle Dave grumbled when he got into the passenger seat, "so I can go home and turn on the sports channel."

"Nice to see you, too," she kidded.

"Don't get wise with me, young lady," he teased right back. "You're not too old to stand in the corner, y'know." He buckled his seat belt and locked the door. "When was the last time you had your oil changed?" he asked from out of the blue. "And how's the air pressure in your tires? Have you checked the windshield washer fluid lately?"

Taylor groaned inwardly. He could be such a worrywart. But he meant well, and she loved him like crazy for it. "I took care of everything last week, remember...the guy at the station told me I needed new wiper blades and—"

"Oh, yeah. Little whippersnapper was just tryin' to rip you off. Good thing you set him straight. He'll know better'n to mess with you again."

She gave an affirmative nod. They drove in silence for a few minutes. Taylor's mind wandered to her morning visitor. She couldn't imagine what her uncle might be thinking...and didn't dare ask.

The instant she pulled into a parking slot in the church

lot, Uncle Dave got out of the car and tugged at his jacket sleeves. "Good golly, Miss Molly. There's Mable Jensen over there. Quick! Hide me before I have to listen to another rendition of her hip replacement surgery."

But it was too late.

"Yoo-hoo," Mable called, waving a lace-trimmed hankie in the air. "Daaay-veeee! I'll save you a seat inside...."

Shoulders slumped, he groaned. "I hate it when she calls me that." Then, forcing a smile, he returned her wave.

"Ratchet it down a notch or two, Unc, or folks will get the impression you're trying to show off."

His brows drew together in confusion. "Show off?"

"The fact that you still have your own teeth." And giggling, she added, "Really, sometimes it's hard to believe you're in the same age bracket as these people. I mean, take Mable, for example. She just turned sixty-five. I know 'cause they wrote her up in the church bulletin. But she acts—"

"Ninety." He stood a little straighter, did a little jig. "Guess I do move pretty good for an old guy, don't I?"

"At sixty-seven, you're younger than me!"

Laughing, Uncle Dave stuck out his elbow. "Will you do me the honor, young lady, of accompanying me to the Ladies' Auxiliary brunch?"

She stuck her nose in the air and feigned a British accent. "Why, thank you, kind suh. Don't mind if I do."

Laughing, they walked arm in arm into the church basement. Immediately Taylor spotted Alex, standing across the room, hands in his pockets and smiling at her. Heart hammering, she felt the corners of her mouth automatically lifting as he headed toward her.

"What're you doing here?" he asked.

"We're here for the brunch. And you?"

"Same."

From the corner of her eye Taylor noticed her uncle's strained expression. She faced him. "Uncle Dave, this is Alex Van Buren, the man whose suitcase got mixed up with mine at the airport."

"David Griffith," he said, a thin smile on his face as he grasped the hand of the taller, younger man. "Thanks for saving my girl a trip to BWI."

Alex shook his hand. "Was my pleasure, sir."

"So," David said, "you two were in Ireland at the same time?"

He nodded. "I spent three weeks there, all by my lonesome. One of the best experiences of my life."

Why did she get the feeling the accent was on *lonesome?* "Three weeks?" Taylor echoed. "Isn't that odd? *I* was there for two...."

"With a tour group?" Alex asked as her uncle's eyes narrowed.

She shook her head. "Nope. I rented a car and drove the west coast, from the southernmost point to the northernmost, then along the Northern Ireland border, back to the airport in Shannon."

Alex's eyebrows rose. *"Alone?"*

"Sure. Why not?"

"'Cause it's dangerous for a woman to travel alone."

Taylor noticed that her uncle's expression changed from suspicious to admiring. She resisted the urge to roll her eyes at both men.

"It's the only way to travel," she insisted. "Especially if you don't like doing typical touristy things."

From the front of the dining hall Pastor Barnes clapped his hands, interrupting all conversation. "Hello, everybody...everybody?" he hollered. "Let's take a moment for the word of God, shall we?"

Like everyone else in the room, Uncle Dave lowered his head. "A moment, ha!" he whispered to Taylor. "If there's anything hot on the food table, it'll be stone-cold by the time he—''

Taylor wrapped his hand in hers, gave a gentle squeeze. ''Uncle Dave...'' she said around a grin.

''Well, it's true,'' he insisted.

Alex crouched near Uncle Dave's ear. ''No problem. I hear there's a new microwave in the kitchen....''

The minister raised his hands just then, and thanked the good women of the parish who'd prepared the food, the youth group for setting up the tables and chairs, the men's club for volunteering to clean up afterward. He gave thanks to God for a lovely summery day.

''Wonder why preachers never get laryngitis,'' Uncle Dave muttered.

''They pray for strong vocal cords?'' was Alex's answer.

''Honestly.'' Taylor sighed as their shoulders lurched with laughter. ''You two are worse than a couple of rowdy boys. You're going to get us—''

A red-taloned hand reached from behind and rested on Taylor's shoulder. ''Shh!'' came the angry demand. ''If you can't show any respect for the pastor, at least show a little for the Lord!''

Taylor narrowed her eyes at her uncle, then at Alex. ''Just wait,'' she mouthed as the pastor said his final, booming ''Amen!''

''Think I'm gonna get into line,'' Uncle Dave said, ''before all the potato salad is gone.'' Nodding, he grinned at Taylor. ''You know it's always the first thing to go.''

''Maybe this year,'' she said quietly, wiggling her eyebrows and grinning, ''it'll be the *second* thing to go....''

Alex laughed. ''Good to meet you, Mr. Griffith.''

''Dave,'' he corrected. ''Good meeting you, too.'' And with that, he was gone.

Alex cleared his throat. ''If you can tell me who the red-nailed lady was, I'll explain, save your good name.''

Shrugging, Taylor waved his offer away. "Mrs. Abernathy is always looking for reasons to scold people. The way I see it, the three of us made her day." Pausing, she tilted her head. "Say...I didn't know you were a member of Resurrection parish."

"I'm not. But my mother is."

"Really? Who's your mother? Maybe I know her."

"If you didn't know her, I'd be surprised." He pointed at an attractive white-haired woman across the way. "She's the president of the ladies' auxili—"

"Helen Martin? But your name is—"

"My father passed away a long time ago, and Mom remarried."

"Small world." Then, tilting her head the other way, she raised one eyebrow, remembering that Mrs. Martin had joined the church just over a year ago. "Why haven't we seen you at services before?"

He clamped his teeth together, as if suddenly something had made him angry. Very angry. "I've been away for a while." Just as suddenly, the friendly smile returned. "And now I'm back." He shrugged.

She wondered where he'd been. How long he'd been gone. *Why* he'd been gone. And what, exactly, had inspired his return home. The questions must have been apparent on her face, because Alex said, "It's a long, boring story. Suffice it to say my hitch in the navy is over, and I'm grounded now, in more ways than one."

Grounded? Did that mean he'd been a pilot? He'd been grinning when he said it, but she couldn't help but notice the smile never quite made it to his eyes. Taylor could almost picture him in a flight suit, standing beside a sleek airplane, helmet under his arm and—

"Why don't we join your uncle in line. I think he may be right. That potato salad seems to be goin' mighty fast."

He offered her his arm, and just as Taylor moved to take

it, Mable Jensen grabbed her elbow. "Taylor! I've been looking everywhere for you. Come with me, dear, there's someone I want you to meet."

Alex's smile dimmed as Mable whisked her away, and he sent the same two-fingered salute he'd sent her in the airport tunnel. She looked away for only an instant, then turned back to ask him to save her a seat.

But in that instant he'd disappeared.

Chapter Two

Alex waited half an hour for Taylor to come back. He sat at the end of a long table, one arm slung over the back of the folding chair beside his own. "Sorry," he told anyone who showed interest in the empty seat, "this one's taken."

Once it sank in that she wouldn't be joining him for the meal, he wolfed down his stone-cold food. The level of his disappointment made no sense, especially considering he'd spent, what, ten minutes in her company? Maybe *this* was the reason he'd always been partial to tall, blue-eyed blondes...because it was less disappointing when they didn't show up?

Maybe, except, what *was* this?

This was ridiculous, that's what. To be fixated on a young woman barely bigger than a minute, well, it just wasn't Alex's style. He'd always been so *cool*, so sophisticated where women were concerned.

He wanted to go home, slump into his easy chair and find an old war movie on TV. So for the life of him, Alex didn't understand why he stayed, why he chatted with other brunch attendants.

That wasn't entirely true. He knew, as he nodded and smiled and talked about the weather, that the sole purpose of his participation in the banal conversations was in the hope they might lead to information about Taylor Griffith.

He was about to ask an elderly woman if she'd seen Taylor when his mother, Helen, spotted him. Smiling, she waved. There was no mistaking what that "look" meant. She seemed as happy as a mother could be, believing he'd taken her advice, finally, that he was making an attempt at getting back on track, into "the stream of things."

Helen had been at him for months, saying he needed to socialize more, get busy building a new life. And that couldn't start, she'd insisted, until he first started talking about the accident. "You could have died in service to your country. That's not something to hide—it's something to be proud of!"

It was a hot button, but out of respect for her, Alex chose not to respond. Besides, he couldn't imagine admitting the truth aloud, not even to his own mother: The mission had been a failure because he'd taken the coward's way out.

A thousand times he'd relived those last milliseconds of the flight, searching his mind for the one thing he might have done differently, the decision that might have saved him *and* the Falcon. It was humiliating, not having a clear memory to help him understand what had gone wrong. That, in itself, Alex believed, was proof of his ineptness as a pilot.

Not an easy thing to admit, when flying had been his life for nearly a decade; when, for generations, all male Van Burens before him had been fliers.

His great-grandfather had tested some of the military's earliest bombers, his grandfather had flown during World War II, his father had served in Vietnam. And each had earned awards and commendations for their bravery. Based on the evidence, Alex could only conclude that the "good pilot" gene had skipped a generation.

And though the man hadn't said so, Alex believed his stepfather felt the same way, too.

Rusty Martin had been a good pilot, a good substitute father. He'd never actually vocalized disapproval of how Alex had handled things that fateful day, but then, he hadn't said he agreed with his stepson, either.

Couldn't be easy, Alex reasoned, for a guy whose best friends—like himself—had been part of the space program for most of their military careers. Poor guy, Alex had often thought, to have a loser for a stepson.

Even the men in his mother's family had a long, illustrious military history. Alex didn't suppose his grandma was any too surprised when her daughter announced her plans to marry a pilot; *she'd* married one, herself. Nor was it a surprise to anyone, when his mom finally chose to remarry, that she picked another pilot.

Alex hadn't expected anyone else to understand the root of his shame, his guilt. But his mother… She'd spent her whole childhood with soldiers, most of whom had been pilots. She'd spent nearly a decade married to his father, another quarter of a century with Rusty. If she couldn't figure out why Alex preferred to keep to himself, why he'd rather not discuss what he believed to be his greatest failure, who *could?*

He didn't need some shrink to tell him why he worked so hard to avoid conversations that started with "So what was it like…" Alex knew full well that a beginning like that was sure to be followed by "waiting to be rescued?" or "knowing you could die?" or "realizing it was you or the plane?"

The questions were reminders of that failure. Besides, he had no satisfactory answers for any of the questioners.

More important than that, he hated being reminded what a coward he'd been during those hair-raising last seconds before the crash.

The first-ever coward in a long line of Van Buren heroes.

Leave it to me to start a whole new tradition....

He knew as well as anyone that avoiding those questions had been harder than answering them. So why was today so different?

Simply put, because *Taylor* was different.

She was the sole reason that today, for the first time since the accident, he'd good-naturedly answered the questions put to him by his mother's church cronies. If talking about what had happened that day would get him close enough to ask if anyone knew where Taylor had gone, it was worth the temporary discomfort.

Turnabout is fair play, he supposed when no one had an answer for him. Not Mable Jensen, not Alex's mother, not even Taylor's Uncle Dave knew where she'd disappeared to. She'd been the only reason he'd agreed to stay for the luncheon, rather than just drop his mother off at the church. Now that Taylor had obviously left, there wasn't much point in hanging around.

After making sure his mom had a safe ride home, Alex aimed himself toward the door.

These days, church activities—church *people* in particular—made him extremely uncomfortable. One fellow's well-intended opinion pretty much summed up how Alex believed everyone else felt: "The Lord performed a miracle out there, or you'd have been shark food, for sure."

What the Lord had to do with it, Alex didn't know, though he hadn't said so at the time. Instead, he'd nodded and smiled politely at the sentiment. He'd never admitted it aloud, but it was true nonetheless—the accident had shattered more than his confidence...it had destroyed his faith.

He hadn't exactly turned into one of those guys who blames God for the bad things that happen in life. But the Almighty had been responsible for letting Alex survive the crash. If He was so all-knowing, wouldn't He have *known* that for a man like Alex, life without flying was no life at all?

Alex said his goodbyes and headed for the parking lot, frowning. If not for the limp, he didn't think anyone would guess what had happened to him eighteen months earlier. Then again, if not for the limp, he wouldn't be home again, trying to build a new life in his hometown. Rather, he'd be on active duty, waiting his turn to run yet another test on yet another F-16.

As he slid behind his pickup's steering wheel, Alex thought about how he'd spent the past hour, answering painful questions in the hope he'd get an answer to a question of his own.

Why he wanted to know where Taylor had gone was a puzzle to him.

And then he pictured her, and the mystery began to unravel.

He shook his head. There had been attractive women in his past. Yeah, he preferred blondes, but there had been a brunette and even a redhead or two. He liked 'em tall, but a few of the short ones had been fun. Taylor seemed intelligent enough, but then, he'd dated doctors and attorneys and scientists....

Key in the ignition, Alex frowned, wondering what was so special about *this* petite brunette. And as the motor roared to a start, he had a feeling the answer had little, if anything, to do with her pale brown eyes or her chestnut-colored hair, her curvy little body or her big bright smile. No, something told him it had more to do with the person who lived *behind* that big, bright smile.

She'd left him feeling the way he had back when he'd

flown to that village in France. No one there had spoken a word of English, and his French began with *oui*...and ended with *oui*. The "stranger in a foreign land" impression had been uncomfortable then, so why was it accompanied by such pleasant sensations now?

Alex slid the gearshift into Reverse and backed out of the parking space, shaking his head. Too much fruit punch, he decided, grinning.

Half a dozen times, as they had stood in her foyer, as they had chatted in the church basement, he'd considered asking if she'd mind if maybe he gave her a call some time.

So why hadn't he asked?

He drove north on Route 40, the image of her fixed in his mind's eye. She was gorgeous, there was no denying that, but she simply wasn't his type, he told himself again.

But if that was true, why had her voice seemed so mesmerizing? And why did he find it necessary to blink and clear his throat when he found himself thinking that, depending on how the light caught her long, curly hair, it could look like anything from mink to velvet to satin?

He adjusted the rearview mirror, a subtle reminder that, as he'd nosed into a parking space in the church lot, his mom had tilted it so she could touch up her lipstick.

Taylor didn't wear lipstick. But then, Taylor didn't need lipstick.

Alex ran a hand through his hair. *You're losin' your ever-lovin' mind, Van Buren.*

He searched for a reason, something to blame for his temporary insanity.

The struggle to align himself with a world that was anything *but* "Navy" was obviously taking a bigger toll than he realized. Why else had he allowed himself to get all smitten by a woman he barely knew? She was everything he didn't want—or need—especially now. So for the life of him, Alex didn't know why he'd spent all that energy, there in the church basement, trying to track her down.

He bounced the heel of his fist on the steering wheel. He and Taylor had spent a few minutes in polite conversation, and he'd enjoyed it. Period. Besides, she obviously spent a lot of time at the church; everyone seemed to know her, and they knew her well.

So why hadn't any of them known where she'd gone?

Makes no difference, Alex told himself. He had neither the time nor the inclination to participate in religious functions, and it was clear as the windshield in front of him that Taylor was a good, devout, church-goin' girl. And since she seemed to spend all her free time doing good, devout, church-goin'-girl things, the chances he'd ever run into her again were slim to none.

End of discussion.

That fact alone should have given him some relief. Instead, a quiet craving grew inside him.

Put her out of your mind, he thought. He and Taylor had nothing in common. Nothing. And even if they did, he had no desire to get involved right now—romantically or otherwise.

Alex noticed that the truck's gas gauge read Empty, and he pulled into the first filling station he came to. It was as he selected octane and began pumping that a small voice said, "Hey, mister. What happened to your leg?"

Alex glanced over his shoulder and looked into a cherubic face. Dimpled fists propped up the boy's chin. Alex guessed him to be four or five.

"Tommy!" the child's mother gasped. "You know better than to ask a question like that. Now, you apologize to the nice man, this instant!"

Tommy's chubby cheeks reddened as he shot a sheepish glance Alex's way. "Sorry," he said grudgingly.

It wasn't the first time Alex had been asked a question like that. At least Tommy's interest was honest. "It's okay, son," he said. "I used to be a pilot, hurt my leg when my plane crashed."

The boy's eyes widened. "Really? Did it explode in the sky, like in the movies?"

Alex grinned. "Sort of. But I was long gone by the time that happened."

Tommy's brow crinkled with confusion. "Gone? Where'd you go?"

That day flashed through his mind. Involuntarily, Alex clenched his jaw. "Had to bail—"

Tommy faced his mother. "Mom, did you hear *that*?"

His mother frowned sternly. "Yes." She shook a finger at him. "And you heard what *I* said...."

The boy turned back to Alex. "Did you have a parachute and ever'thing? Did you float down from the sky and get caught in a tree?"

Alex shook his head. "Wasn't time for the chute to open."

The boy's brow crinkled slightly. "Then how'd you—"

"Tommy, not another word. I mean it." His mother rolled her eyes at Alex. "I don't know what gets into him sometimes. Please, accept my apologies."

"No harm done," he said, meaning it. And winking at Tommy, he added, "Boys will be boys."

Tommy's mother shrugged. "I suppose," she said, then headed into the station to pay for her gas.

"Do you have a little boy?" Tommy asked.

Alex swallowed. He might be a father by now, if he hadn't always put the navy...and flying...ahead of everything else. "No, 'fraid not."

"A little girl?"

"No. I don't have any kids."

Tommy made an "I don't believe it" face and held out his fat little hands. "Well, what's your wife *waiting* for?"

"Don't have a wife, either," he said, chuckling.

"Why not?"

It was a good question. Another one for his "I have no answer for that" list. Well, that wasn't entirely true; he didn't have a wife because, to date, Alex hadn't met a woman he wanted to share his life with.

Not true, his conscience said as the memory of Taylor's pretty face popped into his mind.

"Why *not?*" Tommy repeated.

Alex could only shrug and shake his head.

Taylor would have thought Mable Jensen's nephew seemed like a pleasant enough fellow...if stand-up comedians had been her type.

She didn't know, exactly, what her type was, but it certainly wasn't an overaged hippie who thought it was cool to crack knock-knock jokes by the dozen.

Would've helped if Pete had been a little taller, with big brown eyes, dark shiny waves; if he'd been lean in a marathon kind of way; if he had a wounded puppy-dog expression that made her want to soothe all his troubles away.

Like Alex Van Buren? she wondered, pretending to enjoy Pete's "what do you get when you cross a lawyer with a leech?" joke. When he said, "An agent!" Taylor smiled, even though she didn't get it. Did the punch line miss its intended target because Mable's nephew had laughed at his own joke? Or because she'd been distracted by images of Alex?

The latter, she decided as Pete launched into another ditty. She liked everything about Alex, from the way his dark eyes sparkled when he smiled—which, in her opinion, wasn't nearly often enough—to the mellow tones of his vibrant voice. He'd dressed for the brunch like a man unsure what one wears to such an affair, which told Taylor two things: One, he wasn't a regular churchgoer, and two, he didn't believe in playing it safe.

"Safe" would have been khaki trousers and a dress shirt, loafers, but no tie. Alex, on the other hand, had worn faded jeans and a polo shirt that had seen better days. So had his sneakers. He smelled of bath soap and the barest hint of manly cologne. And he'd cut himself shaving... recently.

"And did you hear the one about...?"

Taylor was in the middle of wishing for a legitimate excuse to walk away from Pete when Trish O'Connor ran up to her, huffing and puffing. "You need to get home right away," the church secretary said. "Your neighbor called and said your cat's on the porch roof, meowing up a storm!"

The woman promised to let Taylor's uncle know where she'd gone, promised to drive him home to save Taylor a trip back to the church.

Pete, Mable and even Alex were immediately forgotten as Taylor headed for her car. Every nerve end in her twitched with fear and dread, yet she resisted the urge to speed. Fast driving had killed her mother. Besides, if a cop stopped her to issue a ticket, it would only take that much longer to get home.

And the more time it took, the more likely Barney would fall off the roof. If there was any truth to the old wives' tale about cats having nine lives, he'd be lucky to have one left, clumsy as he'd always been.

Her car came to a jerky stop when she pulled into the driveway. Sure enough, there was Barney, teetering near the roof's edge, meowing for all he was worth. The sight of his mistress seemed to increase his angst, and he began pacing to and fro, precariously close to the rain gutter.

Taylor raced inside, taking the porch stairs two at a time,

then did the same with the stairs leading to the second floor
of her house.

There, on the other side of her bedroom window, sat
Barney, front paws together, ears twitching, eyes glowing.
Tempted by the sunshine on the other side of the window,
Taylor reasoned, her curious kitty must have fiddled with
the locks that held the window screen in place.

She leaned out the opening and extended her arms.
"C'mere, you silly thing," she crooned. When he stayed
put, she added, "Barney...come here. I'll give you a
treat."

He blinked and meowed...

And flicked his tail. "Come and get me" seemed to be
the silent message he sent his mistress.

Pursing her lips, Taylor made kissing sounds and
snapped her fingers. "Barrrr-neeeee," she sang, "come to
mah-meeeee...."

But he didn't budge. If a squirrel or a bird should decide
to perch in the branches of the tree just beyond the roof,
there was no telling what the cat might do.

All her life Taylor had been afraid of heights. But what
choice did she have? It was either climb out there and grab
him, right now, or wait and take a chance he'd fall.

She eased her upper body through the window and,
trembling, brought up her knee. When it rested on the
warm, sandpapery shingles, she swallowed. Hard. "Please,
God," she prayed, "get the both of us back inside
safely...."

Alex didn't know what prompted him to do it, but instead of turning left at St. Johns Lane, he hung a right. At
the first intersection he made another right, which put him
on Taylor's street. If he remembered correctly, her house
was third from the corner.

If her car was in the driveway, maybe he'd stop by. Just

to make sure everything was all right...since she'd disappeared so quickly from the brunch....

The red compact was there, all right. He noted the relief that coursed through him.

Movement on the roof caught his eye.

What on earth did she think she was doing up there!

He parked on the street, in the shade of the big maple in her front yard. Even from this distance he could hear her, making kissing noises. When he got closer, Alex grinned. "What's up?" he asked as Barney maneuvered nearer the roof's edge.

Taylor only gasped.

"Cat got your tongue?" he added.

"Funny," Taylor said. "Real funny."

But by the look on her face, he reasoned she hadn't found his comment the least bit humorous. On closer inspection, he could see that she was terrified. Of losing the cat? Or of being up so high?

The latter. No, both, he decided.

"You want I should come up there? See if I can get her to come to me?"

"Him. His name is Barney."

"Pardon me," he said, smiling, hoping to ease her tension, "but we were never formally introduced." Waving one arm above his head, Alex said, "Pleased to meet ya, Barn."

He was still grinning when the cat launched itself from the roof, legs flailing, tail twitching, claws extended to get a grip on something.

Alex turned out to be that something.

Ignoring the stinging, piercing pain, he wrapped both arms around the cat and held on tight. "Is the front door open?" he asked, wincing and clenching his teeth.

Taylor nodded.

"Good. I'll meet you inside, then."

Thirty seconds later she was beside him, relieving him of the cat, who made a beeline for the living-room sofa.

"Oh my goodness," Taylor gasped. "Just look at you."

He glanced in the hall mirror. "Mmm, mmm, mmm," he said. "Looks like I've been—"

"In a catfight?"

They shared a moment of nervous laughter, and then she took his hand. "Come with me," Taylor said. "Let's get something on those scratches. We don't want them to get infected."

Her hand was warm. And despite her size, she had an amazingly strong grip. Alex liked that.

For the next five minutes he sat in one of her kitchen chairs, alternately cringing and sucking air between his teeth as she swabbed his cuts with antiseptic. Taylor leaned in, brow furrowed in concentration, as if she were a skilled surgeon and Alex an unconscious patient.

His own mother hadn't fussed over him this gently when he'd skinned his knees as a boy. She'd put Mercurochrome here, bandages there, a slap on his behind and a warning to be more careful next time. And he'd had his share of minor accidents over the years—no surprise, considering what he'd chosen as his life's ambition. A wide variety of nurses had doled out medication, changed the dressings on his wounds. But like his mother, there had been a matter-of-factness to their ministrations.

What made Taylor's attentions seem so…different? Maybe the way her hands shook, ever so slightly, as she touched the swabs to his cuts. Maybe it was the way her voice trembled, just a little, when she asked, "Does that hurt?" and "Am I being too rough?"

And maybe, just maybe, it was the look in her eyes that said even something as insignificant as cat scratches were important…because *he* was important.

Right here, right now, Alex thought he could look into her pretty face forever. If only—

"You were the answer to a prayer," she said, interrupting his thoughts.

"Who? *Me?*"

She tossed the swab into the trash can and recapped the brown peroxide bottle. And pressing one small hand against her chest, Taylor sighed. "I'd been up there..."

She closed her eyes, and when she did, Alex felt as if someone had turned off the sun.

"I don't know *how* long I'd been up there," she finished, eyes wide again. "Seemed like forever!"

Alex said a silent prayer of thanks heavenward, amazed, because he hadn't asked God for diddly in who knew how long, yet he'd asked Him to make Taylor open her eyes. He was even more amazed at the rush of warmth he felt swirling around inside his chest when she did.

"If I'd been up there another minute," she said, laughing, "you'd probably have had *two* people to rescue."

He could think of worse things than having a woman like this beholden to him for rescuing her. Because a woman like this—

Barney sauntered through the room just then, stopping only long enough to give both Alex and Taylor a look that said, "Who are you calling *people?*"

Laughing, Taylor added, "Well, you would've had two somethings to rescue."

He was about to say she was as far from a "thing" as a woman could get when she said, "What're you doing here, anyway?"

You're a magnet, he thought, *and my innards seem to be made of iron ore.* "You left the church brunch just like that—" he snapped his fingers "—without a word." He was beginning to sound to himself like a guy who'd fallen head over heels. Couldn't have *her* thinking that, he decided. And so Alex gave a nonchalant shrug. "Just check-ing, makin' sure you're okay, is all."

She laid a hand on the shoulder he'd shrugged. "Thanks, Alex." And her voice was sweeter than honey when she added, "That was really nice of you." Then, as if she thought maybe *she* sounded like someone who'd fallen head over heels, she spread her arms wide. "Well, as you can see, I'm fine."

You can say that again, he thought. But "I'm glad" is what he said.

She clasped both hands in front of her. Small gesture, really, and yet because it seemed sweet and old-fashioned and feminine all rolled into one, it made his heart pound.

One hand on the refrigerator door handle, Taylor said, "Would you like a soda? Coffee? Tea?"

He chuckled, relieved to have something to focus on besides her dainty hands, her gorgeous eyes. "You sound like the stewardess on our flight back from Ireland."

"Flight attendant," she chided good-naturedly, her fore-finger moving like a silent metronome. "You don't want a ticket from the Politically Correct Police, now, do you?"

Alex slapped himself in the forehead. His intended "Wash my mouth out with soap" was replaced by a "Yeee-ouch!" inspired when he hit one of the still-smarting cat scratches.

She was beside him in an instant, hands fluttering around his wounded face, a worried frown on her own. "Oh, no...you've got this one bleeding again." Taylor grabbed the bottle of antiseptic, slid open the box of cotton swabs. "You really ought to be more gentle with yourself," she scolded softly, daubing the open wound.

She was near enough to kiss, and it took every ounce of self-control he could muster to keep from doing just that. Would her lips feel as soft as they looked? Would those big eyes grow misty, or would she close them and—

"Just because you're a big burly man," she continued, "doesn't mean you have to be so rough with yourself, you know."

Alex swallowed. He didn't know why her innocent comment struck a nerve. But it did. No one had ever been so tender with him. Why, if he didn't know better, he'd have to say Taylor believed he was capable of breaking.

An ugly thought surfaced in his mind.

The accident had all but broken him, physically. But how could she have known that the aftereffects of it had all but shattered his spirit, when they'd spent no more than fifteen minutes, total, in one another's company?

He needed to get out of this place, away from this woman. He had no business feeling drawn to her, not this soon, maybe not at all, ever. It was a good idea, this plan of his to heal on his own, alone. Because alone, he could think. Could reason things out. No way he could do that with her standing there looking at him like some kind of guardian angel.

Getting to his feet, Alex ran a hand through his hair. "Well, thanks for—"

"No," she interrupted, "I'm the one who's supposed to say thanks. You saved Barney, and very likely me, too." She was smiling prettily when she added, "You're our hero!"

He felt the heat of a blush creep into his cheeks. Hero? *If only you knew,* he thought glumly. "Well, guess I'd better get on my way." He forced a grin. "You stay off rooftops now, y'hear?"

Standing at attention, she formed two fingers of her right hand into the Girl Scout salute. "Promise. Once I get that screen back into place, I won't be going near any second-story openings any time in the near future."

"Screen?"

She nodded. "That's how Barney got onto the roof in

the first place. He fiddled with the latches and the screen fell out onto the roof, and…''

Bobbing her head left and right, Taylor clamped her hands together. "I feel ridiculous, being so afraid of high places. Especially since I have no real reason to be afraid of—''

"Why should you feel ridiculous?" He didn't know why, but Alex felt an overwhelming need to defend her. Careful, he warned himself, careful….

"Oh, I don't know," she began softly.

He'd never been afraid of heights. And frankly, he didn't understand people who were. Wasn't afraid of much, and never had been, for that matter. *Fat lot of good your so-called bravado did you over the Caribbean,* came his angry thought.

"I guess," she continued, "I guess it's embarrassing because people, well, you know, they tend to think if they aren't afraid of something, no one else should be, either."

Alex searched for something to say. Something that would comfort and reassure her. "Lots of people have a fear of heights."

It was a lame thing to say, and he knew it. He thought she knew it, too. Why else had she sighed and shrugged and looked away?

What business did she have, looking so gorgeous and womanly and…and sad? Didn't she realize what it was doing to him? How was he supposed to make a quick get-away, keep an arm's-length emotional distance, with her standing there, in reach, looking like…like *that?*

He wanted to wrap his arms around her. Promise that nothing would ever scare her again—at least, not while he was around to prevent it. Wanted to kiss her, to prove how much he meant it.

Alex cleared his throat. *You're outta your ever-lovin' mind, Van Buren.* "Which window?"

"The one in my room."

Great, he thought. Just what he needed. More information to make him want her in his life. Ruffled curtains, probably, and pink stuff sitting on lacy doilies. "Show me. I'll put the screen back into place for you." It was the least he could do. And then he'd make tracks, fast.

Taylor led him upstairs and down the hall, then pointed. "You're a peach to do this." Her lopsided smile became a full grin. "You don't know how much I was dreading going out there to fetch the screen." Laughing, she added, "I was seriously considering closing the window and praying for a strong wind to blow it off the roof."

Alex realized the moment he poked his head through the opening that she'd never have been able to reach the screen from inside. Tiny as she was, she'd have been forced to climb outside, onto the roof, to get it. Wouldn't have been easy, considering how she felt about being up so high. But something told him she would have forced herself to do it anyway.

Gritting his teeth, he realized which of the two of them was most brave. He leaned through the opening, stuck his arm out and took hold of the screen. No big deal for someone who didn't mind heights. But she'd gone out there to save her cat, despite her terror.

Once he'd snapped it into place, Alex said, "Do you have a wrench?"

"Sure. But what do you need with a wrench?"

He wished she wouldn't stand there like that, looking up at him with those big, long-lashed eyes. Being near her was having a peculiar effect on his nervous system. Alex didn't remember feeling this fidgety around a woman before. Didn't remember feeling this fidgety, period.

"Well," he explained, "if I tighten these wing nuts that're holding it in place, Barney won't be able to work them loose next time he has a notion to sunbathe on the roof.''

The luscious pink lips parted, no doubt to ask him how he expected her to take the screen out again, should the need arise. His heartbeat doubled as he remembered that moments ago he'd wanted to kiss her. Remembered that he'd pretty much wanted that from the first moment he set foot in her foyer for the suitcase exchange. But he'd never wanted it more than right now.

Alex swallowed. "If you ever want to remove the screen for any reason," he answered her unasked question, "you can always loosen the nuts...with the wrench."

She smiled. "Makes sense to me," she said, and dashed down the stairs.

"Good. *Something* around here oughta make sense," he said when she was out of earshot.

Barney paraded into the room just then, tail twitching left and right as he eyed the open window.

Alex narrowed his eyes and shot him a warning look. "Don't even think about it, buddy."

The cat shot him a look that said, "The name's Barney, *buddy*." Then, purring, he twined a figure eight around Alex's ankles.

Crouching, Alex patted the cat's head. When he noticed the gouges on the back of his hand, he was reminded of the crisscrossing scratches on his face. "I have a feeling I'll be thinking of you when I shave tomorrow morning," he said. "When I shave for the next week."

He'd be thinking of Barney's mistress, too. Probably for a whole lot longer than a week. The thought almost made him wish he hadn't decided to keep a safe distance from this churchgoing little woman.

Taylor burst into the room just then, carrying a pink metal toolbox. "Don't laugh," she said, plunking it down on the hardwood floor. "I bought it at a yard sale couple years back. Only cost me fifty cents, but it was all dirty and rusty, and the only spray paint on sale at Clark's Hardware that day was—'' she extended both hands, like one of the models who present the prizes on a game show ''—pink!''

It just so happened she was wearing a pink blouse. And pink fingernail polish. The excitement of Barney's adventure had colored her cheeks a pretty shade of pink, and those luscious lips of hers, well, they were pink, too. Alex had a notion to tell her pink was her color. Instead, he opened the toolbox and poked around inside until he found an adjustable crescent wrench.

As he was busy tightening the screen's wing nuts, he heard her clear her throat. She was near enough to touch. Again. Right there beside his left elbow. If he turned, just slightly, he could slide an arm around her waist, ease her to him and—

''So, did you enjoy the brunch?'' she asked.

Alex had to blink to get his brain back on track. Oh. Right. The brunch. Well, yes, he supposed he'd enjoyed it well enough. At least, he'd enjoyed every moment he'd spent with *her*.... ''Food was good,'' he said, hoping to sound noncommittal. But that was all he intended to admit.

She laughed. ''The ladies of Resurrection outdo themselves every time there's an event.'' Then, ''Did you know there's going to be another next Wednesday?''

She hesitated, and he knew she intended to invite him to it.

Knew, just as well, that he had every reason to say no.

For one thing, what did they have in common? And even if he could find something the two of them could share, he had way too many ''issues'' left over from the accident. Wouldn't be fair to haul her through that mess.

Crouching, Alex put the wrench back into the toolbox and fastened its lid. On his feet again, he decided to tell her that he'd sworn off church. Sworn off everything—and every*one*— connected to it. She needed to hear that, because he had a feeling she put the *D* in devout. Besides, he liked his women tall and lithe and blond and blue-eyed, right? Wouldn't be fair to mislead her, not in any way. And he had to find a way to get the words out before she asked him to be her guest.

"I don't suppose you'd like to come," she asked, as if on cue, "as my guest?"

Sunlight glinted from her hair. Hair he wanted to touch, to find out if it felt as soft, as silky as it looked. And there, in the bright light, it was impossible not to notice the pale freckles that dotted her nose, that sprinkled across her ivory cheeks. He wanted to touch those, too. Each and every one of them...with gentle kisses.

Watch it, he warned himself, *this one isn't like the others, not in any way.* And that meant trouble. Reminding himself he had neither the time nor the inclination for romance, Alex straightened, squared his shoulders, lifted his chin a notch. Tell her no, was the thought pinging in his head. Say, *Sorry, but I have stuff to do that night.*

Hands deep in his pockets, he glanced at slightly parted, kissable pink lips, looked into her eyes. Into her big, long-lashed, brownish-greenish-golden eyes and said, "Only if they're serving potato salad."

Chapter Three

Until he'd looked up and seen her there on the roof, Alex had never seen much farther than the end of his own nose. Especially when it came to the needs of others. Especially since the accident.

Oh, he'd done the typical favors for friends and acquaintances, like helping them move from apartments into homes when he wasn't on assignment, letting them use his pickup when he was. Once, when he was stationed in Florida, his next-door neighbor won a trip to the Bahamas. It was Alex who, twice a day, let himself into her apartment to feed her cat. While living in California, he watered a neighbor's roses rather than see the elderly gent's rose club registration fee—and the work he'd put into the roses to that point—go to waste.

He'd never minded doing the favors. Hadn't felt imposed upon by the neighbors who'd asked them of him. But suddenly there was a nagging question in his mind, one Alex doubted he would have asked himself if he hadn't met Taylor.

Would he have volunteered his help if that help hadn't been requested?

He was ashamed to admit the answer was no.

Wouldn't have been hard to admit if the answer had been the result of a hectic schedule. Truth was, he'd simply never thought to offer. And what kind of person did that make him?

Not the kind who deserved a woman like Taylor Griffith....

He shifted uncomfortably in his easy chair, remote control in hand. As the colorful, musical images of TV chefs and sports figures and rumpled detectives whizzed by on the screen, Alex scowled. *Shouldn't have agreed to that date,* he grumbled inwardly. *Only thing you have in common with that woman is...*

As he gave it a moment's thought, his thumb relaxed on the up button. A home shopping host held up a glittering half-carat diamond. The glint and glow of the stone reminded him of Taylor, each spark, each glimmer illuminating yet another facet of her character. The longer he knew her, the more she seemed to shine.

Compared to her, he felt like a chunk of wet chalk.

Somehow, that didn't seem to matter. Whether or not they had anything in common made no difference, either. He liked her. Had, the instant he set eyes on her in that overcrowded plane, liked her more still when they made the suitcase exchange in the tiny foyer of her house. The church brunch, her tender loving care after the cat rescue...every minute in her company was incentive enough to want to spend hours, weeks, months with her.

Alex slumped into his chair, telling himself it was boredom, restlessness, frustration with his life that made him think he was falling for this near stranger. Clapping a hand over his face, he closed his eyes to block the TV's flickering light.

"Shouldn't have said yes to the date," he muttered sleepily. He didn't fight the drowsiness. Maybe sleep would provide a haven from the unsettling feelings Taylor had aroused in him....

Now that she knew what caused his limp, Taylor had to warn herself to be careful. She'd always been a sucker for someone in pain, whether physical or emotional—it's how she'd gotten in over her head with Kent—and Alex Van Buren seemed to have suffered his share of pain and agony, especially lately.

She got a mental picture of him, outfitted in a flight suit, standing beside a fast-flying fighter plane, smiling with the knowledge that he did heroic things every time he snapped the bubble canopy shut overhead.

And he was a hero, no doubt about that.

When Taylor heard about his past, she made it her business to learn more about the accident. An article, buried among reams of information she dug up on the Internet, explained how his F-16 Fighting Falcon had been struck by lightning, causing a complete shutdown of the controls. The plane was one of the manufacturer's latest releases, designed to go farther and faster than any F-16 before it. The test Alex had been performing the day of his crash involved the new agile beam radar and state-of-the-art mission computer. Equipped with bigger fuel tanks to ensure greater range, the fighter was, in Taylor's layman's opinion, an explosion waiting to happen. It was a miracle that Alex had survived.

And she thanked God that he had.

Everything about him brought out the protector in her, starting with the limp...and every masculine emotion that made him try so desperately to hide it. The urge to care for him had swelled up as she'd swabbed the cuts and scrapes put there when he caught Barney. But that hadn't been the first or the only time she'd felt it.

Before she'd even known his name, Taylor had wanted to comfort him as he hobbled past her in the big tube connecting their jetliner to the airport terminal. The feeling had bubbled up again when he left her house that day, limping more because of the weight of his big, bulky suitcase.

One look into his dark, shining eyes was all it took to tell her that something good, something decent lived inside this man. Oh, he did his best to hide it behind a practiced smile and well-timed jokes, but Taylor sensed it all the same. Not such an easy feat when she admitted seeing the same things in the mirror.

Taylor snapped on the light beside her recliner, intent upon reading Sunday's newspaper, cover to cover. She'd made it to the food section when the phone rang, startling her so badly she nearly overturned her teacup.

"Hello?"

"Taylor. It's Alex. Calling about the, ah, that church thing you were telling me about?"

Taylor squeezed her eyes shut. *Please, God,* she prayed, *don't let him back out.* It was a foolish prayer that made her feel like a schoolgirl in the throes of a silly crush. That didn't make it any less heartfelt.

"Don't tell me you're calling to cancel," she blurted out. As if the action might help her stuff the words back into her mouth, Taylor pressed her fingertips to her lips.

After a slight pause, she heard him clear his throat. Already she'd decided it was something he did when uncomfortable, uneasy, uncertain. *Oh, fine,* she scolded herself. *Now you've gone and done it!*

He'd see her as that silly schoolgirl now. And what did a man like that, who'd risked life and limb for his country, want with a—

"No," came his calm, masculine voice, "I was actually calling to find out if we're supposed to meet at Resurrection, or if I should pick you up."

Taylor blinked. Swallowed. "Well, I hadn't really—"

"Because if it's up to me," he continued, "I'd prefer coming to get you."

Brows high on her forehead, she felt herself smile. *Really?* she thought.

"If you have something to do, I'll understand...."

"Do?"

"I know you're pretty heavily involved over there at the, uh, at the church. I just thought maybe you had, um, stuff to set up or something."

She hoped her laughter wouldn't sound too relieved. "No. In fact, I'm not even on the cleanup committee this time."

Yet the minute the words were out, Taylor regretted them. Would he take it to mean she expected to be invited out afterward? For ice cream, or a walk in the park? For a glass of lemonade or a stroll along Main Street?

"Whew," Alex said. "I was kinda hoping you'd say that."

"You...you were?"

He chuckled. "Don't sound so surprised. I'm sure you know you have a way of, ah, growin' on a guy."

So she'd grown on him? "Goodness," she said, giggling. "You make me sound like a wart or something."

"Well, if you're a wart, then I'm Froggy Come A-Courtin'."

She so enjoyed the sound of his laughter that Taylor decided to see to it he laughed a whole lot more often.

"So what time does this shindig start?" he wanted to know.

"Six o'clock. We like to get an early start on weeknights

so the people with kids can get them home and tucked into bed at a reasonable hour.''

People with kids. Oh, how she'd like to be one of those!

"Makes sense," she heard him say. "I'll pick you up at five-thirty, then."

Five-thirty? But it wasn't more than a five-minute drive from her place to the church.

"I'll take you up on that soda you offered when—"

"When Barney tore your face to shreds," she finished for him.

"Aw, it isn't that bad."

She sighed. "The one on your right cheek will probably leave a scar."

"You think?"

There was a hesitation, as if maybe he was checking it out in a nearby mirror.

"Cool beans," Alex said. "I'll have to buy Barney a cat treat."

She was about to ask what in the world he was talking about when he explained. "They say scars give a man's face character."

The image of his handsome, dark-eyed face flashed in her mind. "I think your face had plenty of character without Barney's help," she said, surprised by the timidity of her own voice.

A soundless moment passed. Alex cracked the quiet with a soft "Thanks, kiddo."

Kiddo? she echoed, grinning. "Thanks for what?"

"For being you, that's all. Just for being you." He cleared his throat. "I'll see you Wednesday, then, five-thirty?"

Three whole days without a word from him? She hoped she could stand to wait that long. "Wednesday," she echoed, "five-thirty."

And when he hung up, Taylor punched a fist into the air and hollered, ''C'mon, Wednesday!''

He had every good intention of backing out of the date. He'd even made up a good excuse, to spare her feelings.

Then he'd heard her voice. Heard her say ''Don't tell me you're calling to cancel.''

Every good intention, every well-rehearsed excuse that would explain why he couldn't, shouldn't, wouldn't go to the church social had been forgotten. Alex had hardly been able to believe it when he heard himself say, ''No, I was actually calling to find out if we're supposed to meet at Resurrection, or if I should pick you up.''

Everything about her answer had made it clear that Taylor *wanted* him to pick her up. Why, he'd even thought he could hear a bit of a smile in her voice!

His heart had skipped a beat when she'd agreed to let him pick her up, on Wednesday at five-thirty. Skipped a beat! Like some doodle-brained boy with a crush on his French teacher!

And so it was established that, despite good intentions and rehearsed excuses and pep talks that started out ''You have nothing in common with the woman'' and ended with ''This isn't the time to be starting anything,'' Alex grudgingly admitted that he wanted very much to see her again.

And again.

The only question was, could he keep from calling her every hour on the hour between now and Wednesday?

Taylor let him lead her to the food table, let him hand her a paper plate, plastic utensils, a napkin. ''Say when,'' he instructed, holding a heaping spoon of the coveted potato salad above her plate.

''When,'' she said as it landed with a dull thud.

''Baked beans?''

"Just a few, ple—"

He loaded a spoonful onto the plate, added a thick slice of honey-baked ham and a dollop of fresh ground horseradish. "If you don't want that," he said, pointing at the condiment, "I'll be happy to take it off your hands, er, plate."

Taylor tilted her head and smiled mischievously. "It just so happens I like horseradish."

"No foolin'?" Grinning, he shook his head. "Where have you been all my life, Taylor Griffith?"

As though he regretted his playful words, Alex's face froze in a serious frown. Glancing around the room, he said, "Where would you like to sit?"

Maybe his apprehension was a sign that some woman had broken his heart recently. Or maybe he was one of those guys who'd vowed to remain a bachelor forever, and was now worried that she'd take his comment too seriously.

Taylor pointed at the row of tables nearest the windows. "Let's not sit on an end, though."

"Okay. But why not?"

"Well," she said, staring wide-eyed at her plate, "with the weight of this thing, I'm afraid we'll tip the table over."

"Ha ha," he said, grinning. "Very funny." He indicated a table near the door. "How's this?"

Before Taylor could agree that it was fine, a singsong soprano rang out. "Al-ex-aaaan-derrrr… Yoooo-hoooo, over heeee-ere…."

"Good grief," he whispered, hunching his shoulders, "it's Mable Jensen. Quick, hide me!"

His reaction to Mable was so like Uncle Dave's that Taylor laughed out loud. "Hide you? That'd be like Goliath asking to hide behind David."

Alex raised his chin, sent a polite nod Mable's way, then

quickly sat, putting his back to the woman. "I've been hiding from that woman all my life, it seems. When I was a kid…" He flexed his hands, like crab claws, and shuddered. "She's a cheek pincher, that one."

Reaching for the saltshaker in the middle of the table, he chuckled. "I get it," he said, "David and Goliath." Then he glanced at Taylor's purse on the metal folding chair beside her. "You wouldn't happen to have a slingshot in that thing, would you?"

"Nah," she said, settling herself directly across from him, "had to take it out to make room for my .357 Magnum."

His eyes widened with mock fear. "Lord have mercy on my feeble soul." His mouth slanted in a grin.

"Speaking of the Lord," Taylor said, "would you like to say grace, or shall I?"

Mable stepped up to the table, overloaded plate in one hand, clear plastic cup of tropical punch in the other. "Grace?" she cooed. "Why, I'd love to hear you say grace." One brow high on her forehead, she muttered, "Haven't heard a Christian word out of your handsome mouth in ages, Alexander, so it might just be a good way to learn what kind of upbringing Helen gave you."

He looked cornered, whether because of Mable's intrusion or the invitation to say grace—or both—Taylor couldn't say.

"Mable, m'dear," came a raspy male voice from behind them, "I've saved you a seat."

Mable glanced over her shoulder and smiled when she realized the invitation had been extended by an eligible bachelor. "Why, Homer Bell, you incorrigible flirt. I'm flattered that you waited for me."

Her demand to listen while Alex said grace was forgotten as she moved closer to Homer.

"Saved by the Bell," Alex said, chuckling.

His grin faded when he saw Taylor's hands, still folded at the edge of the table. Only then did she realize he hadn't taken her seriously when she'd invited him to say grace. He looked more cornered now than when Mable repeated the question. But to his credit, he collected himself quickly. "May as well get it over with," he said, smiling.

Funny, Taylor thought, that it never quite reached his eyes.

She watched him bow his head, close his eyes, fold his hands...not in the fingers-laced kind of way, but in the palms-flat-and-pressed-together way. Like a little boy, she thought. The sight plucked a sweet maternal chord in her heart, and she found herself having to resist the urge to brush the bangs from his eyes.

"Lord," he began, his voice quiet and gruff, "thanks for not letting it rain, like the weatherman predicted. Thanks for the potato salad and the nice ladies who—"

He opened one eye a crack. "Hey," came his mock-scolding observation, "you're supposed to be lookin' pious and holy. You know, 'assume the position' and all that when somebody's prayin'. What are you, some kind of rebel?"

Blinking, she bit her lower lip to keep her smile from growing wider, and did as he suggested. The instant she closed her eyes, she heard him say, "That's better. Much better."

Alex cleared his throat. "Now then, where was I before I was so rudely interrupted...by *staring?*"

Lips folded into her mouth to discourage full-blown laughter, she squeezed her eyes shut.

"Ahh, yes," he went on, "thanks for the money this little shindig will raise to help feed the homeless when winter sets in." There was a slight pause, and then he said, "And let's not forget how grateful we are for proper prayer posture. Amen."

Taylor could only grin and shake her head and add "funny" to her quickly growing "Reasons to Like Alex Van Buren" list.

Helen Martin came toward them just then, a food-laden plate in one hand, a paper cup of lemonade in the other. "Hey, you two. Mind if an old lady joins you?"

Taylor scooted aside to make room for her. "First of all, the last thing that comes to mind when I think of you is 'old.'" And it was true, too. Taylor guessed Mrs. Martin to be in her early to mid-sixties, but the woman had never dressed or acted like the stereotypical senior citizen. She seemed to prefer blue jeans to polyester skirts, sneakers to leather pumps, and instead of the hairdo her uncle called "a blue-bubble bob," Helen wore her mostly white hair in a fashionable chin-length style.

Taylor waited for Alex's mother to get settled, then said, "You've been a member of Resurrection Church for a good while. You never mentioned a son." To Alex, she smiled and said, "What were you hiding? Is he a bank robber or something?"

Helen pursed her lips. "He's a fallen-away Christian is what he is, which simply breaks my—"

"Mom," Alex interrupted gently, "I thought we agreed not to get into that in public."

She stiffened. "Well, Taylor *asked*...."

As if Alex hadn't said a word, Helen turned to Taylor and said, "While he was traveling the world, flying high for the navy, he freely admitted that he only went to church on Christmas and Easter, and only then if some *lady* friend dragged him along. I thought surely after..." She aimed a puzzled glance his way. "Come to think of it, this is the second time he's attended a church function since—"

"Mother." Alex leaned halfway across the table and said imploringly, "Enough. Okay?"

Helen held a hand to her chest. Suddenly her smile and

her eyes widened simultaneously, as if she'd just found the answer to the meaning of life. Laying a finger against her lips, she said, "Why, Taylor, dear, I do believe you've had a positive influence on my wayward son!" She laughed, then added, "Isn't that your uncle over there?"

Taylor followed the direction of Mrs. Martin's gaze and spotted her uncle, who frowned as he made his way through the maze of tables. "Uncle Dave," she called, waving. "Looking for a good place to sit?"

He headed their way, every bit as straight backed and energetic as he'd been at forty. "Helen! Hey, there," he said, smiling. "I didn't know you'd be here tonight. You shoulda called. Rusty told me he'd be out of the country for the next few weeks. I could've picked you up, and—"

"Yoooo-hoooo, Daaay-veee," Mable Jensen sang. "Won't you join us?"

Taylor's uncle blanched, and Taylor sent him a sympathetic smile.

Mable sidled up to him. "Do you like my new blue dress?" she asked, blinking flirtatiously.

"Well, sure," he said, "it almost matches your—"

Taylor knew what he was thinking and said a quick prayer of thanks when he didn't say *hair*.

"My dear," he said instead, "it's every bit as lovely as you are."

Mable patted the empty chair beside her. "There's plenty of room. Won't you join us?"

Dave put on his best disappointed look. "Aw now, sorry, Mable," he said, nodding to the table behind her, "but I promised Taylor I'd sit with her."

Mable looked over her shoulder at Taylor, Alex, Helen. "So. You'd rather sit with the big shots. I see." She sniffed, crossing one chubby arm over the other. "Well fine, then, if Homer and I aren't good enough for you, then—''

Alex piped up with ''I hear you still make the best peach cobbler this side of the Mississippi, Mrs. Jensen.'' He wiggled his eyebrows. ''I don't suppose you brought some tonight?''

Almost immediately, her mood brightened. ''Why, yes.'' She batted her blue-shadowed eyes. ''As a matter of fact, I did.''

''Be sure to set aside a big piece for me, will you?'' And winking, he leaned toward her and whispered, ''''Cause you know how hard it is to tear yourself away from big shots....''

She was red faced and grinning like a schoolgirl when she joined her tablemates again.

''I owe you one, son,'' Taylor's uncle said, sitting beside Alex. To Helen, he added, ''The fried chicken is spectacular, as usual. That Rusty, he's one lucky fella.''

''I'm the lucky one,'' Helen said.

But Taylor couldn't help but notice that Mrs. Martin hid a giggle and a blush behind one hand.

Was she...was she *flirting* with her Uncle Dave? No, she couldn't be. Mrs. Martin had been one of Resurrection's most involved parishioners, and seemed totally devoted to her husband. Anyway, even if she had been flirting, Uncle Dave's army buddies hadn't nicknamed him Straight Arrow for nothing.

Are you getting a load of this? was the question in Alex's brown eyes.

She widened hers, as if to respond, *How long has this been going on?*

Alex only shrugged.

''That's some weird sign language you two have goin' on there,'' Uncle Dave observed.

''Now, now, Dave. There's nothing wrong with being

silly when you're young." Helen punctuated her comment with yet another giggle.

"Nothing wrong with it when you're not young," he countered.

Alex crooked a finger, inviting Taylor to follow him. When she stood, he told the older folks, "We're going outside, see if maybe we can catch a breeze." Almost as an afterthought, he said, "Care to join us?"

"Nah. We'll stay near the air-conditioning," Dave said. And in a louder voice, "Besides, I don't want to get too far from Mable's cobbler."

Alex stopped at the dessert table and piled assorted treats on a dinner plate before he followed Taylor outside.

"You don't mind if I grill you about your uncle, since he seems so interested in my very married mother," he said when they were settled.

Taylor frowned. "I suppose not. But when you're finished, hand me the charcoal, will you? Because Uncle Dave has been like a father to me since my dad died."

Wincing, Alex said, "Oh, wow, Taylor, I'm sorry." His frown deepened. "When did it happen?"

She blinked. It had been years since she'd lost her dad, yet sometimes it seemed like only yesterday. This was one of those times. "Long time ago."

"Sorry," he said again. "How'd it happen?"

"Heart attack."

Alex nodded. "I was wondering why I keep seeing you here with your uncle, instead of your parents." He tilted his head slightly, a silent apology.

Taylor decided to change the subject. "Your mom is a real trouper."

"Why do you say that?"

"Well, she never lets any grass grow under her feet, for one thing. When she heads a committee, things get done!" Taylor had always liked Mrs. Martin, had always respected the ladylike way the woman conducted herself. "She's alone an awful lot, but it doesn't seem to faze her. She mows her own lawn, trims her own hedges, prunes her own—"

"All right, I admit it. If I lived closer, or visited oftener, I could help out some."

Strange, she thought, how he'd pretty much echoed what she'd been thinking since her own mother's death. "I didn't mean it that way at all. I only meant I think it's great that your mom is so independent."

He shrugged. "I guess."

Taylor raised an eyebrow. "I take it you don't approve?"

He'd let his real feelings show for a moment, but only for a moment. Laughing to cover it up, Alex said, "Hey. She's a big girl."

"I wish my mom had been more like yours after my dad died. Maybe she would've lived longer."

"You lost your dad *and* your mom?" He looked puzzled. "Good grief, Griffith. Any more surprises I should know about?"

"Surprises?"

"Well, how's a guy supposed to make a good impression on a pretty girl when every time he opens his yap, his big fat boot gets stuck between his teeth?"

A pretty girl? A good impression? Taylor's heart did a flip at the possibility that Alex was as interested in her as she was in him. "All right," she began, "let me give you the down-and-dirty rundown." In a weary I'd-rather-not-talk-about-it-but-since-you-ask voice she said, "My father had his first heart attack when I was a junior in high school. He never really got healthy after that, didn't live to see me graduate from college." She took a deep breath. "And my mother…" How much detail was enough? How much was too much? "My mother was killed a year and a half ago, when her boyfriend's car smashed into..."

Taylor shook her head. She hadn't been anywhere near Route 40 that night, but the images of what must have happened were imprinted on her brain as clearly now as on the night she'd received the tragic news.

Taylor met Alex's eyes. The pitying expression on his face was the very reason she rarely talked about that part of her life. "Your turn," she said matter-of-factly.

Blinking, Alex said, "Huh?"

"For starters, you're an only child?"

He took a swallow of lemonade. "Yeah. Never met my grandparents. Dad died when I was five, and Mom married Rusty on my seventh birthday." He made a Stan Laurel face. "Guess she wanted to make sure I'd never forget their anniversary."

She'd met Mr. Martin a few times at various church functions. He seemed like a nice enough man. "You don't like your stepfather?"

"I like him fine. He was a great dad."

"Then why..." Taylor decided to keep her questions to herself. She didn't like sharing certain parts of her history with others; Alex had the same right to his secrets.

She stood suddenly. "I think we'd better get back inside before people start talking."

He looked mildly surprised, but got to his feet. After gathering up his trash, he tossed it into the wire trash can near the door. "Something tells me we'd have to do more than raid the dessert table to give them 'food' for talk." He grinned, winked, took her elbow and led her inside. "But...I'm game if you are," he whispered into her ear.

She was about to ask what he was talking about when her uncle waved them over.

"What've you kids been up to?"

"Just sharing family secrets," Alex said matter-of-factly.

Taylor tried to hide her shock, while Helen smiled and Uncle Dave nodded as if he didn't give a whit what she and Alex had been talking about.

Alex leaned close to Taylor, said in a soft voice, "Better close your mouth, gorgeous. Horseflies love dark, damp places."

Maybe he'd got that limp, she thought, grinning, when a former girlfriend kicked him in the shin.

Perhaps it was talking to Alex earlier that jump-started her melancholy mood. Maybe it was the weather that conjured up the misty memories.

Summertime had been her mother's favorite time of year, and sometimes, on nights like this, when the humid Baltimore breeze clung like plastic wrap to anything it touched, when crickets chirped and tree toads sang, a quiet melancholy enveloped Taylor.

Sitting in her favorite chair, a stack of photo albums in her lap, she sighed. *Oh, how I miss you, Mom!*

As if he'd read her mind, Barney rubbed against her ankles, then leapt onto her lap and jockeyed for space amid the scrapbooks. Pressing his forehead to Taylor's, he began to purr.

"Okay. All right," she said, hugging him, "you win. I'll look at these later."

The moment she put the albums aside, Barney made himself comfortable in her lap. "You act as if you own the whole house and everything in it, me included," she teased, scratching behind his ears.

And he looked into her eyes, as if to say, "It's about time you figured that out!"

There were a few things she hadn't quite figured out.

Alex Van Buren, for one…

Leaning her head against the chair's cushiony backrest, Taylor pictured him, tall and lean and handsome. She hadn't realized *how* handsome until this afternoon. Not that she hadn't noticed the long lashes, the burnished dark hair, the powerful jaw, the masculine voice. But in the narrow aisle of the airplane, in her foyer, in the food line at the church brunch, they'd been virtual strangers. When he'd stopped by to make sure she was all right on the day he rescued Barney, he'd told her in so many words that he wanted to change that.

Smiling, Taylor acknowledged that she wanted to change that, too. She wondered what her mom would have thought of Alex Van Buren. Too quiet? Maybe. Too serious? Probably. But if she'd looked into his big dark eyes and seen the sadness, the loneliness that Taylor had seen, Amanda, too, would have wanted to find its source…and do whatever was within her power to put an end to it.

Sighing, Taylor shook her head. She'd learned the hard way what happened when she poked her nose in where it didn't belong. Besides, she had no real proof that he was unhappy; not everyone walked around smiling and laughing all the time.

Until a few months ago, *she'd* been miserable, herself. But that was before she'd handed her grief…and her guilt…over to God. Prayer had made Taylor see that, although there might have been things she could have done better, things she might have done differently, she had been the daughter Amanda had wanted, and she'd been loved, warts and all.

The wind picked up, rustling the trees, sending a flurry of leaves spiraling upward, just outside the window. Their quiet pecking against the panes caused Barney's ears to swivel back and forth.

The weatherman had predicted severe thunderstorms for the hours after midnight. Taylor didn't mind the rain. It was the lightning she could do without. Ever since that flight home from Puerto Rico, when she'd looked out the window of the 747 and had seen a bright white bolt slice through the late-afternoon sky, the sight of it struck fear in her.

She hadn't known it at the time, but later, after her mother's wake and funeral, the headline in the local paper had captured her attention: Test Pilot Narrowly Escapes Death In Crash. The story described how the pilot had ejected when lightning blacked out the controls of his F-16...in the skies south of San Juan, Puerto Rico, at four o'clock on February seventeenth.

How eerie, she'd thought after reading the article, because she remembered looking at her watch after the bright bolt had lit up the sky. Her seatmate had seen the flash of light off in the distance, too. "Thank God we're headed north," he'd said. "Funny how things can be such complete opposites."

"What do you mean?" she'd asked.

"Light is usually a good thing, a welcome addition to the world." He nodded toward the spot where the blinding bolt had struck. "But that..." Shaking his head, he'd added, "Light like that can kill."

Something told her *that* had been the bolt of lightning that had nearly killed Alex....

The only light in the living room now had filtered in from the kitchen. This time of day, between dusk and dark, had always been her mother's favorite. Taylor preferred to dwell on that, instead of the strange feeling that had come over her when she'd seen the lightning from the plane's portal.

She hadn't closed the drapes yet, either, and the beginnings of silvery moonglow gleamed from polished wood tabletops and picture frames. The candlesticks on the mantel, the prints on the walls, the deep-muted plaid of the draperies took on a gray hue, like old photographs that had been washed with touches of faint pink, pale blue, mossy green. Even Barney's stripes seemed more pale yellow than orange.

Taylor closed her eyes and slid her hands down his softly furred back. If it hadn't been for Alex, the cat might not even be here, purring contentedly in her lap. He might be…

She shuddered at the possibilities and said a silent prayer of thanks that Alex had come along when he had.

He hadn't seemed the least bit afraid of being two stories off the ground. That in itself didn't make him special; not everyone had a fear of high places.

No, he was special for reasons that had nothing to do with his act of bravery…and *everything* to do with it.

It wasn't rational, feeling this strongly about a man she'd just met, about a man she knew so little about. She credited gratitude; he'd saved Barney—and very likely herself, as well.

But that wasn't entirely true, and Taylor knew it. She'd been drawn to him even as he passed her on the way to baggage claim. Why else would she have fallen asleep thinking about him that night?

Still, it was silly, downright schoolgirlish, to entertain such feelings for a near stranger. Oh, Taylor knew who his mother was, that he wasn't a steady churchgoer. He drove a pickup truck and had lost his father at a young age. He'd survived a lot of painful losses in his years on Earth.

But had he ever been married? Did he have children? Why had his military career ended? And what did he plan to do with his life, now that it had?

Most curious of all…the limp. He seemed self-conscious about it, always taking care to put her on his "good" side, always making sure he stayed a few steps behind her, so she couldn't watch him move.

The physical therapist in her made Taylor wonder if he limped because walking hurt, or because his injury had caused permanent damage, such as bone loss or muscle deterioration. Either way, was he getting treatment? Doing exercises? Taking medications to ease the pain and help the healing process?

She could ask him, straight out, or wait and hope he'd volunteer the information. Her training told her to bide her time; her male patients were particularly sensitive about things that altered their ability to perform routine manly tasks. And walking was about as "routine" as it got.

Maybe one day he'd trust her enough to tell her what specific injury had caused the limp. Meanwhile, she had to find ways to let him know it didn't matter a whit to her if he limped a little, or a lot, or not at all.

Smiling, she remembered the way he'd smirked, a playful gleam in his dark eyes, when she'd gotten all slack jawed at his admission that they'd been sharing family secrets. Almost as quickly as it had appeared, the smile had disappeared and his stoic, no-nonsense demeanor had returned.

Something had happened to convince him he wasn't entitled to moments of enjoyment in life, or in people, either. Somehow she had to find out what. Because once she knew *why* he'd sentenced himself to a life of seriousness and solitude, maybe she could help him with the lesson that had been so hard for her to learn: "The road to nowhere is paved with regrets."

Chapter Four

Every time the phone rang, Taylor found herself hoping it would be Alex. And every time it wasn't, she found herself trying to explain away her disappointment.

Tonight they'd have a real date. No coincidental meeting at a ladies' auxiliary brunch, no last-minute invitation to a Wednesday-night social. The day before, the jangling telephone had startled her so badly she'd nearly overturned her coffee mug. She'd seriously considered reading Uncle Dave the riot act for calling so early in the morning.

Turned out it had been Alex on the phone. Mr. No-Nonsense. The Get-Down-to-Business Kid. "Sorry to call so early," he said in his matter-of-fact way, "but I wanted to get on the list before your weekend was booked."

Get on the list? Taylor almost laughed out loud at his assessment of her social calendar. Other than Sunday services, the only thing "booked" was a trip to the grocery store!

"Thought maybe you'd have dinner with me," he added, "then maybe we could catch a movie?"

"I'd love to," she said without thinking.

Had that been relief she'd heard sighing into her ear?
Taylor hoped so.

"Great," Alex said. "I'll pick you up at five-thirty,
then."

The instant he hung up, it seemed the gears of every
clock ground to a halt. Would Friday night *ever* get here?

Taylor bought new clothes for their date—a kicky just-
above-the-knee skirt of combed cotton and a matching pale
pink sweater set. Since white shoes were part of her physical therapist's uniform, she preferred colorful footwear.
But this outfit called for simplicity, so she bought a pair
of white heels. Bought a white purse, too.

She spent more time than usual on her makeup and
hairdo, trying various shades of eye shadow and an as-
sortment of hairstyles, and ended up with lavender high-
lighting her eyes and white combs holding back her hair.

Now if only she had something to occupy her time for
an hour and ten minutes...

True to his word, Alex arrived at precisely five-
thirty...and brought a treat to thank Barney for the scar
that would lend character to his face. "Sorry I forgot it
last time I was here," he said, crouching to pet the cat.

"Lemonade?" she offered.

Alex stood, checked his wristwatch. And smiling, he
said, "I'd love some, but I made reservations."

Taylor grabbed her purse from the hall tree, slung the
long-sleeved part of the sweater set over one arm.

"You clean up good, real good, by the way," he said
as she locked the door.

She'd never seen him in a coat and tie before. "You
don't look half-bad yourself."

He slid an arm around her waist as they descended the
porch steps. "This meeting of the Mutual Admiration So-
ciety has officially ended." And opening the passenger

door of his pickup, he said, "Sorry it looks so shabby, but I didn't have time to run her through the car wash."

With a nod, she indicated her car, parked in the driveway. "We can take mine."

He glanced at the red sedan.

"I think the last time I ran *her* through the car wash was in 1990," she said, "when she was a week old."

The masculine sound of his laughter was a treat for the ears, and she wondered why he didn't share it more often. Maybe having lived most of his adult life in uniform was the reason for his serious, straight-backed attitude about things, from getting to places on time to speaking one's mind.

Alex made small talk on the way to the restaurant, commenting on how much Charm City had changed in the years he'd been away.

As they sat in the restaurant in Baltimore's Little Italy, awaiting an entrée called gnocchi, Alex told her about all the foreign lands he'd visited while in the navy.

Instead of the movie he'd promised after dinner, Alex drove to a small downtown theater to see what he called an "off-off-off Broadway-type play." The show was mesmerizing, the music memorable. Afterward, he insisted on stopping at Columbia's lakefront before taking her home. "I heard about this great ice-cream parlor," he said, "that looks like something from out of the fifties."

After eating only half of their hot fudge sundaes, they headed for the parking lot. Taylor hummed the theme song of the play.

"You have a beautiful voice," Alex said, draping an arm over her shoulders.

She shrugged. "I used to sing a little."

"Professionally?"

Taylor nodded.

"No kidding." He slowed his pace. "Where? Here in Baltimore?"

"No. I worked for an agency based in Chicago, and they booked me in hotel lounges all over the country." Laughing, she added, "You've heard of 'piano bar ladies'?"

"Uh-huh…"

"Well, I was the 'guitar lady.'"

"Do you still play?"

Another shrug. "No. Not really. Once in a while, I sing at a wedding, and I've done more funerals than I care to recall."

"That's too bad. Seems a waste to deprive the world of a sound like that."

Taylor was glad for the darkness that hid her blush. "I could say the same thing."

"No way! When I sing, birds go deaf. Children run crying to their mamas. Old men's hearing aids start to squeal." He laughed.

"*That's* the sound I'm talking about. You have such a wonderful, robust laugh, Alex." She looked up at him. "Seems a shame to deprive the world of a sound like that."

He helped her into the pickup truck. "So when did you quit singing?"

"Year and a half ago."

And standing in the open door, he asked "Why?"

"Long story."

Nodding, he closed the door, walked around the front of the truck to the driver's side. "We have thirty minutes," he said. "Long enough for a long story?"

She hadn't told anyone about that night in Puerto Rico, when she'd selfishly, coldly refused her mother's final phone call. He sat silent and stiff, staring straight ahead as she spelled it out, detail by ugly detail, and she prayed Alex wouldn't hate her when the horrible tale was told.

Just as she finished, he parked in front of her house, under the big tree that shaded the yard. As he walked around to open her door, Taylor braced herself for a carefully worded yet cool farewell.

He stood in the open door, hands extended, a crooked smile on his handsome face. "Is that offer of a glass of lemonade still open?"

Heart beating double time, Taylor stepped out of the truck and into his arms.

Barefoot and wearing short-sleeved pajamas, Taylor snuggled into her favorite chair and thought about their date last night. Sipping lemonade in the fading light, she nodded slowly. Alex hadn't been referring only to his mother's behavior that day in the church basement. Something told her his resentment went far into the past, cut a lot deeper than that. And, she believed, his serious nature had been born of that bitterness.

But what was its source?

She sighed, put the tall tumbler on a soapstone coaster beside her chair and leaned back, remembering how he'd insisted on buying her a hot fudge sundae on the way home, even though they'd both had a slice of cheesecake for dessert in the restaurant. As they'd sat at the wrought-iron bistro table on the deck of the ice-cream parlor, Alex had used his chin as a pointer. "None of this was here before I joined the navy. Wasn't here last time I came home, either."

"How long ago was that?"

Brows furrowed, he'd stared at the tabletop and absent-mindedly folded his paper napkin into the shape of an airplane. "Too long."

"I remember the uproar it caused," she'd said, hoping to wipe away his expression of regret, "when the county council proposed building this park. People said a man-made lake in the middle of town wouldn't work, that it'd be a waste of taxpayer dollars.''

He'd looked up suddenly and met her eyes. "Then they were fools." With a sweep of his arm, he'd said, "The county got fifty new taxpayers outta all the jobs the lake provided…restaurants, antique shops, boutiques…. Not to mention all the revenue pulled in by tourists.''

Alex had nodded approvingly. "Besides, it's gorgeous the way moonlight shines on the water. And those couples, floating around in paddleboats…" Wearing a lopsided grin, he'd added, "Wonder if they realize their silhouettes against the moon make 'em look like picture postcards?'' He'd seemed embarrassed about his little speech, and had immediately sat up straighter, squared his shoulders.

Taylor walked into the kitchen, put her lemonade glass into the dishwasher and smiled. Who would have thought that inside that solemn warrior type beat the heart of a poet?

Not so surprising, really, when she considered the way he'd held her, there under the big tree. Without saying a word, Alex had made it clear that nothing she'd ever done in the past made a bit of difference to him. With nothing more than a warm hug, he'd told her it was okay. That *she* was okay.

A man didn't become that caring, that understanding, without having learned things the hard way. Something told her that Alex had been on the receiving end of rejection, condemnation, anger more than once. He'd taught himself to forgive others, but had he learned to forgive himself? Taylor didn't think so.

As she headed upstairs, a question rang in her mind: What else lived in the heart of this man…things he didn't feel he could allow people to see? Climbing into bed, she gave her pillow a gentle punch and tucked it beneath her neck as Barney kneaded the empty pillow beside her.

If God answered her prayers this night, she'd have till morning to dream about the secrets that made up Alex Van Buren.

Alex sat at his kitchen table and stared at the palm of his right hand. If he hadn't known better, he'd have said Taylor had left her print there.

Unaware of his grin, he closed the hand, remembering how good it had felt when she'd unexpectedly slipped hers into it as they walked from the ice-cream parlor to his pickup. "You have an awful lot of calluses for a pilot," she'd said, a teasing grin lifting the corners of her mouth. "What do you do in your spare time...build airplanes?"

He'd laughed, given her hand a gentle squeeze. "I tend to whittle the time away. Literally."

She'd turned his hand over in hers, inspected the palm, tracing the lines and calluses. Then she'd looked up at him, the dim glow of overhead parking-lot lamps making her eyes seem more golden than greenish-brown.

Grinning, she'd winked. "Rodeo stuff, I'll bet. You seem like the cowboy type to me."

No one knew about his carvings, and if anyone had ever noticed the calluses the carvings had caused, they hadn't said so. Now Alex shifted slightly on the hard-backed chair, remembering how off balance he'd felt, standing there looking down into her pretty face, picturing the things he'd created from chunks of cherry, pine and oak. Because how had she known he chiseled horses and bucking broncs instead of elephants or buildings...or airplanes?

"Well," she'd said when he hadn't responded, "maybe sometime you'll show me your artwork—and I have a feeling your carvings are works of art, with lots of attention to detail."

Artwork? He'd known, of course, that it took a bit of

an artist's eye to fashion lifelike figures from wood, but he'd never thought of himself as an artist.

In the middle of the kitchen table sat one of his carvings. Alex glanced at the Brahma bull, head low and rear hooves midkick, its rider holding on for dear life.

He picked up the carving, turned it over in his hands. He'd knifed-in the minuscule hairs that made up the cowboy's handlebar mustache, scratched individual fibers into the rider's hemp rope, cut designs on his pointy-toed boots. There were more than two dozen carvings in all, every one a memory of his boyhood summers at the Wild Boar Ranch. In every one—though he planned to show no one what he'd done—Alex had paid a lot of attention to detail.

But how had Taylor known that?

He blew imaginary dust from the feather in the cowboy's braided hat band. Not exactly the best centerpiece in the world, Alex thought, putting the carving back onto the table.

On Taylor's kitchen table, he recalled, were four blue place mats. Beside each, a butter-yellow napkin bound by a satiny ribbon that exactly matched the place mats. The centerpiece? Two ceramic apples…one with tiny holes for pepper, one with bigger holes for salt.

The coziness didn't stop there. Apple-shaped canisters, colorful hand-painted clay pots overflowing with ivy, a big jug filled with soup ladles, wooden spoons and spatulas stood on the gleaming countertops. Something told him those articles hadn't been put haphazardly here and there. He could almost picture her, standing in the doorway, fingertip tapping her chin as she assessed the proper balance for the placement of each knickknack.

Same was true throughout the rest of the house. Every table and wall bespoke the thoughtful effort she'd put into turning what had once been a cold, clinical builder's space into a place any man would love to come home to.

Warm earth tones in the carpeting and draperies were the backdrop for the bright, natural colors of throw rugs and toss pillows. Despite what he'd expected to find the day he'd rescued Barney, she didn't go in for a lot of ruffles and lace, either—another point in her favor—and the proof was everywhere in her house.

When he'd gone into her bedroom to fix the screen that Barney had removed, he couldn't escape her womanly touches. A sensible beige rug covered most of the gleaming hardwood floor. A sleigh bed that looked to Alex like a bona fide antique dominated the center space. The comforter, deep green. And leaning on the headboard, a dozen or more pillows of maroon and cream and navy. Old but elegant tables and dressers stood against the walls, and above them, tasteful landscapes and seascapes in big dark frames. If he had to find a word for it, Alex would have to say "classy."

Alex thought of his own bedroom and frowned. Bare white walls, a wall-to-wall carpet that was somewhere between tan and brown, a bed with no headboard, and a black-and-white-striped bedspread that, like the pillows and sheets, had seen better days.

The rest of his house pretty much echoed the bedroom. Oh, he'd accumulated the necessary furnishings…a couch, easy chair and tables for the living room, a battered but functional dining-room suite, his grandma's old kitchen set…. Suddenly he understood why the place felt cold and stark—it bore none of the contemplative, careful touches that turned a house into a home.

Maybe you should hire Taylor, he mused, *to spruce the place up.*

Maybe he should *marry* Taylor was his afterthought, because if she worked magic like that in a house where she lived alone, how much more might she be capable of if she was doing it all for the man she—

Knock it off, Van Buren. You're skatin' on thin ice here....

Such thoughts were nonsense, and he knew it. What business did he have, feeling this way?

Scowling, Alex shoved back from the table and got to his feet. On top of everything else about his life that didn't seem to be going according to plan, his leg ached more than usual. The doctors had pooh-poohed it, but Alex didn't care—the dull throbbing told him there was one dynamite storm brewing. *Just what I need,* he grumbled, climbing the stairs, *twigs and branches and leaves to clean up in the yard tomorrow.*

The yard. Another place where Taylor had worked her homemaking magic. Bright flowers lined the drive and the walk. Several plants bloomed in clay pots, carefully positioned on the edge of each front step. Still more blossoms hung from baskets attached to the porch ceiling.

There wasn't a weed in the flower beds that hugged the house's foundation. But then, Alex thought, grinning, if he'd been a weed, he would have been afraid to show his head, too, for fear Taylor's nimble fingers would snap him up in a heartbeat.

Actually, he could think of worse fates than being snapped up by Taylor Griffith. *Lots* worse.

The admission raised a question. Why in the world hadn't she married? She sure seemed to be every man's dream. *This* man's dream, anyway, he added, his grin turning into a smile as he limped into his room.

Then again, what did he know? Maybe when nobody was looking, she was a chain-smoker. Or taught pet-store parrots to curse. Maybe she'd been married and—

The very idea made his heart pound with jealousy, because the picture of her in another man's arms wasn't pretty. Not pretty at all.

If there *had* been a man in her past, who was he…and why had she given him his walking papers?

Or had the guy dumped Taylor?

Nah, Alex decided. What man in his right mind would let her go, once he got hold of her? Certainly not *this* man.

Ridiculous, he told himself. Because he didn't know a thing about her. What was her favorite color? Had she seen the movie everyone was talking about? Was she a teacher? A short-order cook? A private eye?

Funny how they'd spent the entire evening talking quietly about everything under the sun, yet he knew little to nothing about her.

He knew her mother's death had cut her, deeply. And he knew she held herself accountable for those last minutes, seconds that might have made a difference, in her life *and* her mother's.

After her heartfelt confession, Taylor had melted against him like honey on a hot biscuit. Words would have been meaningless at a time like that. So he'd offered the hug as his clumsy way of saying, "You're only human, kid. What's done is done, and besides, it wasn't your fault." But it seemed she took it to mean he'd forgiven her her so-called sins. As if he mattered enough to have the power to forgive her!

That he mattered enough…

He climbed into bed and knuckled both eyes. If he knew what was good for him, he'd close the window, save himself a trip later, when the weather turned ugly. The storm was close now—he could tell because his leg ached more than ever. That, and the scent of distant rain hung heavy in the humid air.

Alex wondered if Taylor had locked up tight, as he'd told her to when he left. If he knew what was good for him, he would have picked up the telephone an hour ago; it would have been as good an excuse as any to have another chance to hear that beautiful, musical voice again. Besides, knowing him, he'd lie awake another hour wondering if she was safe, anyway.

But he didn't know what was good for him. And if the truth be told, he'd never known. Wasn't his miserable life proof of that?

He closed his eyes, got a clear picture of Taylor, hair surrounding her gorgeous face like a cinnamon halo, pink skirt skimming her shapely knees. Eyes as big as Bambi's, and a smile that could stop a clock. Rolling onto his side, he exhaled heavily.

Maybe he didn't know what was good for him. Maybe he'd never known.

Maybe it wasn't too late to learn....

A clap of thunder shook the house, waking Taylor with a start.

She could barely move, thanks to the crick in her neck and the pins and needles in both legs. Barney, on the other hand, seemed perfectly comfortable, snoozing on her lap.

She'd gotten up earlier to close her bedroom window when the wind started whistling through the screen, sending the curtains flying and blowing the pages of her magazine open then closed and open again. Unable to sleep, she'd changed into sweatpants and T-shirt and gone downstairs, thinking that maybe a cup of herbal tea and a good book would ease her back into drowsiness.

It had...and she'd been sound asleep in her recliner ever since. Wincing, she stretched to work the kinks from her neck and back. How long had she been asleep? Taylor wondered. She'd come down shortly after midnight. If her aches and pains were any indicator, she thought, it ought to be dawn soon!

Gently she nudged the cat. "Sorry, Barn. You're going to have to move."

Exhaling heavily, he jumped to the floor and was promptly swallowed up by the darkness.

Taylor snapped the light switch.

Nothing.

That last crack of lightning must have hit the transformer down the street. She headed for the kitchen, where she kept the flashlight and batteries. It didn't usually take the electric company long to repair power outages, but Taylor's mother had taught her to play it safe. In addition to oil lanterns and candles, she always made sure to keep a water-filled plastic container on each shelf of the freezer. There was plenty of canned food in the pantry and a hand-crank can opener in the drawer beside the sink. She could go three, maybe four days without electricity and not suffer anything more serious than living without air conditioning in Baltimore's typically thick-as-soup summer humidity.

Another thunderbolt crashed, sending shivers up her back. After flicking on the flashlight, she rummaged in a high cabinet and pulled out an oil lantern.

As she lit it, a gust buffeted the window over the kitchen sink. The lit match doused itself when it landed in the drain. "Don't be such a baby," she whispered, hands over her hammering heart. "It's just the wind."

Taylor remembered the last thing Alex had said before leaving her at the front door. "Lock up tight now, y'hear?"

"What," she'd teased, "you afraid the bogeyman is gonna get me?"

"Never hurts to take an extra measure of precaution."

It was one of her uncle's favorite sayings. Just what she needed, *two* men fretting over her.

Still…it never hurt to be sure….

Taylor carried the lantern through the house, checking every window and door lock, wondering as she did if Alex had locked his own doors and windows. Something told her he had. A guy as solemn and stoic as Alex probably had batteries and flashlights in every drawer...and a generator and gallons of gasoline to power it, as well.

That isn't fair, she told herself. He'd cracked his share of jokes. And hadn't he held up his end of their conversation at the ice-cream parlor?

In the short time she'd known him, Taylor found Alex to be warm...in a distant kind of way. He seemed genuinely interested in hearing about Ellicott City, then and now, but didn't seem at all interested in sharing any details about himself.

In that way he reminded her of Kent, her ex-fiancé.

Accent on the ex, *and thank the good Lord for that!*

Years ago, she and Kent Carnahan had made the finals in a statewide talent contest. She'd entered, along with several other members of the Resurrection choir, mostly for fun. Never in a million years had Taylor expected to win the Best Female Vocalist category.

Kent had earned the Best Male Singer award, and that was how they'd met. The pair spent a lot of time together afterward, competing first in the regionals, then the nationals. Right from the start, Kent had been gung ho to win the top prize: representation by a major U.S. talent agency.

Kent expected to come in first, but until her own win, Taylor had never seriously considered a career as a professional musician, mostly because her work as a physical therapist had always been so fulfilling, but also because she'd never felt drawn to the spotlight.

At least, not in the same way Kent had been. He saw himself as a headliner, singing songs that topped every chart. Taylor, on the other hand, only wanted to save enough money so that she could buy her mother a little shop on Ellicott City's historic Main Street. Amanda had long dreamed of opening a tearoom, where she could serve her fresh-baked crumpets with jellies made from old family recipes. Amanda was a mere ten thousand dollars from reaching her goal when her boyfriend's car crashed....

Taylor tried to shake off the painful memory.

But it was no use. It had been storming in Ellicott City the night of the accident, too. Until that night, she'd never been much bothered by lightning and thunder. Ever since, the very sight of dark clouds made her want to head home, where she could retreat from the world.

Her agitated pacing seemed to intrigue Barney, who walked beside her back and forth across the kitchen tiles. Elbows cupped in her palms, she began to recite the twenty-third Psalm. "The Lord is my shepherd, I shall not want...."

But not even her trusty Bible verse blocked the unrelenting wind and pelting raindrops that rattled the windowpanes. "He maketh me to lie down in green pastures, He leadeth me beside the still waters...."

Thunder rolled slowly, slowly nearer, punctuated by a bolt of lightning that sliced the black curtain of night, brightening the kitchen with a flash of silvery light.

Taylor lurched with fright and pressed her fingertips to her lips in attempt to stifle a scream. "Big baby," she mumbled. "'Fraid of storms and heights and—"

Loud, determined pounding blasted into her thoughts.

There was someone at her door!

She'd put her watch on top of the microwave earlier, and scrabbled for it now. Leaning closer to the lantern's light, she read the round, pearlescent face—3:22. At this hour, it could only be bad news. Hopefully, Uncle Dave would be the bearer, rather than the subject of it.

Taylor raced toward the foyer, bare feet slap-slapping across the hardwood floor connecting the hallway outside the kitchen to the front door. One hand on the doorknob, she used the other to steady herself as she stood on tiptoe to peer through the peephole.

But the electricity was out. Without the porch light, it was too dark to see who it might be.

Biting her lower lip, Taylor took a deep breath and prayed that the good Lord would see fit to keep her calm, rational…. "Uncle Dave?"

"No…it's me, Alex."

Taylor hung the long corded handle of the flashlight around her neck and carefully set the oil lantern on the foyer table. She slid open the chain lock and unbolted the door….

And there stood Alex, looking as if he'd just climbed out of a swimming pool. Rain poured from his hair and clothes, dripping steadily into the puddle between his feet. "Miss Rosie's posies, what're you doing here at this hour?"

Hunching his shoulders, he squeegeed a hand over his sopping face. "Tried to call you, see if you were okay, but your phone's out of order."

"My phone's not working? I know the power's out, but I had no idea the—"

"Um, Taylor…?"

She met his eyes, read the expression to mean he'd like to come inside. "Goodness! Where are my manners?" She opened the door wider. Closing it as he stepped inside, Taylor shook her head. "How long have you been standing out there?

Another shrug, then, "Ten, fifteen minutes, maybe."

"Why didn't you ring the doorb—"

He nodded. "Power's out," they said together.

Was he trembling? Taylor wondered, giving him a once-over. "Good grief, Alex. You're soaked to the skin. What were you thinking, coming out on a night like this?"

He gave a weak little smile and sniffed. "I couldn't sleep. Thought about you over here all alone. Tried to call, see if everything was okay.'' One shoulder rose in half-hearted shrug. ''But...''

''Yes, I know,'' she said, crossing both arms over her chest. ''My phone's out of order.''

''So I thought I'd just drive on over, check things out. Make sure you were all right.''

Taylor's heart swelled with warmth and affection. Not even her worrywart uncle had ever done anything like *this* for her! If she knew Alex better, if it wasn't the middle of the night, if he wasn't soaking wet, she might just throw her arms around him and plant a kiss of gratitude on his cheek.

Speaking of soaking wet, Alex was shivering. And in hot, humid weather like this, it wasn't a good sign. The flashlight beam bobbed to and fro on the foyer floor as she ran around behind him, trying to rub warmth back into his upper arms and back. But it was no use. Not as long as he stood there dripping like a faucet. ''You've gone and caught yourself a chill,'' she scolded gently.

He seemed far more concerned about the puddle he was making on the Oriental rug beneath his feet. ''Sorry about the mess,'' he said.

She waved his apology away. On her way to the powder room down the hall, she told him, ''Don't even give it another thought. It's only water,'' she added, her voice echoing in the tiled space.

When she returned to the foyer, Taylor draped a thick white towel over his shoulders, reached up and hooded his head with another. ''Come into the kitchen with me,'' she said, massaging his hands as they went. The minute they got there, she plunked the flashlight on the table, then ran into the foyer to fetch the oil lantern.

''Sit right here and towel off,'' she instructed, placing the lamp beside the flashlight. ''I'm going to see if I can find you some dry clothes to change into.''

On her way out, Taylor grabbed the flashlight, then turned on the gas flame under the teapot. "And once you're warm and dry, I'll fix you a cup of hot tea."

"Yeah," he said, chuckling between tremors, "fat chance there's anything around here a big lummox like me will fit into."

Hands on her hips, she tilted her head. "It just so happens I have a few things around here that might fit. In fact—" she grinned "—they might be a little big for you."

Alex's grin dimmed as he remembered wondering whether or not she'd ever been married. Maybe the clothes she was going to fetch had been her husband's. An old boyfriend's. A fiancé's. No way he'd wear anything belonging to that—

"It's only a sweat suit," she said, interrupting his thoughts. "Belonged to my father. He used to read the entire Sunday paper wearing this." Taylor shrugged daintily. "I didn't say much when my mom got rid of his other things, but for some reason, I could never part with it."

She didn't wait for a reply. Instead, Taylor darted from the room. It seemed to him she did everything at high speed. She was energy personified. But he wasn't complaining. Her vim and vigor were but a couple of the things he liked about her.

And he liked a whole lot of things about her.

Like the way she'd held on to her dad's sweat suit, for example. Most folks would cling to a diamond tie clip, or a pricey stamp collection that had been squirreled away in a safe-deposit box. Not Taylor! The sweat suit had given her father a certain amount of physical comfort, and she took emotional comfort from the memory of that.

And what about the way she tilted her head, pursed her lips and squinted slightly when someone else was talking, so they'd know she was giving them her full attention. And the way her whole face got involved when she smiled...big, sparkling eyes twinkling, gorgeous lips turned up at the corners.

He heard adorable bare feet thumping down the carpeted stairs, felt his heartbeat quicken in reaction to knowing that, any second now, she'd burst into the room, smiling, flashlight bobbing and eyes gleaming, carrying the musty old sweat suit that had belonged to her father.

Was she...was she *humming?* Not exactly the reaction a guy would expect when he came pounding on a gal's door in the dead of a dark and stormy night. Especially not when his clothes had dribbled and drooled all over her rugs like some sort of swamp thing.

"Here you go," she said, pressing the sweat suit into his hands. "It isn't fancy, but it's sure to beat what you're wearing!" She plopped a pair of white socks on top of the outfit, and grinned.

Alex couldn't help but grin back. "You saved his socks, too?"

"Actually, they're mine." She held up a hand, like a traffic cop, to fend off any protest he might make. "Tube socks. One size fits all, you know?"

Standing, Alex carried the clothes at arm's length to keep them dry. "Okay to change in the powder room?"

Taylor's giggle echoed around the room. "No. It isn't okay. It's so small, you'd end up with bruised elbows and knees to add to your list of complaints."

"Complaints? I don't remember making any complai—"

Another giggle floated around him.

"Make that 'symptoms,' then." She pointed toward the stairway. "You can change in the guest room. Top of the steps, first door on your right."

Suddenly she held one finger aloft. Just as quickly, she'd turned and opened a cabinet door. "Here," Taylor said, pulling a white trash bag from its dispenser, "put your wet things in here, and when you come down, I'll toss them in the dryer."

She laughed then. "Not much point in that, since it's powered by—"

"Electricity," he finished, grinning.

Laying the trash bag and the flashlight on top of the folded clothing, she gave him a playful shove. "There'll be a nice hot cup of tea waiting for you when you get back. The stove, fortunately, is gas."

She'd said it in a singsongy way, as if he needed the added enticement to hurry back. Well, *tea* was not the reason he was looking forward to getting changed. Getting dry wasn't the reason, either.

"Honey and lemon?" she asked as he stepped into the foyer.

"Surprise me," he said, one foot on the bottom step.

She crossed her arms over her chest. "Well?"

"Well what?"

Laughing, Taylor said, "Well, what're you waiting for? You're not getting dry standing there!"

For a reason he couldn't explain, Alex turned and headed for the stairs. He'd never been one to cooperate when told what to do. His mom, Rusty, even his teachers sometimes had had trouble making him toe the line. If they gave an order, he had to know *why* before following it. It was rare that he acted without argument...unless the one issuing commands had more stripes on his shoulders than Alex....

So why had he so quickly and easily done what Taylor told him to do? he wondered, climbing to the second floor.

The question pinged in his head as he walked into the guest room. Laying the flashlight at the foot of the bed, he glanced around the room and began peeling off his sticky, sodden clothes and stuffing them into the plastic trash bag. Only thing Alex could figure was that he didn't mind taking orders from Taylor because it really didn't seem as if she'd been giving orders.

The sweat suit, surprisingly, didn't smell musty at all. Lifting his newly sleeved arm to his nose, Alex recognized the faint scent of fabric softener sheets. He didn't know much about Taylor, but he wouldn't put it past her to pull the sweat suit out now and then and pop it in the washer, just for good measure.

He sat on the edge of the bed to put on the socks. Even in the semidark room, they looked white enough to be featured in a detergent commercial on TV. Right ankle resting on left knee, he flapped the first one and pulled it over his toes.

When he tugged the second sock into place, the mattress shifted slightly, sending the flashlight rolling onto the carpeted floor...and under the bed.

Down on one knee, he patted the rug, feeling for the flashlight's cord. Barney decided to join him at that precise moment. The cat's sudden "Meow!" startled Alex so badly that he lost his balance, rolling onto his side and cracking his head on the iron wheel cover of the old dresser.

Rubbing his temple, Alex growled through clenched teeth, which startled Barney, who cut loose with a blood-curdling yowl.

Alex's reaction was yet another surprised lurch, and *that* made him pull a muscle in his bad leg.

He heard Taylor's tiny feet padding up the stairs. "Alex? Alex," she called, "are you all right?"

The concern in her voice—well, he could have measured it with a scale. "I'm fine," he wanted to say. But he couldn't say it, because he wasn't okay. Dizziness, along with the ache in his leg, made the words stick in his throat.

She knelt beside him, laid a hand on his shoulder. "What happe—"

He knew what had silenced her so suddenly. When he'd touched his temple, his fingertips had come away sticky and damp. Add blood to the sight of him sprawled on the floor, and it was no wonder she'd gone all quiet on him.

She bent lower to get closer to his face. He wanted to get up off the floor, tell her he'd be right as rain. But the room was spinning and her words sounded gurgled, and he knew if he opened his mouth, he'd have a hard time disguising his discomfort.

He'd come over here to see that she was all right. Last thing Alex wanted was to get her looking all worried and distressed.

Like butterfly wings, her hands fluttered around his face. "Alex, you're bleeding," she whispered.

She leaned over him, followed the flashlight's beam and found it under the bed skirt. After she aimed it at his forehead, a quiet gasp escaped her lips. "Lie still now," she said, starting to get up, "while I—"

He tried again to sit up. Another wave of dizziness overtook him as he grabbed her wrists. He'd done it to steady himself, but she mistook the meaning. And the proof came in what she said next.

"I'll only be across the hall," she told him, her voice soft and soothing beside his ear, "to get a damp washcloth. We need to find out how deep that cut is, and I can't do that until I clean up some of the—"

He wanted to hug her when she bit her lower lip, because he knew she'd done it to keep from saying *blood*. If she'd seen the condition he'd been in when they'd pulled him out of the Caribbean, she wouldn't give this little scratch a second thought.

Before he knew it, she was pressing a soft, cool cloth to his temple. How she'd gone across the hall, come back and managed to get him partway onto her lap, Alex didn't understand. But there he was—bloody head, wet hair and all—eating up her cuddling, her fussing, the way a baby chows down pablum.

"You'll be fine," she was saying, "once we get a bandage on this thing."

Why did her voice sound so far away? Why did it seem as if she was speaking into a hollow metal tube? He hadn't hit his head that hard, had he? Alex tried to read her expression, but the way she'd positioned him, everything "Taylor" was ripply and upside down.

"You'll be fine, Alex, just fine," she said again.

Head reeling, he nodded. Course he'd be fine, he thought, grinning, 'cause he was with the girl of his dreams!

"Relax, Alex, relax...."

Relax? *Strange,* Alex told himself, *I don't feel the least bit tense....*

And despite the lightning and thunder raging outside, he went completely limp in her arms.

Chapter Five

"Alex," Taylor said, doing her best to keep her voice from shaking. When he didn't respond, she said it again. "Alex?"

Gently she eased his head to the floor. And grabbing a pillow from the guest-room bed, she lifted him again, slid the pillow under his neck. Legs tucked beneath her, she knelt beside him and sandwiched his big hand between her own.

CPR was a requirement in her line of work. Pressing her fingers lightly against his carotid artery, she closed her eyes. His breathing and pulse seemed normal, and she sighed with relief. If he came to within the next few minutes, he'd probably suffer nothing more than a headache. If he remained unconscious much longer than that...

Taylor held her breath and prayed. "Dear Lord, let him be all right."

Alex gave a weak little smile, as if he'd heard her and, even in this condition, wanted to reassure her. The expression so touched her that Taylor's eyes filled with tears. She pressed her palm against a whisker-stubbled cheek. *Oh, Alex,* she thought, *please be all right.*

Even if he woke in that instant, Alex would need X rays, because there was no telling how much damage the fall had caused. But how would she get him to the hospital? With her phone out of order, she couldn't call an ambulance; tall and muscular as he was, she'd only injure him more if she tried to get him downstairs without help.

The milliseconds ticked by as she tried to decide what to do....

"Wake up, Alex," she said in as sure a voice as she could muster. "Come on. Time to wake up."

He looked so peaceful lying there, like an innocent boy who'd drifted off to sleep after hearing his favorite bedtime story. Gone were the lines around his mouth and eyes, put there by the cares of his world. It seemed almost a shame to rouse him.

If only she had the power to "fix" his world, so that his handsome face could always look this unconcerned.

If only she knew how to turn back the clock, erase every event, every secret that made him hold the world at arm's length, secrets that lined his handsome brow with furrows and dimmed the glow of his brown eyes. It wasn't until a tear slid down her cheek that Taylor realized how very much this man had come to mean to her.

If only she hadn't started falling for him...

Started...or already over the edge?

Wiping her eyes with the backs of her hands, Taylor sniffed and sat up straighter. She had to *do* something, anything, to bring him around. A cool compress might do the trick. But...should she leave him alone long enough to fetch one?

Like a bullet shot from a gun, Taylor raced across the hall, grabbed another washcloth from the linen closet, soaked it with water from the bathroom tap. For good measure, she wet a second, to drape across his forehead when the first warmed from his body heat.

She was beside him again in less than a minute. "Hey, there," she said, "now doesn't that feel good? Nice and cool and soothing…"

He stirred, and she thought maybe he was waking up. "You're going to have quite a goose egg on the side of your head, and won't that look great with all your Barney claw marks?"

His eyelids fluttered and he turned his head toward her, making the bloody cut on his temple more noticeable than ever. Gingerly, Taylor daubed at it with the corner of one of the washcloths, and Alex winced. She took it as a good sign, and continued to clean the wound.

"Alex, if you don't open those eyes of yours pretty soon, I'm going to get the alcohol out…dab a little on that cut. Remember how it stung when I cleaned up the cat scratches?" She forced a phony giggle. "If that doesn't revive you, I don't know what will!"

After the breakup with Kent, she'd vowed never to let herself get too involved too fast. At least, not as fast as she'd gone boots over bonnet for Kent. To her own credit, there had been half a dozen or so young men who'd tried to woo her since the breakup, but she'd managed to keep them at bay without injuring any male egos.

A good thing, too, because if she had let one of them close, and come to care about him, it would likely have destroyed her. Because Taylor had learned something about herself after the split with Kent—she was terrible at dealing with loss. The way she'd moped around after her father's fatal heart attack, the despair she'd felt when Kent left, the months of melancholy she'd sunken into when her mother died…

When she realized it was Alex who'd come knocking at three in the morning, her heart had done a joyous leap.

And when he'd confessed that he'd come clear across town on such dreadful, dangerous night just to make sure she was safe and sound, well, Taylor's already pounding heart had all but leapt from her chest.

Seeing him here now, helpless and needy, awakened every loving, womanly instinct in her. No doubt about it, she was falling for Alex, hard and fast. A scary thought, since she didn't think she had the strength of character to survive another loss.

Maybe he wouldn't leave you, was the hopeful thought that pinged in her mind.

He took a deep breath when she replaced one cloth with the another. "Feels good, doesn't it?" she said, tenderly brushing wisps of brown hair from his forehead.

But then, what reason did Alex have to stay? Like her mother's race-car boyfriend, he'd lived a fast-lane kind of life. If it hadn't been for his aircraft's crash, he'd probably still be testing his limits, risking life and limb, gambling with his life.

Something occurred to her just then.

Was Alex's sad, stolid demeanor the result of not being able to cope with his new, slow-paced lifestyle? If so, it would tell her a lot about him. One thing it would underscore was that if it were within his power, he'd continue testing his limits, risking life and limb, gambling with his life. Limited slightly by his injuries, he'd just need to find other ways to do it.

Well, Taylor thought, turning the cloth over, smoothing it softly across his brow, when Alex was ready to move on—and surely he would be, all too soon—he'd have one less farewell to bid.

Because Taylor had no intention of being close enough to need a goodbye when that time came.

Just then, his hand rose slightly and his eyelids began

to flutter. A soft groan issued from him, and as he attempted to sit up, pain made him cringe.

He flopped back against the pillow. "Taaaay..." was all he could manage.

Taylor knew that Alex was calling her name, and her traitorous heart responded in exactly the way it shouldn't. "I'm here, Alex," she said, leaning closer, one hand on his shoulder, the other combing through his hair. "I'm right here." So great was her relief at seeing him conscious, Taylor wanted to hug him, dot his beautiful face with kisses, laugh and tease him for having taken a nap on her guest-room floor.

It was no comfort to her that she managed to resist the urge. The fact that she'd wanted to do those things told her it wasn't going to be easy, when this storm was over, putting distance between them.

Eyes open now, he met her gaze. In the dim glow of the flashlight beam she could see that he was smiling. Not a smile of recognition, but a smile that looked for all the world like a *loving* smile.

Stop it, she told herself. *Stop it right now!* It wasn't fair to him or her to be hoping for something that could never be. Especially not now, when what he needed was her help, not her schoolgirl-type hopes.

Alex was just thankful not to be alone right now, she told herself. What she'd seen in his eyes, on his face, hadn't been love at all, but rather, simple gratitude.

"Clunked my head on that dresser wheel," he said, squinting one eye. "You wouldn't have any aspirin, would you?"

"Yeah," she said, praying he hadn't heard the relieved tremor in her voice, "but don't you think it'd be better to let a doctor decide what medication you need?"

He frowned, and his voice turned suddenly surly. "Doctor? I bumped my head. I don't need a doctor."

"Alex, be reasonable. You hit your head hard enough to knock you out cold. We have to get you X-rayed and—"

"No way. I'm not going to any hospital."

"But Alex, you might have a concussion. The hospital's only a precaution, to make sure—"

He levered himself up on one elbow. "Listen...I've had more concussions than you have fingers. All a doctor will say is 'Take it easy. Here're two aspirins. Call me in the morning.'"

Sitting up, he made a feeble attempt at smiling, as if in silent apology for his temper flare. "Well, it's past midnight, so technically, it's morning," he said. "So I repeat...got any aspirins?"

She couldn't very well force him to go to the hospital. For one thing, to get him there she'd need his cooperation. For another, he wasn't a little boy, even though in her estimation he was behaving like one at the moment.

"All right, then," Taylor said, her own forefinger touching the tip of his, "have it your way. But for the record, I think you should see someone."

He curled his finger around hers. The eye contact was intense when he said in a gruff, quiet voice, "For the record, your advice has been heard and duly noted. And I *am* seeing someone. Someone very pretty..."

Then slowly Alex got to his feet. "Now," he added as he teetered in the doorway, "where d'you keep the aspirins?"

He'd passed out before, and knew the signs of a concussion only too well.

As a kid, he'd climbed the next-door neighbor's tree to rescue a cat. Turned out the cat knew exactly how to get down. Alex, on the other hand, discovered that without four sets of claws, straight down and headfirst could be mighty painful.

Yep, the symptoms were there. Like the first time, a cat had been responsible and, like the first time, he'd been powerless to prevent it. Alex found himself wishing God had created his skull from steel rather than bone. Then again, metal impacting metal might have done even more damage to his brain than the wheel of that old dresser had.

Which is precisely what he'd been thinking when Taylor had come into the room to see what the noise was all about. She'd looked so upset that Alex wanted to put his arms around her, tell her not to worry, that he had a head harder than a boulder, and in a few minutes he'd be walking the straight and narrow again. He would have said just about anything to wipe that worried frown from her pretty face.

But, true to its nature, the injury rendered him weak and inept, unable to make his limbs or his tongue work.

On the other hand, being momentarily helpless had its perks. Having her warm arms wrapped around him, listening to her angelic voice, feeling her smooth hands on his face wasn't at all unpleasant. Chuckling, he had to admit, not the least bit unpleasant!

He didn't know how long he'd been out. Not long, he supposed, just long enough for Taylor to get a pillow stuffed under his head. *Now, why'd she go and do that?* he complained silently, because it had been so much nicer with his head resting in her lap.

He'd managed to get one eye open, just a crack, but what he'd seen had made him close it again—a tear, glistening silver-white in the flashlight's beam, sliding down Taylor's cheek. He'd found it hard to believe she was crying *for him.* But what else would have put tears in those gorgeous eyes?

Talk about inept! Alex had no idea how to console her. Because no matter what the reason for her tears, he was doomed. If she cried out of concern for him, it meant Taylor cared for him—perhaps a good deal—and that sure wasn't a good thing, not for either of them.

But wait. *Why* was it a bad thing if she cared that much, this soon? He lifted his hand, prepared to wave the question away. It was ridiculous even entertaining the notion that a woman like Taylor would be interested in him...a has-been cowardly pilot with a bad leg and a brooding attitude.

Taylor, he wanted to say, *you deserve better than the likes of me. Get a move on while the gettin's good!*

Weather forecasters never saw it coming. They had predicted that a severe thunderstorm would strike the Baltimore-Washington, D.C., area midweek. It hit on the weekend, instead, sneaking unexpectedly up from the south, causing chaos and havoc in its wake.

Somewhere out in the Atlantic, a hurricane swirled menacingly, pounding the islands and sending inhabitants to high ground. Closer to home, coastal residents from South Carolina to New Jersey busily sandbagged and boarded windows. Even a hundred miles inland, gale force winds and biting rains drove folks inside, where they prayed their roofs would stay on and their basements would stay dry.

Electricity was out everywhere in Taylor's neighborhood, as it was in most every Baltimore county. Phone service had pretty much been disconnected. Listening to the crackle of her battery-powered radio, Alex and Taylor learned that despite the fact that most stores had stayed open later than usual people were fighting over the quickly dwindling supply of water, ice and batteries.

If there was a storm to fear, it was this one.

Yet Taylor, who usually cringed at the mere sight of a gray cloud, sat calmly in the family room, curled up in her easy chair with Barney in her lap. It was hot without air-conditioning, but at least they were safe.

And together, Taylor added, stroking Barney's golden fur.

Alex had wanted to go home the minute she got the bleeding on his temple stopped. But Taylor had insisted that he wait, until daylight at least, before he attempted driving. Even if the weather hadn't been so wretched, he'd have been an accident waiting to happen, dizzy as he'd been. His feeble protests that he could handle the pickup blindfolded had been answered with one well-timed question. "Then what about all the other people on the road?"

He'd settled down after that, and good-naturedly accepted his fate. Alex seemed to feel that since he was stranded at Taylor's house, he might as well make the best of things. And so he sprawled out on the family-room couch, the foot of his bad leg propped on a well-placed pillow on the coffee table while he doodled on a steno pad she'd dug out of a kitchen drawer.

Now and then, he'd doze. But Taylor had learned in her CPR class that a concussion victim had to be awakened frequently. If, upon examination, the pupils were unequal in size, or refused to dilate, it spelled trouble of the brain-injury type. She explained it to him the first time she roused him from a nap. After that, Alex didn't seem to mind that every sixty minutes or so she'd shake him awake to check his eyes in the flashlight's beam.

But then again, he'd agreed to her deal without so much as a word of complaint, too. There'd be no trip to the hospital...unless her hourly checks showed her signs that his condition was worsening. He'd smiled in such a way that, if she didn't know better, Taylor would have said Alex enjoyed being looked after this way.

But she did know better, of course. Because hadn't he

said, right out, that he hated being the cause of all this fuss and bother?

"Look at it this way," she'd told him. "You're giving me something constructive to do till the power comes back on."

And now, remembering the look of surprise on his face when she'd told the joke made Taylor laugh to herself.

"What's so funny?" he wanted to know.

She glanced over at him. "I thought you were sleeping."

Grinning, he linked his fingers under his head. "I was. But how d'you expect a guy to sleep with all this giggling going on?"

She tucked in one corner of her mouth and prepared to tell him the only way he could have heard her one burst of quiet laughter was if he'd already been awake.

"*Now* what's so funny?" he asked before she had a chance to say it.

"Just remembering an old joke is all." She couldn't very well tell him *he'd* been the reason she'd been laughing, now, could she?

"So...?"

Placing Barney on the floor, Taylor turned on the sofa, tucked her feet beneath her and faced him. "So what?"

"So...let's hear this joke." Gingerly he rubbed his temple. "I could use a good laugh right about now."

Now she understood why her mother had always said that even white lies could get a person in trouble; Taylor had to come up with a joke, and fast.

"Knock knock," she said.

"Who's there?"

"Banana."

"Banana who?"

"Banana."

Alex shook his head. "Banana who?"

"Banana."

He inhaled. *"Banana who?"*

"Orange."

"Orange?" He rolled his eyes. "All right, I'll play along…. Orange who?"

"Orange you glad I didn't say banana again?"

Sitting up, Alex leaned forward, elbows on his knees. "You were laughing out loud…at *that?*"

Well, what did he expect on a moment's notice? she asked herself.

"All I can say is, if you think that was funny…" Alex gave her a look that said, *Then I feel real sorry for you.*

"Oh." She crossed both arms over her chest. "And I suppose you can tell a better one?"

His matter-of-fact expression was followed by a non-chalant shrug. "I could do better if I was still unconscious."

Tapping one bare foot on the floor, Taylor grinned and held out her arms. "Okay, funny guy. I'm all ears. Make me laugh."

He gave her a long, penetrating stare. "Could save us both a lot of time if I just had me a feather."

"A feather? What on earth—"

Wiggling his fingers and eyebrows simultaneously, he stood and moved slowly toward her. "Tickle, tickle…"

Taylor grabbed a throw pillow, used it as a shield. "Don't even think about it, mister. I've never liked being tickled."

Two more steps, and he'd be directly in front of her. "Not even as a kid?"

She shook her head. "Not even as a kid."

He perched on the arm of the sofa nearest her chair. "Party pooper."

Maybe that bump on the head had dislodged something old and forgotten in his brain, because of all the words she'd used to describe him till now, *playful* hadn't been one of them.

She'd heard it said that the way to a man's heart was through his stomach. Maybe she could reach "reasonableness" by the same route. "I'm getting hungry. How 'bout I scramble us some eggs and—"

"But there's no power."

"I have a gas stove, remember? And if I can recall what I did with that old stove-top percolator, I can even brew us up a pot of coffee."

She didn't know which had been the magic word...*eggs, stove,* or *coffee.* Taylor only knew that Alex sat back down in a hurry, smiling a goofy grin.

And then she realized he looked a little pale, that he was weaving and bobbing slightly, like a boxer who'd just taken a hard right cross to the jaw.

"Alex," she said, on her knees in front of him, "Alex, look at me."

The smile slanted a bit. "Glad to, cutie," he said, slurring the words a little.

Cutie? She ignored his silly expression, tried to concentrate instead on his condition. When she'd checked the phone not half an hour ago, it was still dead. She could kick herself for not buying a cell phone, as her uncle had advised. If she had one now, she could use it to call for an ambulance. She and Alex may as well have been stranded on a deserted island in the middle of the ocean for all the help she was to him now.

Taylor had to talk him into letting her drive him to the hospital. Sandwiching his hands between her own, she said, "How 'bout letting me buy you breakfast? Maybe the Double T Diner is open...."

He chuckled. "Yeah. Right." Thumb over his shoulder, he indicated the storm, still raging outside. "In this mess? *Now* who's the dizzy one?"

Taylor got to her feet, propped both fists on her hips. "All right, Alex, enough of this tomfoolery. We need to get you to a doctor. Something is wrong. You shouldn't still be having trouble with your balance, and you shouldn't—"

"Tomfoolery?" He started to laugh. "Tom*foolery?* What are you, some kinda throwback to ancient times? If I had a brain in my head, I'd ask you to marry me, 'cause old-fashioned girls like you are frew and free between. I mean free and far betreen. Or is it—"

This wasn't normal, and it terrified her. Tears filled her eyes, because what if, when he'd fallen and hit his head, something more serious than a concussion had happened? What if, because he hadn't gotten medical attention soon enough, that "something" turned out to be irreversible?

"Alex, you're scaring me."

He stopped talking and laughing in the same instant, the silence reminding her of the time somebody had pulled the plug on the jukebox in the school cafeteria, turning the teenaged glee as quiet and echoing as an empty church.

"Aw, gee, Taylor, I never meant...I didn't mean to make you cry." One palm covering his face, he said, "I have no idea what's going on. I'm sorry if this is scaring you."

He looked so miserable that she couldn't help herself. Taylor wrapped her arms around him and patted his back reassuringly. Faking a calm and a sureness she didn't feel, she whispered, "I'm okay. And you'll be okay, too, soon as we get you to the hospital."

His arms slid around her, too, and he held her tight. "All right. If it'll make you feel better," he agreed, "I'll go to the hospital."

Tenderness welled inside her, because again, Alex's concern for her overpowered his own desires. The last thing he wanted was a trip to the emergency room, yet he'd agreed to go, in the hopes it would calm her.

"Hey, let's get something straight here, mister. We made a deal. You promised if things got worse...even a little bit worse...you'd let me take you in for X rays." She pulled back far enough to look into his eyes. "Now I'm going to start the car." She helped him from the sofa arm to its cushions. "You stay put till I get back, you hear?"

He nodded, feeling like a fool and a weakling to boot. He knew as well as she did that what he'd been experiencing for the past hour wasn't normal. He knew because yes, he'd had concussions in the past, plenty of them, and nothing like this ever had happened before.

Alex had no idea what she was doing, rummaging in the closet, running from the laundry room to the kitchen, rattling plastic bags. He only knew his head had never hurt this badly. Not when he'd fallen out of the tree, not when his plane had crashed in the Caribbean.

The uncertainty of his condition scared him. Because he already walked with a limp, and would for the rest of his days. He'd more or less learned to accept that. But how was he supposed to live a normal life with a head injury to boot?

If I make it through this, God, he prayed, *I'll change. I swear I'll change.* He'd stop being such a stubborn idiot and start acting as if he had some gratitude for the life he was living, rather than regrets at the life he'd lived.

He'd put more of himself into preparing for his job, teaching math and science at the high school in the fall. He'd start planning now for his duties as coach of the junior varsity basketball team.

He'd do something about that bland, blank house he lived in. Get something growing in the flower beds, plant a vegetable garden, maybe even figure out a way to make

Taylor see him as something other than a helpless, self-pitying, crippled jerk.

She was breathless when she returned to his side.

"Come on, Alex," she said, tugging his hand until he was on his feet. "Everything's ready, so let's go, okay?"

"Aw, look at you," he said, touching her rain-drenched hair. "You're soaked to the skin."

She smiled up at him. "It's hot, so being wet feels pretty good, actually." And snuggling up close beside him, she draped his arm over her shoulders. "Now, don't you worry. I'm stronger than I look. If you need to, you lean on me, okay?"

Distracted by the flurry of words she'd just spoken, Alex barely noticed that Taylor was leading him to the front door.

"I found a couple other things that belonged to Dad," she said, "so if we get wet going from the parking lot to the emergency room, you'll have something dry to put on afterward."

He saw her flip the lock on the knob just before she closed the front door behind them. "If the power's out at the hospital, they'll be running on a generator...the AC will be on."

What did that have to do with anything? he wondered.

"Last thing you need right now is to catch a chill," she said, answering his unasked question as she snapped his seat belt into place.

So that's what all the running back and forth, the rattling, the rummaging had been about, he realized as he slumped into the passenger seat. She'd been gathering supplies. Smiling, Alex grabbed her hand. "Remind me to remember something when this is over."

Looking over her shoulder to back down the driveway, she said distractedly, "And what would that be?"

I wanna remember to give you a great big thank-you kiss, that's what, he thought, grinning sheepishly.

Chapter Six

Alex leaned back against the pillow and held tight to Taylor's hand. "Small world," he muttered.

"*Real* small," the doctor said. He turned to Taylor. "This old dog you dragged in out of the rain went through basic training with me." Looking at Alex again, he added, "I beat you at every test the navy threw at us, but you won the best girl."

From the corner of his eye, Alex saw Taylor's brow furrow. "Luke, really..."

Luke? Alex wondered how it was that she was on a first-name basis with the guy. "So tell me, *Luke,*" he said through clenched teeth, "how long have you been in Maryland?"

The doctor shrugged. "Oh, four, five years, give or take six months. Did a stint at Bethesda Naval Hospital. When it was time to re-up, Howard County General made me an offer I couldn't refuse. So I didn't."

"Didn't re-up, or didn't refuse?" Alex asked.

"Both." Luke McKenzie winked at Taylor. "Met Taylor at the settlement table...."

Taylor answered Alex's question even before he could voice it. "Luke bought the condo I owned before I bought the house. I forgot to bring his keys to settlement, and—"

"And since she offered to deliver them in person," Luke finished for her, "the least I could do was buy her lunch."

Alex recognized that laugh. It was the one McKenzie had always referred to as his lady-killer laugh.

"I've been trying to get her to marry me ever since."

Alex licked his lips. Swallowed. If she'd been seeing a guy like Luke McKenzie, could she really be as innocent as she seemed? Because McKenzie's reputation as a rogue went even farther back than his own.

He preferred not to think about it. At least, not while his head was pounding like a parade drum. "So what's the prognosis, Doc?"

McKenzie tapped Alex's chart. "Well, according to the X rays, there's no serious tissue damage." He winked at Taylor again. "He always was a hardheaded son of a gun. This time, that was a good thing, eh?"

Taylor gave Alex's hand a gentle pat, as if to say, *ignore him.* "And what about his leg?"

The doctor's brows drew together. "His leg? What about it?"

"The X-ray tech scanned it after he did Alex's head X rays. He seemed to be favoring it more than usual, so I was just curious to know whether or not the fall did any further damage to the leg."

Favoring it? More than usual? Alex ground his molars together and did his best not to punch the mattress. Would this lousy limp shadow and shame him for the rest of his life?

McKenzie took a deep breath "I don't think so," he said, lips thin and jaw muscles working, "but since I have no prior X rays to compare these to, there's no way to know for sure." He focused on Alex. "Which brings up an interesting question. What's the treatment regimen?"

Alex cleared his throat. "Treatment regimen?" he echoed.

Blue eyes narrowed, McKenzie said, "Injury like that requires years of physical therapy...exercise, massage, medication...." He turned to Taylor, his dark expression brightening suddenly. "Now I get it. *That's* how you two met!"

Taylor felt the heat of a blush in her cheeks. "Our association is not of a professional nature," she said. "We're..." She looked at Alex and smiled tenderly. "Alex and I are...friends."

The doctor raised one blond eyebrow. The tightness was back in his expression and his voice when he said, "I see."

The lengthy silence that followed ended when a nurse burst into the cubicle and handed McKenzie a large manila envelope. "CAT-scan results," she explained as he examined the films. To Alex, she said, "How 'bout a cup of juice?"

He shook his head. "Thanks, but no thanks. All I want is out of this place."

McKenzie refiled the test results and headed out of the cubicle. "Not so fast, Van Buren. Nurse...get the man a doughnut and a mug of coffee. If he's gonna be here a while, may as well make him comfortable." Over his shoulder he said, "Taylor, can I have a word with you?"

Alex gripped her hand a little tighter when the doctor added, "In private?"

No one was more surprised than Alex when Taylor leaned over and kissed his cheek. "I'll be right back," she said, smiling sweetly. "Promise."

"I'm going to hold you to it," he said around a lopsided grin. "You're my transportation, remember?"

Ever so gently she brushed the hair back from his bandaged forehead. "I remember."

She found McKenzie waiting for her in the hallway outside the emergency room. Hand on the small of her back, he led her into a small office and closed the door.

He laid Alex's chart on top of a filing cabinet. "Have a seat," he said, perching on the corner of the desk as he gestured to a chair against the wall. Once Taylor was settled, he crossed both arms over his chest. "So, you and Alex are friends, huh?"

"Yes."

"How long?"

Taylor started to answer, then clamped her lips together. Her relationship with Alex was none of Luke's business, and if he didn't watch it, she intended to tell him so. "I thought when you asked to speak to me, you had something to tell me about Alex's condition."

"W-well, ah," he stammered, "partly…"

She sat up straighter and smiled politely. "Then let's start with that part, shall we?"

He chuckled good-naturedly. "All right. Business first." Fiddling with his stethoscope, he nodded once. "I understand his mother left town yesterday morning for a week in the mountains?"

"If that's what Alex said, then I guess—"

"I thought you two were such good friends," McKenzie challenged. "Wouldn't a *friend* know something like that?"

Taylor stood, lifted her chin and chose her words carefully. "I guess that would depend on what kind of friendship Alex and I…enjoy."

The doctor blinked. Blinked again. And then he smiled. "Well, you can't blame a guy for trying," he said with a shrug. "So tell me…are you close enough to take care of Alex for the next forty-eight hours?"

She knew the after-concussion routine. Alex couldn't be left alone until all danger of coma passed. But they'd have to tread carefully here; he wasn't the type to quickly agree to round-the-clock nursing care. She'd put it to him in language he'd understand—either he'd let her take care of him at her house, or she'd move in at his place until he passed McKenzie's medical muster.

"Yes, we're close enough for that."

"Good, good." The doctor stood, grabbed Alex's file and opened the door. "So tell me," he said when she stepped into the hall, "who's gonna break it to him...you or me?"

Taylor smiled. "He wouldn't hit a woman. I'll do it."

Laughing, McKenzie placed a hand on her shoulder. "We go way back, Van Buren and me. I'm not ashamed to say I've always enjoyed givin' him a hard time. Wouldn't have wasted my time, frankly, if he wasn't 'good people.'"

He stood there, just looking at her, seemingly oblivious to the flurry of activity all around them in the E.R. "You make him toe the line, you hear, 'cause you deserve the best. And since I know that's not me..."

"Luke, stop. You're a wonderful man, and someday you'll make some girl a—"

He held up a hand to forestall her protest. "We both know that isn't true. I like being footloose and fancy-free. If I couldn't give up chasing skirts for *you*," he said, "I might as well admit I'm a 'confirmed bachelor.'" He drew quote marks in the air to emphasize his point.

A fingertip to the end of her nose, he added, "If he doesn't toe the line, you let me know." He winked and jabbed his thumb into his chest. "I'll set him straight."

She felt the heat of a blush coloring her cheeks. "Thanks...*Dad*," she teased, "but I think it's a little premature for that kind of advice. Alex and I really *are* just friends.''

''Are you kidding? I saw the way he looks at you. Why, the man's crazy about you!''

It took every bit of her strength not to say, ''You think so?'' Instead, Taylor said, ''You do a pretty good job of hiding it under that suave, sophisticated ladies'-man exterior, but not good enough to fool me. You're good people, too, Luke McKenzie.''

He blushed, and it seemed to surprise him even more than it did her. ''Go on.'' He gave her a gentle shove. ''Tell the big boob he can leave...provided he lets you take care of him for the next couple of days.''

''Will you want to see him in forty-eight hours?''

''Yeah.'' He feigned a grumpy expression. ''Guess I don't have much choice. Took an oath, and all that....'' Chuckling, he pulled a business card from his pocket. ''Call me if anything changes.''

She took the card. ''I will.''

He headed back down the hall, white coat flapping behind him. ''Remember...toe the line,'' he said over his shoulder.

But the thing Taylor's mind was fixed on was what the doctor had said about Alex. *I saw the way he looks at you,* he'd said. *Why, the man's crazy about you!*

Please God, she prayed, *let it be true.*

Because she'd been crazy about him almost from the moment they met.

''We can do this the easy way,'' Taylor said, ''or we can do it your way.''

Alex frowned, put his soda pop on the table beside the hospital bed. ''What's that supposed to mean?''

One hand on her hip, she met his steady gaze. ''It means, Mr. Too-stubborn-for-his-own-good-who's-had-too-many-concussions-to-count, you know very well that you can't be left alone for the next couple of days. So you have three choices-stay here in the hospital, come home with me, or let me come home with you.''

Alex pictured his town house, bleak and bare. And dusty, too. Then he visualized Taylor's place, warm and cozy and well deserving of the stitching on the pillow in her parlor that said Home Sweet Home.

''I can take care of myself, y'know,'' he said as she finger-combed a wayward lock of hair from his forehead, tidied the top sheet on his bed.

''No, you can't.'' She looked him in the eye. ''So what's it going to be?''

He heaved a sigh. ''Well, I sure don't want to stay here....''

''Okay then, your place or mine?''

Chuckling, Alex shook his head. ''Funny, but I never expected to hear that line at a time like *this*.'' He took her hand. ''You're terrific to do this, kiddo.''

She made that cute ''aw, gee'' face he'd grown so fond of and said, ''Hey, what are friends for?''

Maybe, Alex told himself, at the end of these forty-eight hours they'd be more than friends. But if he had even a shred of decency in him, he wouldn't be thinking such a thought. Because Taylor deserved better than the likes of him!

''Luke suggested I get in touch with your mother, but I didn't think you'd want me to. Of course, I can still make the call if—''

''No, you were right. Mom and Rusty haven't had a real vacation in years. Seems to me this is just what the doctor ordered—no pun intended—and I wouldn't think of asking her to come home and baby-sit her clumsy oaf of a son.''

''You're not clumsy.''

Taylor adjusted the collar of his hospital gown in a way

Alex could only define as "wifely." And God help him, he was loving every minute of her fussing. *Two days of this and you'll be so spoiled, you'll smell like day-old fish,* he told himself.

"Just oafish, huh?" he asked, grinning.

"Okay. So maybe you're not Riverdance material. But is it your fault you didn't see Barney in the dark?"

He gave her hand an affectionate squeeze. "So when can we blow this pop stand?"

"Now, if you're up to it. Luke said he'd have the paperwork all—"

"Taylor," he interrupted, "do me a favor?"

She leaned closer, smiled sweetly. "Sure."

"Quit calling him Luke, will ya?"

Brow furrowed slightly, she said, "Well, okay...but why?"

"Let's just say I prefer to keep things strictly professional between myself and the good doctor." *And any reference to a relationship between you and Luke,* he added mentally, *isn't good for my health...or his.*

"Whatever you say." She grabbed her purse. "Do you need a nurse to help you get dressed?"

Did she think he was *totally* incapable? "I think I can manage sweats and tube socks."

Taylor pulled the curtain closed around his bed. "I'll be right here, so if you need me, just whistle."

He couldn't help but think of the old movie classic. "You know how to whistle, don't you?" the heroine asked. "Just pucker up and blow." Pretty as she was, the star of that old black-and-white flick couldn't hold a candle to Taylor.

Sitting on the edge of the bed, he removed the hospital gown and shrugged into her father's sweatshirt. It felt good, warm and soft, against the goose bumps raised on his skin by air-conditioning.

When he got to his feet, a wave of dizziness made him stumble slightly.

"You okay in there?" she called through the curtain.

"Yeah. Fine," he fibbed, steadying himself on the bed's footrest. One by one, he stuck his feet into the legs of the sweatpants. But he wasn't fine. His head hurt more than he cared to admit. His knees were weak, his vision bleary. And his leg ached more than it had in a long, long time.

"Are you decent?"

"Don't know how decent I am," he responded, "but I'm dressed...finally."

Taylor peeked between the pastel-striped privacy panels, her smile so bright Alex wondered why it didn't hurt his eyes. With one quick jerk, she opened the curtain, then rolled a wheelchair up to the bed. "Your chariot awaits, m'lord," she said with a dainty curtsy.

"I don't need that contraption. I can walk just—"

"Hospital policy," she interrupted, one finger in the air. "If you don't sit, they won't release you."

He slumped into the chair. "But I'm too heavy for you to push. I'll bet I outweigh you by two hundred pounds."

She raised one eyebrow. "I'm a lot tougher than I look," she said, aiming the chair at the E.R.'s double doors.

Another wave of dizziness swept over him, and Alex leaned back, rested his head against her chest. When he did, she gave the top of his head a little kiss.

An orderly, heading in the opposite direction, said, "Leavin' us? Well, take 'er easy, Jack."

Jack.

Closing his eyes, he smiled as the tune of an old nursery rhyme played in his head. *Well, Lord,* he prayed, *if I had to fall down and break my crown, I couldn't have ended up with a better "Jill."*

* * *

The power was back on by the time they reached Taylor's house. Barney met them in the foyer, and let it be known with a surly meow and slanted eyes that he didn't much appreciate having been left alone...with an empty food bowl.

"Sorry, pal," Alex said as Taylor closed the front door. "Didn't mean to disrupt your routine."

Taylor laughed. "Just ignore him. It isn't as if he'll starve to death, missing just one measly meal."

"Measly? You call that mound of food you give him twice a day measly?" Alex chuckled. "It's a wonder he doesn't weigh a hundred and five pounds!"

She wrapped an arm around his waist and guided him to the family-room sofa, and he let her. Alex had promised himself as Taylor helped him into the passenger seat that he'd make things as easy as possible for her these next two days. And to prove it, he wouldn't grumble every time she offered to do something for him. In fact, he'd be so cooperative she'd likely think she'd brought the wrong patient home.

"Did you hear that, Barn? He called you a fat cat!"

In response, Barney rubbed his whiskered cheek against Alex's ankle and purred.

Hands on her hips, Taylor said to the cat, "Well now, isn't that a fine kettle of fish. I do all the work, and he gets all the credit."

The word *fish* seemed to renew the feline's interest in eating. Meowing, he walked figure eights around his mistress.

"I'm fine," Alex insisted, grinning. "Go feed the beast before he starts gnawing on my good leg."

Giggling, Taylor fluffed the cushion behind him. "Okay. But first I'm getting you a big glass of water." And pulling a small white bag from her purse, she shook it, adding, "We have to get some of these painkillers into you."

"I don't need 'em," he started to say. But Taylor's grin stopped him. She was no doubt remembering that he'd asked her for aspirins before they'd gone to the emergency room. No point in his pretending he wasn't hurting now....

"After we get you medicated, I'll start a pot of water boiling, brew you a nice pitcher of fresh iced tea."

Somehow she'd figured out that iced tea was his beverage of choice. His heart beat a little harder, because *he'd* figured out that lemonade was Taylor's favorite summer drink. "You don't have to do that. Water'll be just fine."

But Taylor didn't hear him—she'd already rounded the corner, a fuzzy meowing shadow on her heels.

He could hear her in the kitchen, alternately humming and whistling as she filled a glass with water...for him. She was back in a whipstitch, two black-and-white capsules in one hand, a tall blue tumbler in the other. "Here y'go," she said, perching near him on the edge of the sofa. "Down the hatch!"

Remembering his promise to cooperate, Alex popped both pills into his mouth and washed them down with a gulp of cool water.

Taylor relieved him of the glass, put it on the coffee table, in a place he couldn't possibly reach without getting up. But he wasn't about to complain. She'd opened her home to him, and—

"Lie down here," she instructed, plumping a soft throw pillow against the sofa's arm. "You have time for a short nap while I feed the beast and whip us up something to eat."

"I'm fine right—"

She tilted her head and shot him a warning glance, but even as she did, he didn't miss the smile in her big brown eyes. Reminding himself yet again of his promise, Alex lay back and let her slide the sneakers from his feet.

"Let me know if you want the thermostat adjusted,"

she said, dropping the shoes, one by one, onto the floor. "I tend to keep the house a little on the cool side."

Truth was, he'd been chilly since they'd come inside out of the hot, muggy air. He'd noticed a colorful afghan neatly folded over the arm of the sofa. When she returned to the kitchen, he'd grab it and cover up.

As if she'd read his mind, Taylor unfolded it and draped it over him. "Better?" she asked, smoothing it over his chest.

He grabbed her hand. "Much." And touching her fingers to his lips, he said, "Now, stop working so hard. You keep this up, I'll have you worn to a frazzle before suppertime."

She winked. "Not a chance, mister. I'll have you know I take supercharged vitamins." She flexed the bicep of her free arm, as if to prove it. Then, almost as an afterthought, she said, "Want me to get you the remote control? Might be a humdinger of a soap opera on…"

He chuckled. "Nah. I think I'll take your advice, catch a few winks while you work your magic in the kitchen."

Patting his hand, Taylor smiled. "Good idea."

And before he could agree, she was gone.

He closed his eyes, listening as she talked softly, soothingly to Barney. "Did I go away and leave you to starve?" she cooed. "I'm sorry, sweetie, but I had to take care of Alex. It's your fault he hurt himself, you know…."

She'd crooned that way as he awaited the results of his X rays and CAT-scan tests. Alex had never liked hospitals, even when he wasn't a patient, and that old distaste had increased tenfold since his dip in the Caribbean a year and a half ago. But Taylor, with her gentle pats and quiet words of comfort, made him forget all that.

Smiling, he thought, *You broke the mold when You made that one, Lord. There's nobody like her.* At least, no one he'd come into contact with. If there was another woman like Taylor Griffith—and he very much doubted it—Alex had no intention of looking for her.

Suddenly the old adage "A bird in the hand is worth two in the bush" made sense.

A lot of sense.

Taylor slapped together a few sandwiches as the can of chicken noodle soup warmed in the small pot on the stove. Sliced apples and a handful of potato chips rounded out Alex's snack, while six ice cubes cooled his tea.

He was sleeping when she walked into the family room, and she quietly slid the serving tray onto the coffee table. A glance at the grandfather clock in the hall told her she'd have to wake him in a few minutes anyway, to check the dilation of his pupils. She saw no point in waking him now.

Sliding onto the seat of the overstuffed chair facing the sofa, Taylor drew up her legs, hugged them to her chest. Chin resting on her knees, she watched the steady rise and fall of his broad chest.

He had such long, dark eyelashes. And that thick, shining hair of his.

A lock had fallen across one eye, giving him a little-boy quality that stirred everything womanly in her. If not for fear of waking him, she'd brush it from his forehead right this minute!

He licked his lips and, frowning slightly, murmured something unintelligible under his breath.

And Taylor held hers.

Oh, how she yearned to take those few steps from her chair to where he drowsed so peacefully. Under different circumstances, she'd sit on the floor beside him, rest her head on his shoulder, press sweet kisses to his well-chiseled cheek. And tell him the truth that had been growing inside her, almost from the moment he'd bumped into her life...that she—

"Didn't your mama teach you that it's rude to stare?" he asked without opening his eyes.

Though he spoke softly, slowly, the sound of his voice made Taylor lurch slightly. How could he have known she'd been sitting there studying him, if he'd been fast asleep?

"I'm a mind reader," he answered her unasked question. "Plus, you wouldn't believe how clearly a person can see through the slits in his eyes." One eye winked open, one corner of his mouth turned up in a sly grin. "Truth is, I smelled the soup. My growling stomach is what woke me, not the fact that you've been boring two little holes into me for the past five minutes."

Taylor unfolded herself from the easy chair. "Perfect timing. You're just in time for an eye exam." Wiggling her eyebrows, she grabbed the flashlight from where she'd stashed it in an end-table drawer. Kneeling beside him, she turned it on. "Focus on the ceiling…Cyclops."

Smirking and shaking his head, Alex did as he was told. "How much longer do we have to do this?" he asked, frowning as she flicked short, quick bursts of light across his pupils. "My fifth-grade science teacher told me it wasn't visually healthy to stare into the light. Any light. Ever."

"Don't worry," she assured him, laughing, "you'll still be able to see the Orioles play baseball when this is over."

With no warning whatever, he wrapped his hands around her wrists, pulling her near. "Only thing I'm worried about is that I won't be able to see *you*."

Taylor blinked.

And Alex smiled. "What's the matter…afraid I'm gonna kiss you?"

Afraid was hardly the word she'd choose. *Hopeful* was more like it.

She licked her lips. Well, she told herself, it wasn't as

though she hadn't kissed him before. She'd planted quite a few quiet pecks on his cheeks, his forehead and chin as the nurses and doctors worked on him in the E.R. But those had been to comfort and calm him. What was happening now was anything but comforting. Or calming, she added, noting the wild drumming of her heart.

He slid an arm behind her, drawing her nearer still. "You smell like lilacs. Or roses. Something sweet and flowery," he whispered against her cheek.

It wasn't soap—the four-bars-for-a-dollar kind she'd been using for as long as she could remember—but perfume. But she rather liked the idea that he thought she smelled sweet. And flowery. Rather liked the way his big hand warmed her where it touched, too.

"Taylor?"

"Hmmm…" She sighed.

"How 'bout turning that thing off?" He nodded toward the flashlight.

A nervous giggle popped from her lips. "Oh. Sure. Sorry," she said, clicking it off.

He tucked in one corner of his mouth, then said, "Taylor?"

"Hmmm?"

"Gimme that thing, will ya?"

Alex relieved her of the flashlight. She heard it hit the carpet with a quiet *thump*.

"Taylor?"

"Hmmm…"

"Remember that day at the church, when you asked me to say grace?"

She nodded, wondering what that had anything to do with—

"And remember how I had to tell you to close your eyes?"

She nodded again. Yes, she remembered only too well. Taylor swallowed...and closed her eyes.

His other arm went around her, pulling her so close that she could feel the thrumming of his heart against her rib cage. It seemed as if a full ten minutes passed before his lips pressed softly against hers, so softly that at first she nearly opened her eyes to see whether or not he might be teasing her with a feather plucked from the throw pillow.

She heard him sigh, heard a quiet moan that seemed to begin deep in his chest, spiraling upward until it escaped his mouth. One hand on either side of her face, he ended the delicious, delicate contact.

"Taylor?"

"Hmmm..." she said dreamily.

"You're beautiful. The most beautiful thing I've ever seen."

She opened her eyes as a slow grin spread across her face. "Aw, I'll bet you say that to all the girls." Even as she said it, every muscle tensed as she thought of other women he'd held this way, other women he'd kissed....

But Alex shook his head. "I've never said that to a woman in my life." The fingers of his right hand formed the Boy Scout salute. "Honest."

She had nothing to go on but the sincere look on his face, in his eyes. Afraid she might admit, right out loud, that she was falling in love with him, Taylor reverted to what worked best—changing the subject. "Alex?"

His brows rose and disappeared under his disheveled locks. "Hmmm..."

"Did anyone ever tell you you talk too much?"

A sly smile slanted his mouth before he kissed her again.

And Taylor prayed it would last, at least long enough to require her to microwave his soup.

* * *

Alex leaned back against the sofa cushions and patted his stomach. "That was some lunch. I don't think I'll be able to move for a week."

Taylor put the flashlight back into the end-table drawer, then slid the tray closer to Alex. "You sure packed away some food."

"Well, who'd-a thunk you'd make me a trio of sandwiches?"

She shrugged. "I didn't know which you'd prefer... tuna, ham, or peanut butter and jelly. So I made all three." She grinned. "Nobody said you had to eat them *all*." She glanced at the tray. "Was your soup hot enough? I could've nuked it...."

"I know." He held out his hand, and when she put hers into it, he added, "But that would have meant having you leave the room to do it."

She blushed, making him want to take her in his arms and start kissing her again...and again.

"You need a nap," she said, gently shoving him into a prone position. After covering him with the afghan, she grabbed the tray and headed for the kitchen. "I'm in the mood for Italian tonight," she said from the doorway. "How does lasagna sound for supper?"

"Sounds great to me." But then, everything she said sounded great. Everything she did was great. *She* was great.

"I make a pretty mean Caesar salad...."

"Knock yourself out," he said, grinning. "I've never been one to look a gift horse in the mouth."

As she rounded the corner, Taylor whinnied. "Sweet dreams," she called.

Laughing to himself, Alex listened to her quiet humming. The voice of an angel, he thought, closing his eyes.

But he knew he wouldn't sleep. There was too much

Taylor in his head. He didn't know what had gotten into him.

Yes. He did. *Taylor* had gotten into him. At least, he admitted, she'd gotten under his skin. Which didn't make a lick of sense.

He chalked it up to the bump on the head. What else explained the way he'd thrown all caution to the wind? Why else was he behaving like a love-starved teenaged boy?

Under other circumstances, maybe he'd have been able to muster the willpower to keep her at arm's length. If things had been different, maybe he could have kept the promise he'd made himself never to get romantically involved with a woman. If the concussion hadn't weakened him, maybe he would have had the sense to protect her from a guy like him.

A guy like him…

Once, he'd been fairly respectable. Wasn't all that long ago that he'd earned medals and commendations and awards for being an upstanding guy. So what had changed?

The crash, that's what. Nothing respectable about the way he'd bungled things that day! Why, if Taylor knew about the way he'd bailed, the way he'd let the fighter plane go down without a fight—a plane her tax dollars had paid for—she'd be singing a different tune!

No…knowing Taylor, she'd fuss over him like the basket case he believed himself to be. Pity would make her say all the right things. "It wasn't your fault!" and "What else could you have done?" Things his mother had told him, that his stepfather—and anyone else who'd been brave enough to broach the subject—had said. Things he'd never believe, not if he lived to be a hundred.

And with his luck, he *would* live that long…as a lonely, bitter old man.

What more proof did he need that he wasn't the decent,

upright guy Taylor deserved than that he'd allowed her to fall in love with him!

Alex took no pride in that fact, but it was a fact, nonetheless. He could see it in her eyes, could hear it in her voice, could sense it in every loving thing she did for him.

And he'd felt it in her kiss....

Yes, she loved him.

And he loved her right back! But what man wouldn't fall for a woman like Taylor? Should he blame it on the knock he'd taken on the noggin? Her gorgeous eyes? Her lilting voice? Maybe it was that way she had of making him feel like the most important being in the world.

Alex sighed, linked his fingers under his neck and stared at the ceiling, where the long gray shadows of Taylor's birch trees danced. He pictured the trio of trees that grew in her side yard. She'd ringed them with yellow and purple flowers—what kind, Alex didn't know—exactly like the ones encircling the big maple out front.

She seemed to love gardening. And cooking. Fact was, she loved *life*. So didn't she have a right to as much happiness as life could offer? A house with a big backyard, where she could tend her flowers and vegetables, and half a dozen kids could romp under her watchful, nurturing eye.

To complete the picture, she deserved a man who loved life, too...who loved *her* as if it was going out of style. A guy who believed she was the angel who'd hand-placed every star in the heavens.

Could he be that guy?

Closing his eyes, Alex held his breath. He hadn't prayed, not really, in a long, long time. Maybe while he'd been feeling sorry for himself, licking his wounds, God had grown weary of his whining, had given up on him. Maybe He'd heard so much whimpering that He wouldn't even hear his prayer.

Exhaling, he admitted that no, that wasn't the God he'd learned about in Sunday school. That God never turned a deaf ear to His children.

"Father," Alex whispered, "I know I've been a major pain these last eighteen months, but I can change."

He stared across the room, at the neat arrangement of family photographs Taylor had lined up on the mantel. If he did change, could *he* be included there someday?

Crossing both arms over his chest, Alex began listing things he'd already put into motion, things that were proof he'd begun to change.

He'd moved back home, to Ellicott City, for starters. Hired on as a math teacher at the local high school. And volunteered to coach the boys' J.V. basketball team in his spare time.

Maybe, Alex hoped, with Taylor in his life he could round the bend, finish mending his battered ego and his fragile spirit and be the man she so richly deserved.

He ground his molars together, thrust his fist into the couch cushion. "Not maybe," he vowed. *"Definitely."*

Wouldn't be easy, going the rest of the way, but with her rock-steady support and God's unconditional love, he believed he might just make it.

He could make it!

Inhaling a deep, cleansing breath, he smiled as drowsiness overtook him. The last thing Taylor had said to him before disappearing into the kitchen was "Sweet dreams."

Something told Alex that he'd do just that.

Chapter Seven

Taylor was in the kitchen washing the supper dishes the night after the storm when the phone rang. She'd barely gotten a polite "hello" out of her mouth when her uncle announced, "I hear you have a houseguest."

It hadn't been twenty-four hours yet since Alex had appeared on her doorstep, looking like a drowned pup. Must have been tough on poor old Mr. Devries—Taylor's self-appointed private-eye neighbor—to wait out the phone company so he could phone in a report to her uncle. "Good news travels fast?" she asked, smiling despite Mr. Devries.

Uncle Dave chuckled. "Or bad news travels like wildfire...." He paused, and when she didn't blurt out the story, he said, "Well...?"

Taylor sighed, knowing in advance he wouldn't approve of the living conditions here at her place. "I'm not sixteen anymore, Uncle Dave," she began. "I can take care of myself."

"Oh, really?" came his stock answer. "So that's why you invited a total stranger into your home during a hurricane?"

There was no point arguing with him. Instead, Taylor reminded herself that he meant well, that his intentions were good. *Good thing for you,* she told him mentally before launching into the story.

"What about work? Didn't *they* have a problem with your baby-sitting that…that flyboy?"

One well-timed phone call, placed while Alex napped, had made it possible for Taylor to take a day off. The client load had been light lately, anyway, and the receptionist had seemed only too happy to reschedule Taylor's appointments. Which gave her nothing to do but care for her favorite patient.

"He's probably eating you out of house and home."

"Of course he's not."

"Guy's been a bachelor all his life," he said as if she hadn't spoken. "Knowing you, you're cooking up a storm…lasagna, beef stew, sausage and eggs…."

Mr. Devries must have bought himself a telescope recently, Taylor decided, because she *had* made Alex a pan of lasagna. And he'd gobbled it up as though it were his last meal. Just being polite? Taylor didn't think so. "He's been a very good patient, considering," she said, remembering how cooperative Alex had been since their trip to the E.R. "And I'm sure if he had any choice, he'd rather not be here."

Her uncle snorted. "Yeah. Right. I've been a patient of yours, don't forget."

Last winter, when her uncle Dave's appendix burst, Taylor had taken a week's vacation and insisted that he recuperate on the sofa bed in her family room.

"If an ornery old buzzard like me could see how much attention you pay to detail, what's a young fella like Van Buren gonna think? That boy is…"

Is what? Taylor asked herself.

"Is one mixed-up puppy, that's what. Helen tells me he

hasn't been himself since the crash. You're askin' for trouble, kiddo."

Exhaling a silent sigh, Taylor rolled her eyes. "His mom and stepdad are out of town," she said, "and he's only been back home for a short time. When the doctor said Alex needed round-the-clock monitoring, I asked myself what *you'd* do under similar circumstances." She paused, giving him a moment to remember the old army buddy who had spent a year in her uncle's guest room recovering from the death of his wife.

She heard the oh-so-familiar sound that told her he'd given himself a hand-to-the-forehead smack. "Y'got me," he said. "I surrender."

Taylor didn't have to be there to know he was waving one hand in the air, like a white flag. "Have I told you lately that I love you?" she asked, smiling.

"Love you, too, kiddo." He cleared his throat. "So do you need anything? Milk? Bread? Brass knuckles?"

She started to say "We're fine," and caught herself. "Fortunately for me," she said instead, "I went to the grocery store before the storm hit."

"One extra of everything?"

He'd been the one who'd taught her to keep the house well stocked with necessities. "One extra of everything," she repeated.

"Good girl." He paused. "You'll call if you need anything…or if that big lug gets out of line…?"

"Your number is on my speed dial."

"Don't let him run you ragged, now. You have a life of your own to live, and don't you let him forget it!"

Life of her own? Except for work and church, Taylor's life consisted of pulling weeds in her flower beds and brushing Barney to prevent hair balls. "You taught me how to take care of myself, so don't worry, okay?"

"Well, I have a mess to clean up in the yard. You wouldn't believe what that storm did to my peach trees."

Taylor had a mess of her own outside. But it was nothing that wouldn't keep until Alex had made a full recovery. "Don't try to get it all done at once," she warned. "Remember what happened last winter."

He hated being reminded how he'd thrown his back out, trying to shovel three feet of snow from his long, winding drive in one morning, all by himself. "You're gonna make some guy a great wife someday," he teased, "'cause you've got nagging down to an art."

"Hey," she put in, "I learned nagging at the feet of a master."

"G'bye, kiddo. Make that Van Buren fella toe the line, y'hear?"

"Call me when you're finished in the yard, so I'll know you haven't fallen into the brush pile?"

He laughed. "Aw, go make the man an apple pie or something, will ya?" And with that, Uncle Dave hung up.

She'd been repeating it in her head all afternoon—toe the line? Alex hadn't asked for a thing. Unless she counted when he'd asked her to drive him to his town house, so he could pick up a change of clothes. As he rummaged in his dresser, Taylor had stood in the hallway, glancing around his home. No...not a home...just the place where he lived. Nothing here said "welcome."

He'd been about to lock up when he remembered that he hadn't emptied the trash on the night of the storm. Taylor had insisted on taking it outside for him, and forestalled any protests by barging in ahead of him. "Where do you keep your twisties?" she'd asked.

When he pointed, Taylor had reached into the cabinet under the sink. In her own kitchen, this was home to dozens of cleaning supplies, the Crock-Pot, a deep fryer and then some. But except for a brand-new bottle of blue dish-washing detergent and a recently opened box of trash bags, Alex's cupboard—like so many other spaces in his house—was bare. It made her heart ache to see the way he'd been living like a visitor in his own house. Now she knew why he'd so quickly agreed to stay at her place while he recuperated.

Though each end table held a lamp, no magazines, knickknacks, not even an old softball trophy decorated the surfaces. The bookshelves in the living room were empty, save one beat-up edition of Britannica and a raggedy old Webster's. If she had to describe it in a word, she'd have to choose *stark*. Which was precisely why, when she'd come in from stuffing the garbage in a big aluminum can out back, she noticed it at all....

There, in the middle of his kitchen table, a wooden cowboy riding a bucking bronco.

The night he'd taken her to dinner she'd commented on the calluses on his palms, and he'd admitted to being a whittler of sorts. This was one of Alex's pieces, she'd realized.

Taylor had picked it up, gingerly turning it over and over in her hands. "It's beautiful," she'd admitted. A man didn't get hands like that creating just one piece of artwork. "Where are the rest?" she'd asked, glancing around.

Without a word, Alex had led her into the dining room and stood in front of the china closet, where inside, instead of crystal and china, stood more of his creations—horses with and without riders, a two-story log cabin, leafless gnarled trees...

And on the bottom shelf, one perfect foot-tall eagle.

Without asking permission, she'd opened the etched-glass door to get a better look at them. After a moment of scrutiny, she'd faced him. "Alex, you're amazing."

Shoving both hands deep into his jeans pockets, he'd

blushed. "You sing, I whittle." He shrugged. "It's no big deal."

Easing her hands inside the cabinet, Taylor had lifted the eagle from the shelf to admire it, up close and personal.

"You like it?"

She'd met his eyes. "'Like it' is a gross understatement. I *love* it," she'd admitted.

"Then it's yours."

"But Alex," she'd said, gesturing at the statues, "you could sell these. They're every bit as good as works I've seen in art galleries."

"Just something to do to pass the time."

"Pass the time" and "no big deal," indeed, Taylor thought now as she admired his gift to her. She'd treasure it forever. Oh, it was a beautiful piece of art, to be sure, something she'd be proud to display. But that wasn't the reason it immediately became precious to her. *Alex* had carved it with his own two hands; even if what he'd turned out had been a hideous-looking blob, it would always have a special place in her heart.

He'd hemmed and hawed, blushed a little more deeply, then followed her into the kitchen, looking confused as she pulled a dozen sheets of paper towels from the roller above his sink. "What's that for?" he'd wanted to know. "I haven't been drooling in my sleep, have I?"

"I'm going to wrap my eagle in it," she'd said matter-of-factly. "Wouldn't want anything to happen to it between here and home."

Smiling as she remembered it, Taylor believed she'd never forget the pleased little grin her comment had painted on his handsome face.

Earlier, Alex had followed her from room to room as she'd searched for the perfect spot to exhibit his gift. It seemed to gladden him when she decided "the perfect spot" was on the mantel. She wouldn't have thought it possible for his smile to widen, but as she dragged a kitchen chair into the room to adjust the beam of the ceiling-mounted track lighting above it, Alex beamed.

Was he smiling now, she wondered, as he slept upstairs in her guest room? She absentmindedly stroked Barney, who snoozed contentedly in her lap. She carried him nearer the fireplace. "Isn't it the most beautiful thing you've ever seen?" she asked him.

The cat hadn't appreciated having his nap disturbed, and proved it with a heavy sigh as he wriggled in her arms. "Everyone's a critic," she said, bending to put him on the floor. As he sauntered off, Taylor couldn't help but admire the way the eagle looked, noble and majestic, swathed in golden lamplight.

When Alex was gone—and all too soon he'd be well enough to go—she'd have his carving to remind her of their special time together. But not even something as magnificent as the eagle would help her miss him less....

Taylor stepped back from the fireplace and, hands clasped beneath her chin, she sighed, remembering their kiss. She'd been kissed a few times in her past—not nearly as often as Alex, no doubt—but often enough to know there'd been something different about that one, something searching and sad, something watchful and wary. Different, despite the playful way he'd pulled her into his arms, despite his one-liner jokes. If she hadn't known better, Taylor would have said Alex seemed...*afraid* of her. And how could that be, when he'd lived his whole adult life courting danger!

He was a brave, honorable man, as evidenced by the life he'd lived, daily risking life and limb for his country. He put his all into everything, like the way he'd pointed out the unique architectural features of the old buildings in Baltimore's Little Italy, the way he'd recited fascinating facts about the city's history, the way he'd hewn minute details into every realistic-looking feather, into the serious-looking face of the wooden bird now perched stoically on her mantel.

Took a lot of heart to live life that way. Taylor knew, because her father had been a man like that; her uncle Dave, too. Must have taken something horrible, something truly dreadful, she decided, to strike fear into a heart like that.

The crash of his fighter plane? Immediately she dismissed that notion, because wasn't the occasional accident part of the job of a test pilot? How many times had she read in the paper about other pilots who'd died so that the military would have the data it needed to keep soldiers safe should the country need to go to war?

She got a mental picture of Alex, battered and struggling in the choppy waters of the Caribbean…. The thought sent a cold chill through her, and Taylor said a quick prayer of thanks that he'd managed to stay afloat until the Coast Guard could rescue him.

A woman? Something told her it would take more than a broken heart to break a man like Alex.

Was he broken?

It made no sense, and she had no evidence to back up her assessment, but something told her that's exactly what he was: a broken, lonely man.

She sat on the floor in front of the fireplace and looked up at the determined expression on the face of Alex's carving. In nature, where survival of the fittest ruled all creatures, the eagle had no choice but to be stealthy, steadfast, stubborn. Its steady-eyed scrutiny reminded her of its creator; in unguarded moments, Alex, too, could look ruthless, determined, single-minded. Easy to understand in the eagle's case, when anything less meant certain death. When the wild birds soared from the mountaintops in search of food, what did they fear most…predators? The weather?

What did *Alex* fear?

He was so driven, so doggedly decisive about even the most mundane things, that she could only assume that he feared failure. Feared it greatly.

The assumption raised another, more disturbing question.

Why?

The nightmare woke Alex with a start. Gasping for breath, he sat on the edge of the bed. He grabbed a tissue from the dispenser on the nightstand and blotted perspiration from his forehead.

He had still been in the hospital, recuperating from the first of a dozen operations, when it all began. In his pain-riddled sleep-state, he'd mistaken his feeding tubes and monitor wires for parachute cords. The struggle had been so intense, so fierce, that he'd disconnected nearly everything, including the "nurse call" button and the TV's remote.

Within moments, an orderly had secured his wrists to the bed rails, his torso to the mattress. Later he mused that the dose of tranquilizer the young man had injected into him must have been large enough to subdue an elephant, because Alex hadn't opened his eyes again for nearly forty-eight hours. Not such a bad thing, he remembered thinking when he came to, because not once during his drug-induced sleep did the nightmare return.

Later, his roommate told Alex that the ruckus he'd kicked up had awakened every patient at their end of the hospital floor. According to the kid, it had taken two muscle-bound orderlies, a doctor and a nurse to silence his bellowing with meds and restraints.

The roommate's rendition of his behavior was verified by the night nurse, corroborated by the in-home nurse hired by the navy to care for him those first weeks after his release from hospital. Quiet nights, she'd said, were rare.

A neighbor in Alex's Norfolk apartment building concurred. "Sounded like somebody was bein' murdered in there," the retired officer had said. "Nearly scared the wife right out of her cold cream and curlers!"

To date, his nightmarish conduct had alarmed about a dozen people. Alex didn't relish the idea of making Taylor number thirteen.

She hadn't come running, which told him the dream had been quieter than usual. Either that, or fussing over him had so completely worn her out that she'd fallen into a deep, undisturbable slumber....

A wave of guilt washed over him at the thought. When this was over—and surely by tomorrow he'd be well enough to leave—he'd have to do something to prove how much he appreciated all she'd done, and the "glad to do it" attitude with which she'd done it. He'd be up the rest of the night if he followed his usual after-nightmare pattern, so there'd be plenty of time to think of what to do....

A terrible thirst overtook him, making him yearn for a sip of Taylor's refreshing iced tea...tea she'd made especially for him. Stepping into the sweatpants he'd brought from home, Alex started down the carpeted stairs in the socks she'd given him earlier.

The house was dark, the silence so complete that it made him miss the lilting tones of Taylor's voice. Much as he wished it could be so, Taylor couldn't be at his side keeping him company round the clock. Especially not at two forty-five in the morning. He couldn't help smiling a bit, despite his dream-provoked jangling nerves, because he knew full well that if Taylor *could* have been there for him, every minute, she would have been.

No sooner had he completed the thought than Alex heard the faint strains of violins. The sound, along with a dim light, spilled softly from the family room, puddling on the gleaming foyer floor.

He rounded the corner, fully prepared to ask her if she ever got tired, to inquire about the source of her boundless energy. But what he saw froze the words in his throat, froze his stockinged feet to the floor....

There was Taylor, sitting cross-legged on the white shag carpet she'd placed near the hearth, staring up at the mantel, where the eagle he'd given her stood in a halo of incandescent light.

From his vantage point Alex had a three-quarter view of long, silken waves that poured down her back like a minky waterfall as she swayed to the rhythm of the hushed, symphonic music. Sometime while he'd slept, she'd changed from her jeans shorts and polo shirt to white stretch pants and an oversize T-shirt.

Surely that serene expression hadn't been induced by his carving…had it? His offer to give it to her had been last minute and thoughtless at best, a feeble gesture of gratitude at worst. If he'd had any idea that his pathetic attempt to thank her for all she'd done would have this effect, he would gladly have given her the bronco rider, the dogwood tree, the log cabin, as well.

Alex believed he could have stood there, watching her, until he toppled over from sheer exhaustion…if doing so hadn't made him feel like a Peeping Tom. He had no right to spy on her this way, even if she was a delight to behold. But could he back off, make his way down the hall and into the kitchen undetected? He believed he owed it to Taylor to try.

And so he backpedaled down the hall, continuing his efforts at silence even after he'd entered the kitchen. Slowly he reached for a glass in her tidy kitchen cupboard. Easing the refrigerator door open, he grasped the handle of the iced-tea pitcher, then gingerly grabbed a handful of ice cubes from the bin in the freezer. And managed to do it all without making a sound....

Until he began pouring liquid into the tumbler.

Distracted by images of Taylor staring at his wood carving as though in a trance, he let the tea flow over the rim of the glass, from the counter to the floor. The icy sensation clinging to his white-socked feet made him lurch, causing him to upset the tumbler. It landed on the Formica with a clatter, making him drop the pitcher, which hit the floor with a plastic *clunk* before rolling and bobbing and coming to rest against the cabinets' shoeplate with a hollow *thunk*.

So much for peace and tranquility, he thought, shaking his head at the coppery puddle surrounding his feet. As he grabbed the nearest kitchen towel and squatted to sop up his mess, Taylor rushed into the room and flipped on the light.

"Alex," she cried, racing to his side, "are you all right?"

Shading his eyes from the brightness, he tried to smile. "Yeah...except for being a major klutz."

She hunkered down beside him, one hand on his shoulder, and relieved him of the drenched terry-cloth towel. "Here," she said gently, "let me do that."

Alex didn't object. Seemed pointless when he knew as well as she that left to his own devices, he'd only make a bigger mess. Sitting at the kitchen table, he peeled off his soggy socks. "Sorry..."

She grabbed another towel from a drawer. "It's not tar, y'know."

Hands resting on his knees, he sighed heavily. "Yeah, but you still have a sticky mess to contend with. And at three in the morning, yet."

"It's no big deal," Taylor told him as she worked. "Nothing a little warm water and soap won't fix." She glanced at the apple-faced wall clock. "Besides, it's only two forty-five."

She paused then, and gave him a scolding frown. "What're you doing up at this time of night, anyway? You should have been asleep hours ago."

The way things usually played themselves out, it took hours to get back to sleep after being awakened by the nightmare...if he got back to sleep at all. "Woke up," was all he said, "and couldn't get back to sleep."

"Was it the music that woke you? I hoped it was soft enough...."

"What music?" he asked. "I didn't hear any music." He grinned, but his heart wasn't in it.

Brow furrowed with concern, she crossed the room, stood in front of him. The fingertips of one hand, slightly damp and chilled from the wet towel, lifted his chin. "You're not in any pain, are you?" she asked, leaning forward to peer deep into his eyes. "Because there's that prescription for pain pills in the—"

"No," he interrupted, "no pain." At least, he told her mentally, not the kind you mean.

She continued to study his face. "Dizzy?"

Dizzy over you, he thought. But "No" was all he said.

Straightening, she tilted her head, rested one fist on her hip. On her very curvy hip, Alex thought.

"Luke..." Eyes wide, she bit her lower lip. "I mean, Dr. McKenzie gave you something to help you sleep. You want me to get one of—"

He shook his head, took her hands in his. "Taylor, I'm fine. Honest," he said, giving her a gentle shake. "Guess I'm just not used to being pampered and fussed over this way. All this lolling around has made me fat and lazy."

Tilting her head the other way, she smiled. "Fat, my foot. You have the physique of a marathoner."

That made him laugh. "So you admit I'm lazy, then?"

She reached out and smoothed the collar of his T-shirt. "Hardly. I don't know a single lazy marathon runner."

Heart beating double time—because of her nearness, because of the way she was looking at him, because she'd gone and touched him in that loving, wifely way of hers— Alex gave in to the urge to pull her onto his knee. "Exactly how many marathoners do you know?"

Taylor settled in as if his lap had been made exclusively, expressly for her and her alone. "Hmm," she said, squinting one eye. "Now that you mention it, I don't know any...personally, anyway...but I've seen plenty of them on TV."

He watched as she blinked her big, long-lashed eyes, watched her smile softly and fought the temptation to draw her closer still, pick up where they'd left off yesterday afternoon on the family-room sofa....

She squeezed his upper arm. "Big strong guy like you, all these hard muscles," she said, "Man doesn't get a bod like this by being lazy."

Alex laughed. "You're mighty good for a guy's ego." *Mighty easy on the ole peepers, too,* he added silently. "Better watch out, or you'll have to hire a handyman."

"A handyman?" she asked. "Whatever for?"

"To make keyhole shapes out of all your doorways, so I'll be able to fit my big head through 'em."

Her smile vanished, and in its place came the dreamy, schoolgirl look he'd seen on her face earlier in the family room, when he'd caught her gazing at the eagle carving.

"Does that mean you'll be stopping by now and then, even after you're all better?"

He loved it when her voice got all whisper soft that way. If she'd asked him to lasso the moon with that voice, he'd have jumped right up and gone hunting for a long sturdy rope.

Yeah, she'd fallen in love with him, all right. The proof

was written all over her lovely face, rang loud and clear
in her musical voice. If he had a decent bone in his body,
he'd stand her on her pretty little feet, right here and now,
and get as far away from here as his bum leg would take
him. Not for his sake—Alex rather liked the idea that
someone as good, as trusting, as gorgeous as Taylor had
fallen for him—but for her sake, because he believed she
deserved better, so much better than a guy like him.

On the other hand, she was a big girl, wasn't she? If she
wanted to waste herself, her time, her *love* on the likes of
him, who was he to argue? He reminded himself that he'd
been one hundred percent sincere when he'd said that
prayer, asking God to help him change, so he'd be worthy
of Taylor. And hadn't his mom taught him that no prayer
ever went unanswered? "God says 'yes,' and 'no,' and
'wait,'" had concluded his mother's lesson.

Tension knotted in his gut, inspiring a second prayer, an
addendum of sorts to the first. *That change we talked
about, Lord? Let it happen fast, will Ya, 'cause I'd hate
Your answer to be no.*

While he'd been mind wandering, Taylor had sat there
alternately blinking and biting at her lower lip...a pink and
very kissable lip. Alex figured it to mean she'd read his
silence as his way of telling her that when he left here
tomorrow, he wouldn't be back.

Nothing could be further from the truth, and he wanted
her to know that as surely as he did.

He drew her closer, so close that the overhead light
made fringed eyelash shadows on her freckled cheeks. In
his college English lit class, Alex had earned a reputation
as class clown because he'd so often poked fun at the po-
ets. Now, luxuriating in the radiance of her love, he
thought he understood a little better why the writers' son-
nets often focused on a woman's outward beauty. *Lord,* he
thought, *You outdid Yourself when You made this one.*

She'd asked if his keyhole joke meant he'd be back. Their lips were nearly touching when he answered, "You couldn't keep me away with a whip and a chair."

The instant the words were out, he felt every muscle in her relax. Relief sparkled in her dark eyes, joy widened her mouth.

She licked her lips. Big mistake, he told her silently, if you don't want to be kissed. Then he admitted he'd be the one making a mistake…if he *didn't* kiss her.

The last time he'd taken her in his arms, he'd held her as if she might break, or disappear like the angel he thought her to be. This time Alex kept nothing back. He'd acknowledged that Taylor had fallen in love with him. What he hadn't admitted until now was that he loved her, too, more than he imagined it possible to love a woman. Correction, he thought; more than he imagined it possible for *any* man to love a woman.

"How 'bout an overprotective uncle and a hyperactive cat?" she teased. "Would that keep you away?"

Alex shook his head, made an upside-down smile. "Not even if one of 'em had personally trained a man-eating pit bull."

And he meant it, from the bottom of his Taylor-swelled heart.

The last patient of the day had just left, and Taylor passed the final hour of her workday tidying the workout room. She hadn't been able to concentrate on anything—or anyone—all day, because her mind kept whirring with memories of Alex. So it was no surprise, really, when she tried to replace the wide paper roll on the exam table with one intended for the paper-towel dispenser at the scrub sink. Rolling her eyes and sighing at the silly mistake, Taylor thanked God everyone else had gone home and there'd been no witness to her silliness.

Her distractedness had begun three days ago, immediately following Alex's departure. The house seemed so big and empty without him.

Her heart lurched every time her home phone rang…and immediately sank when the callers turned out to be volunteers soliciting donations for one charity or another, salesmen inquiring about the condition of her roof and storm windows, the cable company wanting to know if she'd like to add new channels to her service.

She'd talked to her pastor's wife about the bake sale that would take place on the weekend. Talked with her uncle Dave about the leaky faucet in his kitchen sink. Talked with Luke McKenzie about Alex's condition.

But she hadn't heard a peep from Alex.

She'd believed him when he'd stood on the front porch, hands in his pockets and smiling that one-dimpled grin of his as he said, "Well, thanks for everything. I'll, ah, I'll call you. Soon. Okay?"

Of course it was okay, and she'd told him so!

Had she been too enthusiastic? Had the intensity of her response frightened him?

At first it had been easy, resisting the urge to call him. Now, as she vacillated between worry that his condition had worsened and fear that he was deliberately avoiding her, Taylor was having a tougher time of it. And so she did the next best thing.

"Mrs. Martin?" she said, forcing a cheeriness into her voice that she didn't feel. "It's Taylor Griffith."

"Taylor!" Alex's mother said. "How nice to hear from you, dear. I've been meaning to call and thank you for what you did for Alex while Rusty and I were away."

Was that what he'd told his mom? That Taylor had taken good care of him? If he thought that, then why hadn't he called?

"It was nothing. Really. I was happy to do it." Only

too happy, she added mentally. She cleared her throat. "I was just wondering if you were planning to bring anything to the bake sale on Saturday."

"As a matter of fact, I promised to make my so-called famous marble fudge cake."

"Sounds delicious!" What other chitchat could she make that seemed legitimate, that made sense, before asking Helen Martin if she'd seen her son? "I'm baking brownies, myself."

"Oh, that's marvelous, dear. I've had your brownies...they're always such a hit, especially with the children." She hesitated, as if she sensed that the bake sale hadn't been the primary reason for Taylor's call. "Alex tells me you make a mean Caesar salad," she said.

Taylor could almost picture the woman's smiling face, felt her own cheeks flush in response. What else had he told his mother? Surely not about those unforgettable kisses...

On second thought, maybe they *had* been forgettable. At least to Alex. If they'd meant as much to him as they'd meant to her, wouldn't he have done as he'd promised, and—

"He's been having a lot of trouble with his leg," Mrs. Martin said, interrupting Taylor's thoughts. "Alex is a very proud young man, so I'd be surprised—no, shocked—if he's called. He has a terrible time admitting when he's in pain." She sighed. "But I expect you found that out last week, didn't you, dear?"

Had that been the reason he'd been avoiding her? She had learned that he didn't like talking about his physical discomfort. Still, he wouldn't have had to talk about his leg if he didn't want to. She hadn't been *that* much of an ogre while taking care of him, had she?

"I'm sorry to hear he's having problems," Taylor said. Which was equally true. She wondered again what Alex was doing for the leg. Medication? Exercise? Both? *Neither, knowing him*... "Well, I still have some paperwork to do before I leave work, so I'd better get busy or I'll be here all night."

"See you Saturday, then," Mrs. Martin said. "Be sure to save one of those brownies for me, you hear?"

"Only if you promise to save me a slice of your cake!"

As she hung up the phone, Taylor muttered, "Small talk." She'd never been very good at it, as evidenced by the stumbling, fumbling way she'd said goodbye to Alex's mother.

Her hand was still resting on the receiver when the phone rang, startling her so badly she nearly knocked the whole unit off her desk.

Much as she'd have liked it to be Alex, the likelihood was slim to none, so there wasn't much point in striving for a merry greeting. "Hello?" she said dully.

"Um, ah, Taylor Griffith, please..."

Heart hammering, Taylor swallowed. "Alex?"

"Hey," he said, sounding truly pleased to be talking to her. "I didn't recognize your voice."

She coughed. "Sorry. Frog in my throat."

"Reason I'm calling is to see what you're doing on the Fourth."

"The Fourth of July?"

He laughed. "Yeah. That'd be the one."

The date was only a week away...a *whole week* away. Taylor and her uncle had plans to attend the annual Freedom Day parade down Main Street. Afterward, they'd head for the church picnic, and from there, the fireworks at the Columbia Mall, same as last year. She rattled off the itinerary and held her breath, hoping he intended to ask if he could join them.

"Oh. Well, then, I guess—"

"You're welcome to come along," she blurted. More than welcome, she added mentally.

His voice brightened. "Hey, that sounds good. What time is the parade?"

"Nine o'clock sharp. But the only way to see anything is to get there early, claim a section of sidewalk by eight."

"In the morning?"

It dawned on her that standing for an hour, waiting for the first band, then waiting another hour as the rest of the marchers paraded by—especially on concrete—might be difficult for Alex, what with his bad leg and all. "Some folks like to sit right on the curb, but Uncle Dave always brings lawn chairs."

"Smart," Alex said. "That way, kids can see over your heads."

Kids? It surprised her that he'd think of such a thing, but Taylor didn't admit it aloud. Instead, she simply added it to her already lengthy "Why I Like Alex" list.

Chapter Eight

Taylor had never put more time and effort into getting ready for a date. For reasons she couldn't explain or rationalize, from the moment Alex suggested taking her and Uncle Dave to breakfast before the parade, she'd started planning her outfit.

On the phone the afternoon after he'd hurt himself in her guest room, Helen Martin had told Taylor how unlike Alex it was not to have every step planned; since his accident, it was as if he'd become a different man.

She explained how he'd been the invited guest in the Hollywood mansions of several TV and major motion picture producers, providing down-to-earth realism and clarity to the stories they'd film for nationwide audiences. "Why didn't you tell me?" Taylor had asked when she'd finished talking with his mom.

And he'd shrugged, as if he really didn't think it was any big deal, traveling with the movers and the shakers. "Didn't see much point in it," Alex had said. "You were the one with the glamorous career."

That he saw her that way had made Taylor laugh. "A

two-bit lounge singer," she'd pointed out, "who never cut a record...and never wanted to. But important people actually asked for your advice!"

"It was a question of availability." He'd shrugged again. "If it hadn't been me, it would've been somebody else who didn't have a flight that day." And he'd smiled to add, "The major difference between you and me, Taylor, is *you* have the talent to entertain a roomful of people. I think that's downright glamorous!"

He seemed to see her as anything but ordinary, and although Taylor disagreed completely, there was no denying how flattering his assessment had been. And while he'd proven himself to be a feet-on-the-ground, rational-thinking kind of guy, she certainly didn't view him as ordinary. Not by any means. Precisely why no average outfit would cut the mustard, not when the person she wanted to impress was Alex Van Buren!

Now, after stepping around the pile of shoes on the floor outside her closet door, she shoved aside the clothes mounded in the middle of her bed and picked up one item at a time. The red gingham blouse with black jeans? she wondered. Or a white poet's shirt with tan shorts? Strappy sandals over bare feet, or tennis shoes with athletic socks?

She sighed, knowing it depended on Baltimore's undependable weather. It wouldn't be Charm City if it was anything but hot and humid on the Fourth, which made deciding tougher still. Groaning aloud, she grabbed the remote and turned up the volume on the TV. Barney yawned and stretched, as if scolding her for disturbing his nap.

"Oh, pipe down," she said, ruffling his golden fur. "Any second now, that noisy commercial will be over, and when it is, you can go back to sleep."

As if he understood that Channel 13's early-morning forecaster would indeed quiet things down a mite, Barney arched his back, walked around in a minicircle and made himself a nest in the middle of Taylor's pillow.

Before the car dealership ad began, the station's weatherman promised to report on the weekend weather. "And you'd better make good on your promise, Marty, ole pal," Taylor said as she doubled up a pair of socks. Maybe, armed with the information Marty Bass would provide, she'd finally be able to choose something to wear.

"Well," she said to the TV, "a girl can hope...."

A map of Maryland filled the screen as the station's theme music played in the background. Marty Bass stepped into view, cowboy boots gleaming and the sleeves of his Western-style shirt rolled up at the cuffs. "Sorry folks," he said, looking apologetic, "but things don't look too good for the Fourth."

Taylor threw the balled-up socks at the set. "Aw, Marty," she complained, "say it ain't so."

As the Maryland map morphed into a colorful animated display of Baltimore and surrounding counties, he said, "Looks like we're in for some serious rain, maybe even a thunderstorm or two." Marty adjusted the knot of his silver-and-turquoise string tie.

This time Taylor aimed a soft-soled slipper at the broadcaster. "You're not my favorite weatherman anymore, Marty," she griped. "Gray skies would be fine, but thunderstorms?"

"The front that's moving in," Marty continued, pointing at the chart, "looks like it's gonna stall over the Atlantic. And if that happens, well, we could have some pretty severe weather well into next week, that's what!"

Severe weather? But how could that be? The city had barely recovered from last week's gale-force winds!

"We could be in for a repeat of last week—" he echoed her thoughts "—right down to thirty-five-an-hour gusts."

Well, no way she'd let a little wind and rain spoil her

favorite holiday. But a *little* wind and rain hadn't been what Marty had forecasted. "But…it'll clear up before the celebrating starts, right, Marty?"

As if in answer to her question, the weatherman said, "Nope…ain't gonna be purty, folks, so my advice is…stay tuned to Channel 13 for the latest on cancellations and postponements."

He returned to the news desk and joined his bearded coanchor. "And now," Marty said, holding his Channel 13 mug aloft, "stay tuned for 'Coffee With.' Our guest this morning will be romance writer—"

Disgusted with Marty's gloomy forecast, Taylor turned off the TV. *Romance writer, indeed,* she fumed. There was nothing romantic about a stormy Fourth of July.

She could almost hear her uncle Dave. "Don't be such a Gloomy Gussie," he used to say when childhood disappointments made her pout. "A poked-out lip won't get you anything but chapped." It had been good, solid advice that had helped her solve a multitude of girlish problems. What could it hurt to try it on for size now?

Maybe Marty had misread the printouts from the national weather bureau. Maybe the jet stream he'd referred to so many times would dip, or rise, or do whatever it was that jet streams did when they weren't creating havoc around the globe.

Uncle Dave's advice wasn't working, and Taylor sighed, because she could count on one hand the times Marty Bass had incorrectly predicted the weather, and he'd been with the station for decades.

She glanced at the mountain of outfits jumbled on her bed and shook her head. She couldn't recall ever having made a mess like that, especially not on purpose, and never in preparation for a date. As she hung a white blouse on its hanger, her uncle's suggestion rang in her memory. Taylor laughed to herself, thinking that if Marty's July

Fourth weather predictions *were* right, at least she'd have plenty of time to clean things up!

"I hate Fridays that end on a sour note," Luke McKenzie grumbled as he scribbled something in Alex's file.

"Sorry to rain on your parade," Alex joked. "Pun intended."

McKenzie grimaced and sat back in his creaking leather chair. "I hear there's a comedy club down on Water Street. Maybe you ought to audition."

"Be a little tough doing stand-up," he shot back, "considering…"

The doctor ran a hand through his hair, visibly affected by Alex's comment. But rather than respond to the blatant sarcasm, McKenzie harrumphed. "You always were stubborn as a mule." Frowning, he shook his head. "I can't for the life of me figure out why you waited so long to have this checked out."

"Don't lecture me, Mack. I'm not three years old." He patted his thigh. "Besides, it isn't *your* life at stake here, now, is it?"

McKenzie leaned forward, clasped his hands on the desktop and narrowed his eyes. "I don't think you get it, Alex, m'boy. Are you aware just how serious this might be?"

Alex held one hand aloft to forestall any further reprimands. Of course he'd known what the symptoms might mean. Why else would he have avoided an examination all these weeks? "Doesn't get much more serious, way I see it."

"Look," McKenzie said in a gentler tone, "if I'd been in your shoes, I guess maybe I'd have done the same thing." And before Alex had a chance to say it, McKenzie did. "But I wasn't in your shoes. I have no idea what's going through your head right now, but for the love of Pete, man…''

He stood suddenly, tossed his ballpoint onto the blotter. ''You thickheaded, defiant…'' Both palms pressed flat on the desktop, he leaned closer. ''You could've trusted me with this, Alex. I haven't been your doctor of record for very long, but we were friends once, remember?''

Alex nodded. He'd more or less known that, from the first sign that things weren't right, and so he admitted it with a slow nod. ''So when do we do it?''

McKenzie flopped into his chair, picked up the handset on his phone and pressed the intercom button. ''Sandie…get me Dr. Bricker, will ya? Don't let that secretary of hers give you any guff, you hear? You tell that harebrained little twit that this is urgent…an emergency, 'cause that's exactly what it is.''

Urgent.

Emergency.

Alex exhaled a sigh of frustration. Yeah, even he would have to agree that the possibility of losing a leg was critical. Heart pounding with fear and dread, he could only sit there feeling stupid and helpless. *You think you feel helpless now,* he thought, shaking his head, *just wait a week, till after…*

He couldn't complete the thought. Oddly, the surgery didn't scare him half as much as the prospect of telling Taylor about it. Sweet, beautiful, giving Taylor, who'd handed him her heart without giving it so much as a moment's thought, without the typical tests and trials and proof that had been demanded of her predecessors. Those gals had said all the right things, had donned the proper facial expressions and postures as they spouted their carefully practiced lines…lines that had one purpose and one purpose only—to coax him into making them Mrs. Alex Van Buren.

Taylor, without benefit of script or practice, had told him with her actions what kind of man she believed him to be...the kind who'd protect a heart like hers for as long as he lived and breathed. The ache in his own heart was easily ten times greater than the one in his leg. If he hadn't deserved a woman like Taylor before, what made him think he'd deserve her *afterward?*

If. In Alex's opinion, the biggest word in the English language.

If he hadn't crashed the F-16 and become disabled, *if* he'd gone to McKenzie when the symptoms first appeared, maybe then he would have had a ghost of a chance, at least, with a woman like Taylor. Maybe he would have asked her to marry him, and maybe, just maybe, she'd have said—

"Alex? Alex, you okay?"

Hard to tell how long he'd been woolgathering. Looking up, he met McKenzie's worried eyes. "Yeah. Sure," he said around a stiff grin. "Why wouldn't I be okay? I mean...what's a leg in the overall scheme of things?" He shrugged. "At least the other one's healthy, right?"

The doctor didn't seem to appreciate Alex's attempt at humor, as evidenced by his scowl. "You wouldn't be in this pickle if—" This time McKenzie silenced himself with an upheld hand.

"Don't worry, Doc. The thought's crossed my mind a time or two since your diagnosis." He smirked. "Or should I say prognosis?"

McKenzie opened his mouth to reply, but the hissing of the speakerphone stopped him. "It's Dr. Bricker," came his secretary's crackling voice. "Shall I put her through?"

Grabbing the handset, McKenzie pressed a forefinger to the nosepiece of his round gold glasses, sliding them nearer his forehead. "Ready when you are...." He swiveled so that his chair faced the wall, putting his back to Alex.

And Alex knew why. McKenzie had never been very confident in his "poker face." He listened to the muffled conversation for a moment, then stood and walked stiff-legged into the waiting room. Hands deep in his pockets, he paced back and forth in front of the row of metal-trimmed chairs separating the receptionist's station from the waiting area.

He stopped, slid a hand along the rough gray upholstery, then glanced around at chipped white plastic tabletops and faux wood bookshelves. He couldn't help but wonder what his old navy buddy was doing with all his money—not spending it on office furniture, that much was sure. That fact surprised him, because hadn't McKenzie told him in the E.R. the other day that a couple of the Orioles and several Ravens football stars were patients of his...?

He'd no sooner completed the thought than the doctor himself appeared in the doorway, looking more glum than Alex had ever seen him look. He gave a quick, formal nod. "C'mon inside, Alex."

Lips taut, he smiled. "Dr. Bricker doesn't let any grass grow under her feet, does she? Don't tell me, let me guess...she's scheduled O.R. time for me already."

The doctor opened his door wider. "Let's talk in here, all right?"

He'd been the last patient of the day, and the waiting room was empty, except for the secretary and receptionist. Before long they'd both be headed home, too, so Alex didn't understand the importance of his hearing the news behind a closed door.

"Alex...?"

Shaking his head, Alex unpocketed his hands and limped into the office. "Least you could do is buy a guy a cup of coffee," he said as McKenzie closed the door, "before you tell him you're gonna chop his leg off...."

*   *   *

It had been Alex's idea to pick up Taylor and her uncle at seven and treat them to breakfast before the parade. So at seven-fifteen, she began to pace. It wasn't like him to be late. Sending a silent prayer for his safety heavenward, Taylor decided to give him fifteen minutes more before she called his house.

At seven-twenty, she considered the possibilities. Maybe he'd been one of those who'd lost power during last night's thunderstorm. Maybe he'd forgotten to set his alarm.

Maybe something has happened to him, she thought, biting her lower lip as she said another prayer on his behalf.

By seven twenty-five, she was nearly beside herself with worry. Admittedly, she hadn't met him all that long ago, but she'd learned enough in the short time she had known him to understand that he took punctuality very seriously. He'd said as much the first time he'd picked her up, when he'd arrived right on schedule. "It isn't just rude to be late, it's a sign of vanity and self-centeredness."

"Vain?" she'd said. "Self-centered?"

He'd nodded in that matter-of-fact way that was so distinctly Alex. "Folks who are habitually late have a deep-seeded need to be noticed. What better way to ensure you'll be the center of attention than by making everyone wonder where you are?"

"Well said, Dr. Freud," she'd teased.

In response, Alex had patted his bad leg. "Ole Hitch 'n' Hobble here gets me more than enough notice...."

An unexplainable, eerie chill snaked up Taylor's spine at the thought of his leg, despite the oppressive July heat. She felt unable to wait another moment.

Just as she grabbed the handset, the telephone rang. "Oh, thank You, Lord!" she whispered, relief and joy mingling in her heart. "Well, it's about time!" she sang into the mouthpiece.

"My, my," said Helen Martin, "but you're bright and cheery for such a gloomy morning."

"Oh. Mrs. Martin." Taylor swallowed. She'd expected it to be Alex, calling to say he'd been delayed because of a flat tire, because he'd forgotten to gas up the pickup truck, because he'd forgotten to set his alarm. "What can I do for you?"

The woman's weary sigh filtered into Taylor's ear. "It's not what you can do for me, dear. It's what you can do for Alex."

For Alex? Taylor held her breath.

"He's at home, feeling very glum...not that I blame him...."

Glum?

"H-he's all right, isn't he?"

"Well, not exactly..."

Taylor's heart hammered and her mouth went dry. Toe tapping, she waited for the woman to get to the point.

"He had some bad news yesterday afternoon, Taylor, and I'm afraid he's not taking it very well." She paused, cleared her throat. "Not well at all."

"Bad news?" Taylor wrapped the coils of the telephone cord around her forefinger, pacing back and forth as far as the line would allow. "What kind of bad news?"

"Well, I'm not sure I should be the one to tell you. Alex might not..." She sighed again. "He might not appreciate it if I told—"

"Mrs. Martin, I don't mean to be disrespectful, but how can I help Alex if I don't know what's wrong? I promise to be tactful and discreet. I wouldn't hurt him for the world and—"

Alex's mother interrupted to say, "I know that, dear. Anyone with eyes knows that."

Taylor stopped pacing, midstep. *Anyone with eyes knows what?*

"Dr. McKenzie did some X-ray tests on Alex's leg while he was in the E.R. for the concussion, as a precautionary measure." She took a deep breath. "It seems there's some…some…"

It was all Taylor could do to keep from slamming down the phone, driving fast as she could to be with him. Whatever was wrong, surely the two of them could face it better together.

"Mrs. Martin? Are you all right?"

"I'm sorry, Taylor. It's just…Alex might well be a grown man, but he's still my only child. I thought I'd faced the worst test of my faith when his plane went down, but this, this…" On the heels of a sob, Helen Martin said, "I don't understand. What could God be thinking, doing this to my boy? Hasn't he already suffered enough?"

Taylor's heartbeat rattled her rib cage as she considered the implications of what Mrs. Martin *wasn't* saying. Possibly the injury Alex had sustained to his leg in the crash hadn't healed properly, and scar tissue had caused further damage, or…

Or he had something worse.

Something like cancer.

The word struck fear in her soul. She closed her eyes. *God, no…not that,* she prayed.

"Dr. McKenzie has called in a specialist. They'll perform exploratory surgery day after tomorrow. And Alex…well, Alex is…"

Terrified, Taylor finished silently. And who could blame him! "Don't you worry, Mrs. Martin. He's toughed out worse. He'll pull through this. You'll see."

Who was she trying to convince with that little pep talk—Mrs. Martin? Or herself?

"But you didn't see him, Taylor."

Taylor cleared her throat, waiting.

"Rusty and I stopped over there just now, to take him

some sticky buns. I baked them first thing this morning. They're his favorite, you know.'' She sniffled. ''He didn't answer the door, so I had to use my key. Me, his own mother!

''When we went inside, we found him, just sitting there in his recliner, staring at the television. It wasn't even turned on, Taylor, and yet there he sat....'' She blew her nose before going on. ''He wouldn't talk to us. Didn't say a word. After a few minutes, he said, 'Mom, Rusty, go away. Please. I need time to think...alone.'''

It took all of Taylor's control to keep her own tears at bay. Right now she needed to be strong. For Mrs. Martin. For Alex.

''I've never seen him looking so defeated. I'm afraid he won't consent to the operation.''

''Oh, he'll consent, all right,'' Taylor said emphatically. ''He'll consent if I have to put the pen in his hand and make him sign the release papers myself!''

She got a mental picture of Alex as his mother had described him, slumped in a chair, gazing vacantly, and her heart ached. ''I'm on my way,'' Taylor said. ''I'll just call my uncle first, tell him—''

''You don't know how much I appreciate this. I wouldn't put you in such a position, but something tells me if anyone can talk any sense into him, *you* can.''

How could Mrs. Martin know a thing like that?

''We'll wait to hear from you,'' his mother said. ''Just knowing you'll be there...oh, *thank you*, Taylor!''

Taylor hung up and called her uncle to let him know about the change in plans, then grabbed her Orioles baseball cap and stuffed her hair under it. ''Lord,'' she said aloud as she slammed the front door behind her, ''guide my words, and open Alex's heart to hear them....''

Alex hadn't thought it possible to suffer worse humiliation than what he'd experienced after the crash. Losing the fighter had been tough enough, but to be forced to forfeit his pilot status…he'd sooner have drowned in the drink that day.

He pressed thumb and forefinger into his eyes, blocking out what little light managed to squeak through the room-darkening wooden blinds. Hopefully, the pressure would be enough to keep the tears at bay. What kind of man had he become, that a little bad news could get him so down, could send him so close to the edge? *Are you really so spoiled,* he wondered, *so soft that you can't take it on the chin anymore?*

With his free hand Alex absently kneaded what remained of his thigh, thinking that he'd gladly endure pain ten times as bad as he'd been experiencing these past few weeks…if it meant he could keep the leg.

At first he'd blamed it on all the walking he'd done in Ireland. When it didn't let up upon his return to the States, he'd chalked it up to moving into the new house, then the exercises he'd been doing to ready himself for the teaching job he'd be starting in the fall. And finally, the spill he'd taken in Taylor's guest room….

Deep down, he'd known all along that the soreness was different somehow, that the throbbing hadn't been even remotely similar to anything he'd experienced after his collision with the Caribbean. But he'd decided to tough it out, as he'd done so many times before.

Why? Because he'd met Taylor, that's why, and felt as if someone had turned on a light inside him. He hadn't wanted to so much as consider the possibility that anything could darken his world again. She made him feel alive, whole again, and more like a man than he'd felt since before the accident.

For some crazy reason, the pretty little nut seemed to think he was an okay guy. And for whatever oddball reason, she acted as though she enjoyed his company, even when he was grumbling about a concussion-induced headache. What a fool he'd been to think he had a chance with a woman like Taylor...energy personified. Every move she made, every word she said proved what a vital, healthy, vibrant human being she was.

He felt taller, stronger, smarter, somehow when she was at his side. But then, what man *wouldn't* feel like a powerhouse, standing beside a li'l gal barely bigger than a minute!

His heart did a peculiar flip-flop every time those big doe eyes of hers lit up...at the sight of *him*. He'd thought he'd left that gut-wrenching, breathless schoolboy feeling behind him long ago. And yet, every time she smiled that "I think you're terrific" smile...at *him*, his stomach lurched as if he were a passenger on the Sooper Dooper Looper at Hershey Park.

If he'd been so aware of her admiration, why had he felt the need, every time they'd walked together, to stay a half step behind her? He *knew* she didn't give a whit about his limp....

He could tell by her seemingly genuine enjoyment of even his most ridiculous jokes, by the way she listened intently as he described his interest in the stock market, that she wasn't embarrassed to be seen in public with him, that she didn't see him as a hobbling, faltering oaf.

False male pride? Pretense at dignity? It made no sense, no matter how he puzzled it out. But the truth was, Alex had been uncomfortable enough for both of them, despite the way Taylor chattered nonstop, letting him set the pace, pointing out things of interest so he'd know her focus was on him and not his awkward gait.

An ugly truth began to surface in his mind.

If it shamed him to be with her when his biggest gripe had been the limp, what would he feel like in a few weeks

when, thanks to the so-called medical professionals who'd
decided the only cure for his problem was amputation, he'd
trade his faltering stride for a seesawing hip-hop?

And if he loathed walking with Taylor now, beautiful as
she was, how much more would he despise rolling along
beside her…in a wheelchair!

Luke McKenzie had pointed out that the wheelchair
would be only a temporary inconvenience. Taken by itself,
it wouldn't have been so terrible, if it didn't have to be
replaced at some point…

By a prosthesis.

That's just great, was Alex's grim thought, *a wooden
leg!*

All right, okay, so according to McKenzie the thing
would look and operate almost as well as his real leg, and
it would be made of lightweight plastic, not wood. That
didn't change the fact that it would still be months before
the wound healed enough to even *think* about such mea-
sures; that it would take months, perhaps years, before he
learned to walk with the hideous contraption strapped to
his miserable, gnarled and twisted little stump. Meanwhile,
McKenzie assured him, Alex would gradually progress
from wheelchair to walker to crutches. He could hire someone to build a ramp, "to make it easier to get into your
house…."

Some assurance!

He'd come through that other mess a year and a half
ago without much complaint. But then, how hard had it
been to accept his condition, when the injuries never threat-
ened his manhood? Because despite the agony of post-op
pain, despite the grueling physical therapy, he'd pushed
himself hard, bound and determined to bounce back on his
own, without drugs, without help from anyone.

The doctors hadn't sugarcoated it, saying flat out that
he'd be lucky, at the conclusion of his six-month stay in

the hospital, to go home in a wheelchair. He'd dug in his heels, literally at times, and proven them wrong...and in record time, too, surprising not only the nurses and therapists and the surgeons themselves, but his fellow patients, as well.

What if he let the surgical team take his leg, and things didn't go as well this time? What if he'd used up all the fight God had given him in the last medical go-round?

He would become a helpless slug, that's what, crawling through life, dependent and needy and...

Taylor's pretty face flashed in his mind. He'd rather die than have her see him like that.

Taylor had been standing on Alex's porch in the pouring rain, persistently ringing the doorbell, for nearly fifteen minutes. "I know you're in there," she called through the door, "so you may as well let me in."

A slight shuffling sound on the other side of the door gave her hope that he'd decided to do as she asked.

"What're you doing here?"

His voice, gravelly and gruff, underscored Mrs. Martin's assessment of his condition, making her more determined than ever to get inside that house. "You promised me bacon and eggs," Taylor said, forcing a laugh, "and I aim to collect!"

"You talked to my mother, didn't you?" Anger put a hard edge on the sadness of his tone.

Feeling helpless, Taylor grasped the handle of the screen door and pressed the release button, only to find it had been locked. He'd shut her out, literally and figuratively. As she listened to the seemingly endless silence, she prayed, *Lord, help me know what to do, what to say, to help him....*

"Taylor, I—I don't...I can't see anyone right now."

Tears burned in her eyes when she heard the hitch in

his otherwise smooth baritone. "Alex, don't do this. Let me help you."

Did this latest silence mean he'd reconsidered, that any second now she'd hear the unmistakable sound of the opening door?

"I don't need your help," he growled.

Ignoring his hostility, she said, "Then why are you locked in a dark house on a rainy day, alone?"

She could almost picture him, standing there shaking his head and frowning, as he considered what he'd say next.

Nothing could have prepared her for the defeat so evident in his tone when he said, "If you really want to help me, you'll do as I ask." He cleared his throat. "Just go away, Taylor." Another hesitation, and then a sandpapery "Please?"

Closing her eyes, Taylor prayed for all she was worth. "Tell me what to do, Lord," she whispered to herself. "Surely You don't want me to leave him here, alone? Surely You want me to—"

Suddenly she opened her eyes, knowing exactly what it was that the Lord wanted her to do.

Racing down the front porch steps, she ran to the end of the block. Sidestepping puddles and fallen leaves, she turned the corner, running full-out until she stood in the alley separating Alex's town house row from the row behind it.

If memory served her correctly, there hadn't been a padlock on the gate of the tall stockade fence surrounding his backyard. And, if she remembered right, he'd said something about a key, hidden on the ledge above the back door. As she eased quietly through the gate, she prayed, "Don't let him have locked that screen door, too."

By now, she imagined, he'd probably be wondering what she was up to. Her car was still parked in front of his house, after all. If only she'd thought to drive it around the block and park it in the alley, Alex would have no choice but to assume she'd taken him at his word, leaving when he'd asked her to.

As things stood, if he figured out what her plans were before she managed to get her hands on that spare key, no telling what he might do!

At five foot two, there was no way she'd be able to reach it up there, high atop the aluminum frame. But Taylor didn't have the luxury of the time required to search for something tall enough, sturdy enough to increase her height.

She noticed a finger-thick, four-foot-long branch that had fallen during last week's storm, the perfect tool to help her knock the key from its hiding place.

It took several jumps and jabs before the key landed quietly in the sodden grass beneath her feet. Securing it tight in one palm, she wrapped the fingers of her free hand around the wrought-iron door handle, and sent a prayer of thanks heavenward when it opened without resistance.

On the fourth attempt, she managed to slide the key into the keyhole. And after what seemed like a full minute, she heard the unmistakable *click* of the releasing dead bolt lock.

Finally, thankfully, Taylor was inside, shaking from baseball cap to sneakered feet.

The instant she saw him, standing slump shouldered and grim faced in the archway between the kitchen and the laundry room, Taylor ran to him and, mindless of her rain-slicked jacket and dripping baseball cap, threw her arms around him.

"I love you," she blurted, dotting his cheeks, his chin, his lips with kisses. "I love you, do you hear? So don't you ever, *ever* shut me out again!"

Alex put all he had into keeping his cool, into trying not to return her hug, not to respond to her kisses. But it was no use. Heart hammering, he swallowed the sob aching in his throat. "Taylor," he groaned, holding her at arm's length, "what're you doing here?"

"I already told you," she said, standing on tiptoes. "You promised me breakfast, and—"

"I mean," he interrupted, "how'd you get in here?"

She looked up at him through lashes made darker by dampness. Rain? he wondered, heart pounding, or tears?

"You told me where you hid your spare key," she said, voice quavering, "when we came over here the other day to get you a change of clothes." She lifted her shoulders. "The day you gave me the eagle, remember?"

Yeah, he remembered, all right. Remembered how her gushing praise of his so-called artwork had rendered him stupid, red faced and stammering as she admired the rest of his carvings. Remembered how he had admitted to himself, standing not ten feet from where he stood now, that he loved her.

Alex had to get her out of here, fast. Because if he let her continue standing here in his arms, big brown eyes staring up at him from under the brim of that soggy, black-brimmed cap, he was doomed.

"I guess you didn't hear me just now," he said, surprised at the cragginess in his own voice, "when I told you to go away, when I said I didn't want...couldn't see anyone right now...."

She looked down, and when she did, he was reminded of how, even on a blue-skied day, when clouds passed in front of the sun he felt deprived of its warmth as well as the light.

Gently, tenderly, she smoothed his shirt collar, tidied the flap covering his left pocket. Her hand came to rest there, over his hard-beating heart. Surely she could feel it, pounding against her palm.

"I heard you," she whispered, meeting his eyes at last. He watched a bead of rainwater trickle from her hair onto her forehead. Unconsciously Alex wiped it away with the pad of his thumb. "If you heard me, then why—"

"You know perfectly well why." One well-arched, delicate brow rose slightly. "You're going to make me say it again, aren't you?"

"Say what again?" But even as he asked the question, Alex knew what she was talking about. He held his breath, telling himself he'd been hearing things seconds ago, that it had only been wishful thinking when he'd assumed that she'd said—

"I love you, Alex." Her dainty hands slid slowly upward, came to rest on his shoulders. And giving him a gentle shake, she repeated it, emphasizing each word individually. "I...love...*you.*" She punctuated it by lightly jabbing a forefinger into his chest. "Do you get it?"

He looked at the ceiling. "Yeah. I get it, all right. It's proof positive that you're out of your mind." Meeting her eyes, he put as much sternness into his voice as he could muster. "Do *you* get it?" he asked, mimicking her finger-to-the-chest move. "You don't have a clue what you're saying, what you're letting yourself in for."

She lifted her chin and feigned a smug, know-it-all expression. "Says you."

"Wha—?"

Narrowing her eyes, she said it again. "That's right, says you."

One corner of his mouth lifted in a wry grin, despite himself. "Izzat so."

She nodded, and with no warning whatever, disengaged herself from his arms and nonchalantly closed the back door. "Rain's blowing in here, making a mess on your floor," she said, shoving the scatter rug back and forth with her foot to sop up the puddle.

Then, as if she were the lady of the house, she grabbed the teapot from the stove, filled it with tap water and placed it on a front burner with a quiet *klunk.* "I don't suppose you have any honey," she asked, opening and closing cabinet doors, "do you, *honey?*"

The term of endearment made his pulse race, made his palms damp. She'd been on the brink of tears just moments ago. But look at her now, he thought, trying her best to sound upbeat and chipper, for no reason other than to lift his fallen spirits. If he had a shred of decency in him, he'd boot her out of here before the water in that teapot rose one degree in temperature.

He reminded himself that his future was uncertain, grim at best, because whether he decided to go ahead with the surgery or not, he'd be a basket case. And he didn't want her around to witness that. Period.

It was the last thing he wanted to do, but the very thing he believed he *should* do. Equally important, it was what she deserved. "Taylor," he said, in a calculatedly cold and distant voice, "go home."

His words stopped her...but only for a fraction of a second. He'd cut off his own leg rather than hurt her feelings, but if that's what it took to protect her from the long, difficult times that lay ahead, so be it! He crossed his arms over his chest, to show her he meant business.

She didn't respond right away. Maybe, if he was lucky, she'd do as he asked....

Slowly she turned to face him. "If you think for one minute that I intend to go back out into that downpour just to fetch you some honey," Taylor said calmly, matter-of-factly, "you've got another think coming."

If she was so all-fired sure of herself, then why, Alex wondered, was her lower lip trembling? And why were her eyes turned down at the corners?

But Alex knew the answer.

Taylor had been telling the truth, the whole truth and nothing but earlier when she'd said she loved him. And

he'd have done just about anything if it were possible for
him to admit his feelings, too.

She swallowed, clasped her hands in front of her, like a
little girl praying. For what? he wondered. But he knew
that, too.

The bill of her baseball cap partially shaded her face,
making it impossible for him to know if the sparkling drop-
let on her cheek was a remnant from her time out in the
rain, or a tear. It wasn't until another drop slid down behind
the first that he had to admit she was crying.

Hanging his head with shame, Alex sighed. *What am I
gonna do with you?* he thought. He didn't realize until she
crossed the room and wrapped her arms around him that
he'd spoken the words aloud.

"You're gonna love me," she said, one cheek pressed
against his chest. "Just love me, okay?" Snuggling closer,
she sighed. "Just love me, and everything else will fall
into place."

Alex removed the baseball cap, tossed it onto the table,
watching awestruck as her mass of gleaming chestnut-
colored waves tumbled over her narrow shoulders, spilled
down her slender back. He filled his hands with it, as if to
memorize the satiny thickness of it, buried his face in it to
imprint its crisp, clean scent onto his brain.

She'd hit the bull's-eye, all right, because he loved her.
Loved her like crazy. But he'd never tell her. How could
he, and still respect himself?

What she needed was a virile, healthy man who could
give her all the things she so richly deserved, rather than
a one-legged cripple who'd bog her down and—

"Alex?"

She had the most amazing, musical voice. He wondered
what it must have been like being a part of the audience
back in the days when she sang for her supper. He'd probably always regret not having asked her to sing for him,

because he had a sinking feeling chances like that were as gone as his leg would soon be. Alex closed his eyes, determined to remember the sound of that wonderful voice, because—

"Um, Alex?"

Oh, but she could be like a puppy to the root.... "Hmm?" he said around a smile.

"I know your mother raised you better...."

He leaned back a bit to look into her face. Into her incredible, lovely face. "Sorry," he admitted, "I'm afraid I don't get it. Raised me better than wh—"

Blinking lashes spiky and clumped by tears, her dark eyes gleamed. "She wouldn't approve of you being deliberately rude."

Shaking his head slightly, he repeated, "Rude? Sorry, but—"

"I've said 'I love you' a hundred and fifty times since I got here." She shrugged. "Doesn't seem all that unreasonable for me to want to hear you to say it *once*."

Grinning at her deliberate exaggeration, he did a mental countdown. She'd said it five times exactly, if he included what she'd just told him. He knew precisely how many times he'd heard those magical, marvelous words, because each time, he'd had to remind himself to inhale, to exhale, had felt his ears grow hot and his cheeks flush red.

Did she have any idea what she was doing to him, standing there all petite and warm in his arms, looking up at him, wearing an expression that said as clearly as her voice had that she loved him wholly, no matter what, and always would?

Did she realize that it was *because* she'd take him healthy, limping, one legged...that he could never tell her what she wanted to hear?

Chapter Nine

For the past ten minutes Alex had been sitting in his beat-up recliner listening to the pleasant sounds of domesticity going on in his kitchen. The fingers of his right hand drummed the end table while his left massaged his aching leg. He wondered if she'd ask what McKenzie and Brickman had planned for him. And if she did, how much should he tell her?

When his mother had stopped by earlier, he'd told her flat out that he didn't want to discuss the reasons she'd found him sitting alone in the dark on the Fourth of July. But then, she'd made a career out of reading his mind, so he wasn't all that surprised when she wriggled the information out of him.

How much of what he'd admitted to her had she shared with Taylor? Surely not all of it; his mom had her share of stereotypical female traits, but "blabbermouth" wasn't one of them. But along with her maternal mind-reading skills, she'd honed "hint-dropping" to a fine edge, too. Knowing her, he figured that carefully chosen words had implied what family loyalty prevented her from saying.

Taylor came into the room just then, balancing mismatched earthenware mugs and spoons on an old baking tin that had belonged to his grandmother, as had most of his kitchen utensils. He hadn't needed to invite her to make herself at home. She'd done that quite easily on her own, it seemed, right down to the paper napkins on the makeshift tray.

Sometime in the process of rooting around in his cabinets in search of the things she needed to make them each a cup of tea, she'd taken the time to step outside and cut a few blossoms from the wild rose shrub that climbed from his neighbor's yard into Alex's. She'd removed the label from the can of tomato soup he'd made himself for supper last night. Rinsed and polished dry, it made a more than suitable vase for the cardinal-red blossoms that stood between the chipped mugs.

"Find any honey, *honey?*" he asked as she slid the tray onto the bare-topped coffee table.

Kneeling on the floor between his chair and the table, she met his eyes. "Now, you didn't really expect that I would, did you?"

In truth, he knew *he'd* never bought any, but it was hard to tell what his mom might have shoved into the cabinets on one of what she liked to call her "missions of mercy."

"I did find some sugar, though...." Widening her eyes, she added, "In the refrigerator!"

He could only shrug. "Mom seems to think that dry goods should be refrigerated. Keeps 'em from getting invaded by—" he drew quote marks in the air "—little black bugs."

Taylor wrinkled her nose. "Here? In the suburbs?"

"It's a habit she picked up when we were stationed down south."

She put a napkin on the end table beside his chair, placed his mug on top if it. "I noticed at dinner the other night that you drank your coffee black. Same goes for tea, I assume?''

He'd have eaten the tea bag dry, tag and all, if she'd asked him to with that look on her face. Lord, but he loved the way her eyes lit up when she smiled! In place of an answer, he asked a question of his own. "Ah, how do you take yours?''

"I didn't know you were Irish.''

He had no earthly idea what she was talking about, and said so.

"Didn't you notice when you were over there the way the Irish tend to answer questions with questions? It's a charming, entertaining trait.'' Head tilted the other way now, she added, "But I have to admit, it's not very time efficient....''

Where had she learned to smile that way? he wondered. Was she born with that rosy glow, or did she get it out of a tube, like the gals in the makeup commercials on TV? Something told him that everything about her was the genuine article.

Oh, how he'd miss her when—

How long she'd been sitting there, sugar bowl and spoon poised above his cup, Alex could only guess. Inspired by her playful grin and twinkling eyes, he spouted, "Ah, maybe just half a teaspoon...''

She measured it out and stirred it before attending to her own drink. He noticed she added two heaping spoonfuls of the sweetener to her tea. How did she stay so slender? On the other hand, it sure explained where she got all her energy. "You do that all the time?''

Her expression said *Do what all the time?*

"Put that much sugar in your tea, I mean.''

She nodded, as if to say, *Doesn't everyone?* But when she spoke, she said, "Enough small talk, Alex. Time to spit it out. Fill me in.'' Eyes closed, she held up her hands, like someone being robbed at gunpoint. She opened her eyes and aimed a well-manicured pointer finger at him. "And remember, I'm tougher than I look."

That much he already knew. She'd survived her father's death, her mother's and, thanks to his mom, he knew Taylor had been dumped by an old boyfriend. Yeah, life had toughened her up, all right. The problem, as he saw it, was she didn't need any more toughening up.

Alex hesitated, uncertain how much information to provide, how to dole out what he did decide to say. "What, ah, what did my mother say?"

She exhaled a sigh of frustration. "There you go again, answering a question with a question!"

It seemed to Alex more an afterthought than a planned action when she scooted closer, knelt in front of his chair and draped her folded hands over his good knee. "Barney has plenty of food and water," she said, one brow raised in silent warning. "I can stay for hours and hours...."

He had a strong suspicion that, despite her mischievous grin, Taylor wasn't kidding. "I just don't want to worry you, is all," he began haltingly.

"I learned this much waiting for my dad to come out of surgery—what I don't know is far more worrisome than the truth." She patted his knee, her friendly invitation to begin.

Lifting the mug, Alex pretended to sip the hot tea, and took his time about it, too. Because he didn't want to spill the beans. Especially not when he had no idea who'd be responsible for cleaning them up.

She tapped his knee and whispered, "Um, I think you should know I recognize a stall tactic when I see it."

She had him dead to rights, and he knew it. "Okay. But one more question first?"

"All right." She held a forefinger aloft, her way of saying *just one*....

"Why do you want to know...whatever...?" Alex tried to underline the *whatever,* sloshing tea onto his hand when he did. It wasn't all that hot, but he muttered under his breath anyway before putting the mug onto the napkin with a *thud.*

Taylor grabbed a dry napkin from the tray and calmly blotted the dampness from his hand. "Back in a sec," she said, getting to her feet.

"Where are you—"

But before he could finish, she'd dashed from the room. Alex tried to remember a time when he could move that fast. When he was in basic training? On the high school track team? At the age five? *Never,* he admitted. At least, not without a well-defined purpose.

He was about to ask himself what Taylor's mission might have been when she darted back into the room, dampened paper towels in one hand, dry ones in the other. "What's that for?"

"The sugar in the tea will itch when it dries." She washed his hand, taking care not to miss the short webs connecting his fingers.

And he let her. Why? Alex had no idea, especially when he'd decided before she came pounding on his door that he didn't want her involved in this whole hospital-surgery-recuperation thing, didn't want her feeling duty bound to take care of him—before, during, or after. But, much as he hated to admit it, Alex liked the way she took care of him. Liked it a lot. It wasn't so much what she did as the way she did it, as if it fed something inside her every time she performed even the smallest, most insignificant favor.

If he had a single brain cell functioning at the moment, he'd take back his hand, get on his feet and politely escort her to the door. He'd thank her for stopping by, and promptly lock the door behind her, take the phone off the hook and make preparations to move...to Alaska, to Australia, someplace where she couldn't find and tempt him into doing the exact opposite.

"There," she said, interrupting his thoughts. "All clean and shiny." After dropping the paper towels onto the baking tin turned serving tray, she dusted her hands together. "So, go ahead…tell me—"

"Not so fast, pretty lady. I know a little something about stall tactics, too, y'know."

Brows high on her forehead, Taylor looked every bit as innocent as she had a right to. "You agreed to let me ask one last question," he reminded her.

Brows in their proper position now, she nodded. "I guess I did, didn't I?"

"Well?"

She sighed. "The answer is really quite simple. I want to know about anything that affects you."

He scrubbed his clean and shiny hand over his face. "That's what I don't understand, Taylor," Alex said, meeting her eyes. *"Why?"*

And she sighed again. Shrugged and sent him the tiniest smile. "I love you."

Chin touching his chest, he groaned. He'd been afraid she might say that. "For the life of me," he admitted, "I don't understand that, either."

She wedged herself onto the cushion beside him, between his hip and the arm of his chair, and rested her head on his shoulder. "You want an alphabetical listing? Or would you prefer numerical?"

Unconsciously his arms went around her and he kissed the top of her head.

"There are hundreds—no, make that thousands—of reasons why I love you, you big nut." She looked him in the eye. "I have an idea that a different list would save us a lot of time…."

Nose-to-nose as they were, she was more than close

enough to kiss. *Time* was the last thing on his mind at the moment. "Huh?"

"I could list things I *don't* love about you," she explained, "and that'd take no time at all, because I love everything about you."

Unable to bear another moment of the pure, perfect love pouring from her eyes, Alex tried to glance away. But she bracketed his face with both hands, forcing him to look at her. "Why is it important for you to know why I love you, Alex?"

"Because," he said, his voice gruff and low, "the next few months aren't gonna be easy, and I don't want—"

She laid a finger over his lips, effectively silencing him. "How 'bout we look at it this way. Let's say, for argument's sake, that this isn't about what you want at all. What if we said it was about what I want."

Gently he wrapped his fingers around her willowy wrists. It didn't take a genius to figure out the meaning behind her suggestion. Oh, but she was something special! "What you *think* you want, you mean. Do you have any idea what you're setting yourself up for?"

Leaning back, Taylor peered at him through narrowed eyes. "Of course I do."

"I don't think so."

"So you're saying I don't know my own mind? That I'm silly? Immature? Incapable of making life-altering decisions?"

"Well, not exactly."

"What exactly?"

He got a mental image of himself hobbling around on crutches, stump dangling in midair. Shaking his head, he tried to blink the picture away.

"What, Alex?" she said, drawing him nearer. "What is it?"

He hadn't said a word, so what on earth was she babbling about?

"Just now," she said, answering his unasked question, "you looked as though you'd seen—"

She bit her lip, telling him that she'd figured out *exactly* what he'd seen pictured. Taylor cuddled as close as the chair would allow. "Oh, why don't you just spit it out, Alex. I know you feel it. I can see it in your eyes. I can hear it in your voice. So get it over with, so we can get on with things."

He could play dumb, pretend he didn't know what she wanted to hear. But much as he wanted to say it, Alex couldn't allow himself to. It simply wouldn't be fair, asking her to waste her life on the likes of him. Not when she could have more, so much more.

It took some doing, wedged in beside her as he was, but Alex managed to get to his feet. His body felt cold in all the places where her warmth had been. Instinctively he realized this was how his whole world would be once she was gone. And like it or not, he had to do whatever it took to make that happen.

"There's nothing to get on with," he said. "So why don't you go back on into the kitchen, fetch your cute little baseball cap and go home, where you belong."

She stood wide-eyed and blinking, hands clasped under her chin.

"I mean it, Taylor. If I'm gonna to do this…this *thing*…then I'm gonna do it alone."

Her voice was a mere whisper when she said, "What do you mean, *if?* It isn't like you have a lot of options. Not if you want to live."

Alex only shook his head. He didn't have the energy, or the heart, for that matter, to tell her that doing nothing was but one of his options.

She misunderstood his silence, read it to mean that he'd dug in his heels, intended to walk the go-it-alone route.

"Alex...why?" Taylor took a step closer, and he took a step back. But she ignored it and moved forward another step. "Why would you want to do it alone?"

He raised his arms in helpless supplication, let them drop heavily to his sides. Didn't she see? It wasn't what he *wanted*. It was what he had to do, for her sake!

"Look at me, Alex."

Her voice sounded stronger now, more like the Taylor he'd fallen in love with. A good thing, he thought, because her strength would give him the courage, the conviction to stick to his guns.

"Alex...?"

Don't look up, he warned. One glance into those dark, mesmerizing eyes, and his decision was as good as doomed.

"Look me in the eye and tell me you don't love me, that you don't want me to be there beside you through this...this *thing.*"

He stared at the carpet between his feet. Until that moment, he hadn't realized he'd forgotten to put on shoes that morning. Or socks, for that matter. *You're a mess,* he told himself, *inside and out.* It hit him like a brick to the skull— he'd needed her from the get-go, for reasons that had absolutely nothing to do with his health. But to accept what she was offering, he'd also have to acknowledge the sacrifices she'd be required to make.

Alex clamped his molars together, narrowed his lips. "Will you get your baseball cap...it's on the kitchen table...or should I?"

"I don't care about that stupid hat! Keep it, throw it away, *eat* it for all I care!"

He looked up, but only long enough to see if she still wore her windbreaker. When he determined that she did,

Alex once again riveted his eyes to the floor. "Okay, then…I'm gonna go over there and open the front door, and when I do, I want you to—"

Peripheral vision told him Taylor was headed straight for him. He tried to sidestep her, but she moved too quickly for him.

"I'm not going anywhere, you big idiot." She wrapped her arms around his waist. "You can stand there muttering insane nonsense, but you can't make me take it seriously."

Chin resting amid her soft curls, he closed his eyes, closed his arms around her. "Ah, Taylor." He sighed. Was she aware what a weak, unprincipled man she'd fallen in love with? He hadn't always been that way. When had the changes taken place? Taylor tightened her hold on him, all but making him forget that the question regarding his worth as a man deserved an answer. "What're you doin' to me?"

"I'm not doing anything *to you*," she said into his chest. "I'm doing it *for me*." Tears pooled in her big eyes when she looked up at him, and her voice wavered when she said, "Maybe you don't need me, but I sure do need you."

He watched a sparkling, silvery tear drop down her cheek.

"Please don't send me away, Alex."

She bit her lip, and he knew she was struggling to regain control of her emotions.

Gathering her close, he breathed a long, shuddering sigh. He knew for a fact he'd never been loved like this before. Knew just as well that it wasn't likely he'd ever be loved this way again. *Maybe you don't need me,* she'd said, *but I sure do need you.* Alex understood her better than she realized, well enough, at least, to have figured out that she'd substituted *need* for *love*…for his sake. There was only one reason he could come up with to explain why she'd do a thing like that—Taylor didn't really believe he loved her at all. She'd hinted at it earlier, with all her talk about seeing it in his eyes and hearing it in his voice, but it had been false bravado prompting her speech, nothing more.

In trying to protect her from the pain he'd be going through in the next months—possibly years—ahead, had he hurt her instead?

Lord, he prayed, *tell me what to do....*

"Thank you," she whispered.

"Thank you?" he repeated. "I always knew you had a screw loose," he said, "and now I have proof."

Sniffing, she looked into his face. "I'm going to quote something you said just a few minutes ago—'huh?'"

Chuckling, he said, "Well, think about it, pretty lady...I'm a miserable mess of a human being, and you've volunteered to stand by me, no matter what...yet *you're* thanking *me*." He looked deep into her eyes. "Care to explain that?"

She gasped, scraped a fingernail across his pocket. "Oh, look...I've gotten mascara on your shirt. I'll have to take this home with me, give it a good dose of—"

"If they gave awards for asides, you'd win, hands down."

"Maybe, but you'd come in a close second."

What lay ahead wouldn't be easy, but it sure would be more fun with her around to keep him centered. "So... why'd you thank me?"

A proud little grin lit up her face and she said matter-of-factly, "Because I asked you not to send me away, and you didn't."

Drawing her near once more, he shook his head. "No, I guess I didn't, did I?"

"One more thing to add to my 'Why I Love Alex' list."

Cupping her chin in one hand, Alex gently tilted up her face to receive his kiss. Their lips were touching when he

said, "You're a crazy, mixed-up, gorgeous li'l thing, do
you know that?"

Her answer? A slow nod.

He saw the affection beaming from her eyes, saw pure
devotion, too, rooted in unconditional, uncompromising
love.

Moments ago, before his brief but heartfelt prayer, he'd
thought he owed it to her to keep his feelings for her to
himself, thought she deserved that measure of protection.

Now, he realized, the best way to accomplish that was
with the truth. "I love you, too."

When Alex had finally shared his terrible secret, Taylor
had not shed a tear. There'd be plenty of time for that later,
alone in her room. What he needed now was to see that
she had complete faith…faith that he'd be cured, faith
she'd stand by him until he was.

It hadn't been easy talking Alex into coming to her
house. But she'd pointed out that since they'd missed
breakfast, the parade, the picnic, there wasn't much sense
in missing the fireworks, too. Especially when they could
watch them from her deck…

Nor had it been easy leaving him alone in his town
house, even when he'd promised to head for her place the
moment he'd showered and changed into fresh clothes.

Just for good measure, she'd thrown two added incen-
tives into the invitation—steaks and baked potatoes,
cooked on the gas grill…and her own ineptness. She hoped
God wouldn't hold it against her for saying, "I just bought
the thing and I'm scared of blowing the house up when I
try to light it."

"So use the broiler," he'd suggested, a pretty good indicator, Taylor thought, that without her coaxing, he would
have continued to hole up in that dreary house, all by himself.

"Sorry," she'd said, compounding the fib, "but it's broken." Taylor had made it clear that she intended to cook outside, with or without his help. "Do you want it on your conscience if I land in a treetop?"

He'd quickly admitted that he did not, and promised to meet her at her house in an hour. Which gave her enough time to stop at the grocery store for meat, potatoes and salad fixings.

As an afterthought, she grabbed the ingredients for hot fudge sundaes. When the fireworks display ended, she would fix them each a big bowl of the gooey stuff. Maybe the treat would remind him of the wonderful time they'd had at the ice-cream parlor a few short weeks ago. The memory would give her something to hope for and look forward to; would it have the same effect on Alex?

The minute she walked into the house, the question was forgotten as Barney began prowling through the grocery bags. "No treats in there for you this time, fella," she told him. "But maybe if you're good, you can have a scrap of my steak later."

Tail flicking, Barney pranced from the room as if to say, "I might grace you with my company later, and then again, I might not."

But for the first time since she'd brought him home, Taylor paid little or no attention to the tabby's mood. She had a lot of work to do, and very little time to do it....

Starting with her appearance.

After a quick shower, she decided to let her curls air dry, and changed into a kicky little skirt of gauzy cotton and a short-sleeved white blouse. Plain white flats and silver wolf earrings completed the outfit. She added a dab of eye shadow the same shade of lavender as the skirt, a touch of blush and a hint of lipstick.

Next she prepared the salad, and when that was finished, Taylor set the glass-topped table on the deck. Satisfied that it looked every bit as appealing as a restaurant offering, she positioned the padded chaise longue near the stairs, so that when Alex lay back on it, he'd have an unobstructed view of the fireworks. A small wrought-iron table beside the chair would give him a place for soft drinks and snacks, and then a citronella candle in its center would discourage mosquitoes.

Adjusting the stereo dials to a station that played classical music, she aimed the speaker toward the French doors. Here, in the family room, the euphonious notes were slightly on the loud side, but from the deck it would be just right.

Glancing at the clock, she heaved a relieved sigh. Finished, and with five minutes to spare.

Almost as if on cue, the doorbell rang, sending her heartbeat into double time.

He looked so handsome standing there on her front porch that Taylor wanted to throw her arms around him.

And so she did.

"Good to see you, too," he said, chuckling slightly. "I, ah, I brought you something."

She stepped back to allow him to present her with a large white paper cone filled with fresh flowers. "Alex, what a nice surprise." She could feel her face redden in a blush. "Let me find a vase," she said, turning quickly to hide it from him, "and we'll use them as our centerpiece."

Hands in his pockets, Alex followed her into the kitchen. "Place looks great, as always," he said. "But then, I've learned to expect perfection from the likes of you."

In the kitchen, standing in the glare of the light above the sink, there was no hope of hiding her flushed cheeks. And so she busied herself by searching for the right vase, her kitchen shears and the powdery mixture she kept on hand to ensure the blooms cut from her garden lasted as long as possible.

She couldn't help but notice the bouquet had more than the customary number of daisies in it. But how could he have known they were her all-time favorite flowers? Spreading the blossoms across the countertop, she began arranging them in the tall, cut-glass vase.

"They had roses," Alex said, standing to her left, "but something told me you weren't a roses kind of girl."

Pulling a daisy from the bunch, she met his eyes. "As a matter of fact, when I have a choice, *these* are the flowers that're always first on my list."

He slid the bloom from between her fingers and turned her to face him. Snapping off all but an inch or so of the stem, he tucked it behind her ear. "Beautiful," he rasped, sliding a knuckle across her cheek.

The intensity of his gaze set her heart to thumping harder still. She'd promised herself, as she got ready for his visit, to put a little less pressure on him. He needed her full support, especially now, with everything that was happening to him.

She turned her attention back to her arrangement. "You ain't seen nuttin' yet. After we eat, I'll get a flashlight, show you God's magnificent creations in my gardens...."

"Okay. Whatever you want to do is fine with me." He leaned both elbows on the counter beside her, looked up into her face. "But just for the record, the most magnificent thing God ever made is standing right here, beside me."

She didn't know what to say, confronted by such blatant compliments. What could have happened, between the time she'd left his house and the time he'd arrived here, to explain this drastic change in him?

Eyes on her work, she said, "What a nice thing to say, Alex."

Her side vision told him he was nodding, smiling. She didn't know what to credit for his brighter outlook, but she knew who. *Thank You, Lord,* she prayed.

"Are you hungry?" she asked, poking the last flower into place in the vase.

"I wouldn't turn down a steak, if a pretty girl offered me one."

Grabbing the vase, she headed for the deck. "Keep that up," she said, grinning over her shoulder, "and I really will have to hire a handyman."

Chuckling at the reminder of their time following his concussion, Alex went outside with her. "Turned out to be a nice night."

Positioning the flowers he'd brought in the center of the table, she nodded. "It sure has, thank God!"

"Course, this is Maryland. If you don't like the weather, wait five minutes…"

"And it'll change," they said together, laughing.

"I'm going to pour us both a nice tall glass of freshly squeezed lemonade. Would you mind starting the grill while I'm inside?"

"Wouldn't mind a bit."

As she passed him on her way through the French doors, he grabbed her hand. "Have I told you how pretty you look tonight?"

Taylor rolled her eyes and smiled. "Only half a dozen times, in half a dozen different ways."

He gave her hand an affectionate squeeze. "Well, stuff like that…" He shrugged and let her go. "It bears repeating, I guess I wanted to say."

"You look very handsome tonight yourself," she pointed out. "Pale blue is a good color on you."

Alex tucked in one corner of his mouth. "No fair fighting flattery with flattery," he said as she stepped into the kitchen.

"What's good for the goose is good for the gander."

"Yeah, but let's not forget…*I'm* the gander."

"Silly goose," she said, laughing as she closing the door.

As she dropped crescent-shaped ice into tall tumblers, Taylor couldn't help but think of the obvious change in him. He seemed happier now than before the doctor's diagnosis. Maybe her prayers had been answered, and Alex had found his way back to the Lord.

He'd told her during one of their first meetings that as a boy he'd wanted to be the pastor of a small rural church. But, feeling the pressure of family tradition, he'd given up the dream and followed in the heroic footsteps of Van Buren men. It was a shame, she thought as she filled their glasses with lemonade, that he hadn't been given a chance to pursue his dream. Because in her estimation he had all the right qualities required of a good preacher.

Taylor didn't think the cancer—if indeed that's what it turned out to be—was a wake-up call from above. Surely God, in His infinite mercy and love, could have found a gentler way to rouse Alex from his spiritual lethargy than the loss of his leg.

Almost as if he'd heard his name mentioned, Alex poked his head inside. "The grill's lit. Anything else you need me to do?"

She grabbed their drinks. "You could hold the door."

"That rain was just what we needed," he said, holding the door, then closing it behind her.

"I'll say." She handed him a glass. "It cooled things down and got rid of some of that oppressive humidity."

Alex sipped the lemonade. "Will you answer a question for me?"

She sat at the table. "Sure, if I can."

"Is there anything you *can't* do?" He held the glass up. "This is perfect." With a grand sweep of his free arm, he indicated her yard, still visible in the dimming twilight. "That's perfect." He nodded toward the house. "Ditto."

He stepped nearer the table and touched a daisy in the flower arrangement. "Double ditto." And lifting her chin on a bent forefinger, he grinned so that only the dimple in his right cheek showed. "How do you say 'ditto times ten thousand'?"

Pulse racing, Taylor could only blink silently up at him, because she had no idea how to respond to his nonstop approval. "Will you answer a question for me?"

"Sure," he copied, "if I can."

"Did you take a nap before coming over here?"

"No, why?"

"I thought maybe you'd fallen out of bed."

"Haven't fallen since..." With his chin he indicated the house. "Well, you know."

"Bump your head in the shower, then?"

"Ah, no-o-o-o-o..."

"Bump it getting into the pickup?"

He shook his head.

She tapped the tip of a pink-polished fingernail against her bottom lip. "Something sure is different about you. I just can't seem to put my finger on it."

Chuckling, he took her hands in his, pulled her to her feet. "You're right. There is something different about me. I'll give you three guesses."

"Haircut?"

He pulled her close. "Nope."

"New aftershave?"

"Uh-uh."

"I give up."

He drew her nearer still. "By my count, you have one more guess left."

She lifted her shoulders, grinning. "Sorry. Fresh out of—"

Alex silenced her with a soft, slow kiss, and Taylor returned it with equal ardor.

"Guess I'd better put the steaks on," he said after a moment.

Much as she hated the delicious kiss to end, she agreed. "Guess you'd better, if we want to give our full attention to the fireworks."

"Oh, don't you worry your pretty head about that. I know exactly where my attention will be when the sky starts exploding with color."

"Mmmm," was her dreamy response. "I see I've gone and fallen in love with a poet."

Oh, how she loved the sound of his laughter!

"I wasn't a poet until I met you." And as if to prove it, he kissed her again, longer, harder, with more feeling this time...if that was possible.

"I, ah, I'd better get the steaks."

He let her walk away, but his expression made it apparent he was none too happy about it.

"I have to put the potatoes in the microwave if we want to eat them with the steaks."

He winked. "Need any help?"

She shook her head.

"Hurry back, then," he said, settling onto the chaise longue.

Inside, as she punched the buttons to set the microwave's timer, her heart continued to pound. She loved him as she'd never loved any man...as she never *would* love any man. He was right for her, Taylor knew, because she'd prayed about their relationship long and hard, almost from the first day they'd met. With every *Amen,* she found a new reason to like and respect him, and read those reasons as God's stamp of approval. The most pressing question, at first, was whether or not he'd return to the Lord. Without any proof, she believed he would, if for no other reason than that she'd prayed for it almost as fervently as she'd prayed about her alliance with him.

At some point in the near future, she'd have to broach the subject with him. Hopefully, by that time, Alex would have a better idea what his faith meant to him. If not…

She preferred to focus on *her* faith, on her belief that God would not misguide her. He'd answered each of her prayers with a signal that drew her closer, ever closer to Alex.

Could she have read the signals wrong? Possible, Taylor supposed, but not likely.

She hoped.

Because her whole future, her happiness, depended on being right….

Chapter Ten

It was as though God and nature had made a silent pact with Taylor and Alex, for the rain disappeared and the clouds opened up to reveal a deep black sky. "Looks like an Elvis painting," he observed. "A really pretty one, with ten million stars behind the..."

"Star," they finished together, laughing.

Beneath that inky, glimmering canvas, they sat and prepared to eat filet mignon, twice-baked potatoes and a tossed salad.

"Would you like to say grace?" Taylor asked, folding her hands.

The whole time he'd grilled the steaks, he'd been afraid she'd ask that very question. What was it with her, he wondered, wanting to pray at ice-cream parlors, restaurants, even hot dog stands? "Nah, I think since it's your house, you should do it," came his well-rehearsed response.

In place of the "you do it," "no, you" game they'd played every other time, she quietly lowered her head and closed her eyes as Alex said his own private little prayer: *Thank God!*

"Lord God," she began, taking his hand, "we thank You for the minimiracle You've give us in the way of beautiful weather. Oh, how we love You for seeing to even the teeniest of our needs!"

Eyes closed, Alex smiled and gave her hand an affectionate squeeze, because he didn't know another person on earth who'd say "teeniest" to God.

"Thank You for making all this healthy food available to us...."

She hesitated, and he was tempted to open one eye, to find out why, when she continued, "For the handsome barbecue chef who cooked the steaks to perfection—"

"For neighbors who care," he put in, half laughing.

He could hear the smile in her voice when she echoed, "For neighbors who care. We ask that You continue showering us with—"

"No pun intended," he interrupted, "'cause we won't mind a bit if You decide to hold off on the rainy forecast...."

He heard the "teeniest" giggle before she went on, "With good health, and faith in Your abiding love."

"Aye-men!" he said, flapping his napkin across his lap.

He asked her about her work, and Taylor told him that the idea to become a physical therapist had dawned when a high school classmate was involved in a serious car accident.

"She broke both her legs, a couple of fingers and her collarbone," Taylor explained. "Mind you, this is back in the days when they kept you in the hospital for weeks following an accident like that. I visited her every day after school.

"The doctors told her she'd probably never walk again,

which terrified her, because since kindergarten she'd been a dancer...with Broadway dreams.

"Anyway, one day," she said, sprinkling her potato with salt, "Claudia wasn't in her room, so her nurse took me to her. We found her in a room that looked more like a workout gym than anything I would have associated with a hospital. I stood beside the door, fascinated as this big burly guy led her through a series of exercises, explaining what each one was for and the results they'd produce."

Taylor sighed and, smiling a wistful smile, said, "She made it to Broadway, and do you know who she credits?"

He looked into her excited, beautiful face, and though he knew the answer, Alex said, "Who?"

"Her physical therapist, that's who! That man made a real difference in Claudia's life. I wanted to do work like that."

Made perfect sense, from his point of view, that she'd chosen a career that made use of her gift for nurturing. "Must not have been easy for you, though, tiny as you are."

Taylor nodded emphatically. "True. I had to buy myself a weight set, so I could build up my upper body." She flexed a bicep. "Didn't want my weakness to be the reason someone didn't get the full effects of physical therapy!"

His experience with the profession hadn't been nearly as positive as her friend's. Alex was about to tell her that if he'd had someone like her on his team after the crash, maybe he'd have recuperated better, faster. Maybe he wouldn't be facing amputation a day and a half from now.

"So, how was your steak?" he asked, wondering how she managed to keep that gorgeous figure when she packed away food like a linebacker.

She opened her mouth to answer when a golf ball landed with a soggy *plop* in his salad bowl.

Gasping, Taylor dropped her fork to the glass tabletop

with a noisy clatter and sat back, one hand pressed to her chest.

He could have told her it was no big deal—just a little Caesar dressing that would come out in the wash. But it was too late for that. Alex could almost see the thoughts taking shape in her pretty head—dip napkin in water, wipe guest's shirt, apologize for interruption, above all, calm down!

With thumb and forefinger he picked up the dimpled ball. "Now, that's what I call a hard-boiled egg," he said, nodding thoughtfully. "You might wanna remove the shell next time, though."

For a split second she only stared at him. And when her wide-eyed expression softened into a warm, sweet smile, Alex gave himself a mental pat on the back, because his joke had earned its intended reaction.

He reached out to take her hand, but she was already on her feet, acting out the scene he'd just pictured in his head.

"Oh, Alex," she began, "your poor shirt. And it's linen, too." She dragged her chair next to his. "Linen is like a sponge for something oily, like salad oil…. Well," she said, covering her forefinger with a corner of her napkin, "you'll just have to leave it here, so I can soak it." Frowning, she clucked her tongue. "Who would have thought anyone would be playing golf in the dark," she added as she attempted to blot up the greasy spots with the napkin-coated finger. "And on the Fourth of July, for goodness sake!"

He barely heard a word after *Alex,* because her face was mere inches from his. He wanted to take her face in his hands and silence her nonstop nervous chatter with a kiss.

And so he did.

He couldn't help but notice the way she relaxed—not only verbally, but physically, too—when he pressed his palms against her cheeks, when he pressed his lips to hers.

Was he crazy, or had he been responsible for the calm
reaction his touch inspired? Because if Alex could believe
for a minute that he was actually *good* for Taylor, then—

An ear-piercing whistle shattered the mood. "Wooo-
wooo, Taylor!" a woman hollered.

Taylor tried to look in the direction of the voice, but
Alex's hands, still pressed to her cheeks, wouldn't allow
it.

"Way to go, Taylor!" a man bellowed.

Alex chuckled. "Um, does this happen often in your part
of town?" Under his hands he felt the heat in her cheeks.
Because of the kiss? Or embarrassment at the interruption?

"Well, no, not exactly. I've found golf balls while mow-
ing the lawn...small price to pay for the gorgeous view, I
suppo—"

"I'm talking about your built-in audience over there."

Grinning sheepishly, Taylor giggled. "That's Lauren
and Dick Buroker. They've been trying to set me up ever
since I moved in, it seems." She looked toward the house
next door, gave a friendly little wave.

His gut tightened at the thought of her out on the town
with another man. "Blind dates, huh?" he said through
clenched teeth.

Taylor shook her head and whispered, "*Bad* dates."

Relief surged through him at Taylor's admission. And
he would have said so if Lauren hadn't yelled, "It's about
time!"

"Wa-a-a-ay about time," her husband echoed.

Without taking his eyes from Taylor's, Alex fired back
in a loud voice, "Ditto..."

As their lips met this time, the opening fireworks display
flared in the sky, leaving Alex to wonder which caused the
hammering of his heart...the neighbors' applause, the ka-
leidoscopic explosions overhead, or the vibrant woman in
his arms.

Suddenly he realized that life without her would be the way the sky had been earlier—dull, drab, dreary.... The keen edge of fear sliced through him, because he didn't want to go back to that life, ever. He'd wasted a lot of time worrying about what she thought of his limp, when all along the proof that it didn't make a bit of difference to her was right there, under his nose. *He* was the only one who gave a hoot if he had two legs, or one, or none at all....

"You'll never leave me, right?" he said on a ragged sigh.

"Never."

She'd said it without a moment's hesitation, and while that should have comforted him, it didn't. Because what if, after she had time to think about what she'd said, Taylor decided she didn't have what it took to be nursemaid to a disabled person? What if she realized—

"Alex?"

"Hmmm?"

"Wipe that worried look off your face. My fickle teen years are far behind me." She kissed the tip of his nose. "I'm pushin' thirty, y'know. I know what I want."

He marveled at her ability to read his emotions simply by looking into his face. He hadn't exactly been overly religious these past few years, but he knew who he had to thank for this gift called Taylor. *Thank You, Lord!* he thought. "Well," he said, "you look like a teenager."

She winked. "It's the low lighting. And the Maybelline... Eighth Wonder of the World..."

Life with Taylor would be a lot of things, but boring wouldn't be one of them. "So you love me, huh?"

"Yeah." She shrugged, simulating indifference. "I guess."

He chuckled. "But...why?" A strange déjà vu sensation blanketed him the moment the question was out of his mouth. He had a feeling he'd asked that before, but for the life of him, he couldn't remember how she'd answered.

"Why wouldn't I love you?"

His heart felt twice its normal size when he heard that. He didn't feel lucky enough to press her for details. Because what if, in searching for reasons, she came up with one that made her rethink how she felt about him?

Don't rock the boat, baby, he told himself, just accept it. *And thank the good Lord for it.*

Standing, Taylor threw the napkin onto the table, then took his hand and led him to the chaise longue. "Make yourself comfortable."

"I *was* comfortable," he said, "Perfectly comfortable."

"You'll be more comfortable there." She pointed to the chair.

Ignoring the burning pain in his leg, Alex settled onto its padded seat and held out one hand. "Join me?"

"Don't mind if I do," she said, snuggling in beside him.

Alex tucked his left arm behind her and, because there wasn't room for it anyplace else, she rested her elbow on his stomach. "Comfy?" she asked, head against his shoulder.

"Very." Fact of the matter was, his leg was killing him. And the right arm of the chair was digging into his hip. Half an hour of this, and he'd be lucky if he could stand at all, let alone walk. The discomfort reminded him of high school and Saturday nights at the movies, when he'd slide an arm across his date's shoulders and not move it again until the film ended. He wondered if it would take ten minutes for the pins and needles to dissipate, as it had back then, or if advancing age would make it more like half an hour.

"This is my all-time favorite holiday," Taylor said.

"Not Christmas?"

"What's not to like? Jesus's birthday, special celebrations, decorations..." She leaned closer and whispered from the corner of her mouth, "But just between you and me, it's not nearly noisy enough."

Laughing, he remembered that only a moment ago she'd pointed out how grown-up she was. Yet there she sat, reacting to the light show with all the energy and enthusiasm of an eight-year-old.

Her face reflecting shades of pink, gold, blue and green, Taylor pointed as several moon-shaped fireworks erupted above. "Rib-rackers! My favorites!" As the smoke cleared, she said, "Isn't it phenomenal?"

In all honesty, the only "phenom" he could name was cuddled up close beside him.

"I don't mean the display itself," she continued. "I mean the fact that someone figured out that if they started with a lift charge of some kind, stuck it in a launch tube with black powder, added a time-release fuse..."

The excitement in her voice might have been contagious...if he hadn't been so distracted by how beautiful she looked, lit up by the vibrant glow from above. "I'm gonna want to be very polite around you from now on."

"Polite?"

"Well, I don't want to mess with anyone who knows as much as you do about explosives."

Laughing, Taylor said, "My fifth-grade science fair project was titled 'All about Pyrotechnics.'"

"Let me guess. It won a blue ribbon."

She nodded. "At my school and at the county level. Made it as far as third place at the state level, too."

"No kidding?"

She met his eyes, but only long enough to say, "No kidding." The bright splashes in the heavens had immediately recaptured her attention.

Alex shook his head. "I'm impressed. I can barely remember how old I was in fifth grade, let alone the details of my science fair project.''

"You know what's really remarkable?''

"You're remarkable,'' he said, kissing her temple.

And she kissed his cheek. "They're still making fireworks pretty much the way they made them hundreds of years ago.''

He smiled. "You don't say.''

"Well, at least where the main ingredients are concerned. I think it was around 1800 when they started substituting potassium chlorate for potassium nitrate.''

"Is that right?''

"Phenomenal,'' she said again, gaze fixed on the sky.

Alex had absolutely no interest in what was going on up there. He was far more intrigued by the phenomenon in his arms.

"Hey, did I just feel a raindrop?''

He held out his free hand. "Yeah, I think maybe you did.''

"Aw, no fair. If this keeps up, they won't be able to do the big finale!''

The rain was falling harder, more steadily now, dampening the deck, the chaise, everything but his spirits. *She's like a big kid,* Alex thought, grinning. "The show's more than half over. Considering what your ol' pal Marty said, we were lucky to see this much of it.''

"You make a good point...'' She gave him a playful elbow jab to the ribs. "Mr. Maturity...'' Taylor made a move as if to get up.

"Where do you think you're going?''

"To clear the table, for starters.''

Narrowing his eyes, Alex said, "If I'm so mature, how come I'd rather stay out here, dodging raindrops?''

"You don't want to get stuck doing dishes?'' She batted her eyelashes.

He knew she'd intended it as a fun and friendly thing. But her blinking stirred something tender yet passionate deep inside him. *Ah, Taylor,* he thought, gazing longingly into her eyes, *do you have any idea how lovely you are?*

"I think you're pretty good-lookin', too," she said with a smile.

Had he spoken his thoughts aloud again? Or had she read the emotions on his face again?

Taylor stood, held out a hand to him. "I'm soaked to the skin and the wind is kicking up," she said. "Didn't think it was possible to be cold on the Fourth of July, but…" She did a little jig, and shivered.

Laughing at her antics, he got to his feet. But the moment he put his weight on his bad leg, he winced with pain.

Taylor grabbed his arm. "Alex…?"

"I'm okay," he huffed, feigning a smile.

"You don't look fine. You look like you've just run a one-minute mile…barefoot on broken glass."

"You oughta be a writer," he said, "with that fertile imagination of yours…." He swiped a hand across his damp forehead. If he couldn't tell the difference between raindrops and perspiration, neither could Taylor…he hoped. This was her favorite holiday, and he hated the idea of ruining it for her.

She pressed her little body tight against his, slung his arm over her shoulder. "C'mon, big guy," she said, "lean on me. And don't give me any of that 'I'm too big' nonsense. Remember, I'm tougher than I look."

Alex didn't argue.

Slowly, step by step, they made their way inside. She helped him to the family-room sofa, a big, deep-seated thing with lots of loose pillows. Taylor tossed the back cushions onto the floor, pressed one against a double-wide arm. "Lie down," she instructed, rubbing her hands together. "You're gettin' a massage, mister."

Despite the pain, Alex laughed. "Massage? Don't be ridicu—"

"Need I remind you that I'm a professionally trained, certified physical therapist?" She donned a deep, James Bond-kind of voice. "Massage is my business, my only business…." In her own voice she added, "We can do this the easy way, or we can do this your way."

Alex was determined not to make a face when he bent the leg to lower himself onto the couch. He gave her a Stan Laurel smile, just to prove all was well. "Okay, but don't you think we oughta get the dishes inside first?"

"You're halfway to paradise…." Taylor pointed at the cushion where she wanted him to lay his head, and mouthed the words "Now lie down."

He honestly didn't know if he could. At least, not without grunting or grimacing. Should he do it in stages? Yeah, that's the ticket, he told himself—seated position to fetal position in one fell swoop.

As he eased himself onto his side, Taylor shoved the coffee table out of the way, then got onto her knees next to the sofa and laid a hand on his thigh. "Tell me if it hurts, even in the slightest, okay?"

As if that was possible, he thought, grinning. How could she possibly hurt him, tiny as she—

"Yee-ouch," he hissed through clenched teeth.

Wearing an upside-down smile, she did a perfect Bullwinkle imitation. "Sorry, don't know my own strength!"

Despite funny faces and comedic imitations, Taylor was all business for the next fifteen minutes as she gently worked his leg's largest muscle. He wouldn't have given a plugged nickel as a bet on whether or not this would do him any good in the long run. But he had to admit, as she slowly, methodically worked her way around the knee, to the calf, down to the ankle, that it felt mighty good. The warmth of her touch, the soft rasp of her palms against the fabric of his trousers had a tranquilizing effect—the massage itself…or the lovely creature giving it to him?

She leaned nearer his face and, smiling sweetly, whispered, "Alex…" She kissed his chin. "I want you to relax." Kissed his cheek. "Let every muscle go completely limp."

He pointed to his mouth. "I'll be a regular dishrag…with the right incentive…"

One brow rose high on her forehead as she patted his hand and smirked. "All in good time, Mr. Maturity, all in good time."

He wouldn't have thought it possible for her to reach his back, not while he was lying on it. But she knew her stuff, all right. And in moments, the muscles of his lower back felt as slack as a wet noodle.

"Close your eyes, Alex."

"Why?"

"Because it makes me nervous when patients watch me work."

"You? Nervous? Ha," he teased. "You just don't want me to see you slide the wallet from my back pocket. Besides, I'm not your patient. I'm your—"

"Fat lot you know," she shot back. "Besides, you keep your wallet in your right front pocket."

He lifted his head off the pillow. "How'd you know tha—"

She batted her eyelashes, the same way she had on the deck earlier, making his heart beat double time, making his pulse race. Again.

"It pays to be observant," she said.

Now, how could he disagree with that, when he'd observed all sorts of details about her, like the way she preferred toffee to chocolate, and the fact that she liked country-and-western music every bit as much as she liked classical, the way she scraped the nuts off her hot fudge sundae the moment she found out how much he liked them.

Hands on his shoulders, she alternately pressed fingertips and thumbs into the tendons connecting his neck to his head. What that had to do with the pain in his leg, Alex didn't know. But what she was doing felt so good, he wasn't about to complain.

She worked her way around to the back of his neck, to the base of his skull and, combing her fingers through his hair, massaged his scalp.

His forehead was next, then his eyebrows, and before he knew what was happening, the pads of her thumbs had eased his eyelids shut. If she kept this up, he'd be fast asleep another minute from now....

Taylor continued working his leg muscle long after Alex fell asleep. In his relaxed state, he looked more like an innocent young boy than a man with the weight of the world on his shoulders. Surely there had been a mix-up, a mistake at the hospital lab. How could a man as strong, as vital as Alex have cancer? She'd read and reread the articles written shortly after his fighter had crashed. It hardly seemed fair to heap another setback on him; hadn't he already suffered enough?

She sat on the floor beside the sofa, palms flat on his chest and chin resting on her hands, content to watch the steady rise and fall of his broad chest. He was beautiful, in a neoclassic way—thick dark hair, thickly lashed brown eyes, a tall, well-toned body.... If she dared admit such a thing to him, Alex would likely blush and stammer and shake his head in denial. Amazing, when she thought about it, that when he shaved every morning he didn't see in the mirror what she saw every time she looked into his wonderful, masculine face. But then, wasn't his humility just one of the hundreds of things she loved about him?

Gently, so as not to wake him, she traced one of the fading scratches Barney had inflicted on him the day of the ladies' auxiliary luncheon. He'd told her how he hoped one of the scrapes would leave a scar, to give his face character. Amazing, she thought again, because how could he not see the qualities—integrity, honesty, honor—carved by every smile line, by every furrow of worry? Warmth and affection bubbled up as she recalled the way he'd sucked air through his teeth when the tip of her medicine-soaked cotton swab had dabbed the cut. *Careful what you wish for,* she thought, following the curve of the weeks-old wound, *'cause in this case, you got it.*

He stirred, waving one big hand in front of his face, as if to discourage a pesky mosquito. Smiling, Taylor wondered what he'd say if he knew *she* was the pest? She considered drawing out the playful game, tickling his cheek, then waiting for him to wave her away, but she didn't want to wake him; no telling when he'd relax enough to sleep again.

Just over twenty-four hours ago, Alex had confided back at his town house, Luke McKenzie had told Alex that the mass they'd found was cancer, that in all likelihood he'd lose his leg. Tears stung her eyes as she looked into his sweet, serene, sleeping face. She knew little to nothing about his background, but surely he'd never done anything to deserve a punishment like this!

But that was a silly, immature thought, and Taylor knew it. God wasn't disciplining Alex for a wrong committed in the past. Didn't He promise to protect His children? Mentally she recited Psalm 33:20. *Our soul waiteth for the Lord; He is our help and our shield.* But maybe, just maybe, Alex was meant to learn from the experience, to grow and mature in faith.

Suddenly she felt a little guilty, thinking such a thing. Because how could she possibly know the state of Alex's faith? He might well be stronger, more devoted and loyal to God than any so-called good Christian she could name.

But he didn't go to church.

And he didn't seem comfortable saying grace before meals.

Did he pray when he was alone? Did he pray at all? And if he did, what did he pray for?

The real question, the only one that made any difference, really: Was he a Believer, in body and soul, in heart and mind? If the answer was no, then what?

She loved him, more than she'd loved Kent, more than she believed she'd ever love anyone…except God. But if Alex hadn't given the Lord a promise of some sort, could she love him still? *Should* she love him then?

He stirred just then, as if the questions in her mind were disturbing his peaceful sleep. One big hand rose, came to rest upon his chest. She laid her cheek on it, and, closing her eyes, she sighed, knowing how hard life could be, yoked to an unbeliever. But she loved him, and he loved her….

She had much to be grateful for—memories of happy times with her parents, her own good health, a job she enjoyed, a solidly built little house. She had Uncle Dave, numerous friends and Barney. What she didn't have, what she hadn't managed to find, was the love of a good man, a decent man, who'd share his world and even his everyday cares with her….

Except for the "religion" thing, Alex had already done that. So now the question was, had God put Alex into her life to love and protect her as no one before him had…or the other way around?

Alex sighed, long and deep, rested his free hand amid her curls. He was smiling ever so slightly. *What are you dreaming of, sweet Alex?* she asked silently. *Are you dreaming of life with two strong, healthy legs, a home filled with children who adore you, a wife who thinks you hung the moon?*

Though he couldn't possibly have known what sort of thoughts had been flitting through her mind, the question made her blush. He hadn't said a word about marriage. Why, he hadn't even suggested they date one another, exclusively. Those unspoken questions...they described *her* dream.

But she couldn't help herself, because yes, she loved him, with every cell in her body, with every fiber of her soul. And while he hadn't talked about the future, she believed Alex loved her, too. After he recuperated from the operation, got back on his *feet*...he'd need her more than ever if worse came to worst, and plural became singular....

Taylor saw only one problem on their horizon—this "religion thing." But other couples had managed to get around it; why not her and Alex? Because really, a hard life *with* him would be better than an easy life *without* him...wouldn't it?

He tousled her hair. "What're you looking so serious about?" His voice, slightly hoarse from his nap, cracked on the word *serious*.

Taylor shook her head, unable to imagine his reaction should she admit the silly, schoolgirlish things she'd been thinking, should she tell him the petty worries she'd been considering. "Did you have a nice rest?"

"Yes," he said, levering himself up on one elbow, "I did...*Irish*."

She looked puzzled. "But Griffith is a Welsh name, not..." Grinning, she remembered that she'd called him to task for answering a question with a question. "Touché." Then, "Pleasant dreams?"

"Pleasant enough." He patted his leg. "Thanks, by the way."

"Pain's all gone?"

He shook his head. "Feels a whole lot better than before."

She got up, perched on the edge of the couch and rested a palm on either side of him. "Wish I could have made it *all* better."

He wiggled his eyebrows and grinned mischievously. "Well, y'know what they say...."

"Who?"

"'Who' what?"

"Who's 'they'?"

"Oh," Alex said. "That who."

Taylor giggled. "So...what do they say?"

"I forget," he said, laughing.

"You're such a tease. Seriously, what do they say?"

"Seriously, I forget."

"Uh-huh. And my name is Sophia Loren."

Chuckling, he drew her near. "You're much prettier than Sophia, even in her heyday. And what they say," he whispered against her lips, "is that the best way to cope with pain is to do something to distract yourself from it."

"Oh, they do, do they?"

He nodded.

"And where did 'they' teach you this bit of sage advice?"

"Hospital. Last time I was, ah, in."

"After the plane crash, you mean?"

Another nod. And then he frowned. "Say, what d'you know about it?"

Taylor feigned a pompous little sneer. "Oh, I did some investigating...found a few articles, did a little reading...."

"And?"

"And what?"

Chuckling, he rolled his eyes. "We're not gonna start that again, are we?"

"Start what?"

He hugged her tight. "Taylor?"

"Hmmm…"

"Anybody ever tell you you talk too much?"

Before she could even think up a response, he'd blanketed her lips with his.

Surrounded by his arms, by his love, Taylor reveled in his kiss. If it turned out he wasn't a Follower, then she'd just pray him into one; night after night, day after day, week after week, until she developed calluses on her knees if that's what it took, until one day he admitted his love for the Lord.

They woke to the sound of the grandfather clock counting off the early-morning hour.

"Good grief," she said, stretching to work the kinks from her neck, "I feel like I'm about a hundred and fifty years old."

Alex winced as he sat up. "Well, Granny," he said in an old-man voice, "don't you worry none, 'cause you don't look a day over a hunnert."

Smacking her lips, Taylor frowned. "I'm going upstairs, wash my face and brush my teeth. That extra toothbrush you used last week is still in the guest bathroom if—"

He raised both eyebrows. "Could you be any more subtle?" he said behind a hand.

Blushing, she stammered, "I—I didn't mean…I just thought…"

And then she recognized the teasing glint in his dark eyes. "I'll put on a pot of coffee first. Give me ten minutes, and I'll make you a big country breakfast."

"Bacon and home fries? Eggs, easy over?"

"The works," she said, grinning.

Half an hour later, he shoved his plate away. "I'll bet I've gained ten pounds since I met you." Hands on his stomach, he jiggled it. "Look at this thing!"

"Flat as a pancake, hard as a washboard."

"Not for long, the way you cook."

"It's my duty as a red-blooded American female to do what it says in *The Smart Woman's Rule Book*." She held one finger aloft and pretended to quote from it. "'Feed your man till he's roly-poly, so no one else will want him.'"

"You're kidding, right? There's really no such book...is there?"

From the startled look on his face, it seemed Alex considered its existence a genuine possibility. "Are you kidding? Last time I was in the bookstore, it was all sold out!"

"C'mere, you little nut," he said, grabbing her hand. And once she settled on his lap, he wrapped his arms around her. "So what're you gonna tell people when they find out we spent the night together?"

Gasping, she gave his shoulder a playful shove. "But you...we...I—I..."

He hugged her tighter. "Aw, I didn't mean to get you all tongue-tied...although you can bet I've made a mental note how it's done, just in case, of course."

Ignoring his little aside, she said, "My mother used to say 'Your reputation is like your head—you only get one.'"

Grimacing, Alex repeated it, then laughed. "Well, it's plain as the nose on your face where you get your nuttiness from."

"But Alex, you made a good point. Your truck has been in my driveway all night. What will people—"

"I never should've said it. It was stupid."

He sounded truly contrite. Looked it, too. Taylor was

about to admit she'd been teasing when he added, "I didn't mean to get you all upset. I'm sorry. Honest."

Head bobbing from side to side, she sighed. "I've just been pulling your chain, and that was mean. I'm sorry." Unconsciously she finger-combed the bangs from his forehead. "*God* knows we're innocent. Doesn't matter what the rest of His flock think."

He popped a golden-brown potato wedge into his mouth. She didn't understand the naughty gleam in his eye, but knew if she waited, she'd find out what caused it.

"I thought you devout types walked a straight line."

"Straight line?" She'd play along, at least for the moment. "Whatever do you mean?"

"Well, you know, like you think bad behavior is contagious or something."

"Contagious? Sorry, I still don't get it."

"Okay. Look. It's like this—if folks think you've sinned, that forces them to think about your sin, which means they're sinning in their hearts, and that, of course, is a sin!"

She stared at him in silence for a moment, then pressed the back of her hand to her forehead in Scarlett O'Hara fashion. "I do declare, I believe ah'm about to swoon from all this talk of sin."

Alex kissed the tip of her nose. "There's nobody like you."

"And isn't *that* a blessing!"

She got to her feet and started stacking the breakfast dishes. "Speaking of blessings, it's nearly eight...if we don't lollygag, we can make the nine-o'clock service."

His mouth formed a grim line as his brows drew together. He pulled himself together quickly, though, she noticed as he smiled up at her.

"Lollygag?" He looked left, right, met her eyes again. "Where did you come from?"

"A time machine," she teased, "and it was set for the year 1863. It's been a trial, I tell you, adjustin' to y'all's fast-paced lifestyle, truly, a trial."

She carried the dishes to the sink. "So what do you think?" she said over her shoulder. "Should we try for nine, or wait for the eleven-o'clock service?"

The sound of his chair scraping across the floor made her turn. His fun-loving expression was gone, and in its place a no-nonsense look that troubled her more than she cared to admit.

"I know I said I love you, Taylor," he said, his voice deep and serious, "but let's not get carried away with this 'we' stuff. Got it?"

Chapter Eleven

Taylor had told herself it didn't matter whether or not he was a Christian. So then why was her heart beating like a parade drum?

In truth, it was more about his "I know I said I love you" line than anything else. Did it mean he hadn't meant it, or that he was sorry he'd said it?

Unable to face him, she turned toward the sink and began stuffing the plates and silverware from breakfast and last night's supper into the dishwasher. She didn't believe it was her place to judge him, not in areas of faith, not in the way he lived his life. If he didn't want to attend Sunday services, he must have a good reason. And even if he didn't, what business was it of hers?

"I'll probably get ready soon as I'm finished here," she said, doing her best to sound as if she didn't care one way or the other whether or not he joined her. "So...what're your plans for today?"

She heard him heave a sigh, and without turning around, she knew somehow that as he pocketed one hand, he was running the other through his hair.

"No plans, really."

It wasn't a good idea for him to be alone today, not with surgery scheduled first thing in the morning. "I have some hot dogs in the freezer. I could pick up some buns on the way home from church, open a can of baked beans, toss a—"

"What time's dinner?"

His voice sounded so sad, so distant. She wanted to go to him, wrap him in a loving embrace and promise him everything would be all right. But something told her this was neither the time nor the place for that. Later, after church, after he'd had a shower and some time alone to think, maybe things would look different to him.

"How's one o'clock sound?"

"Sounds good to me."

Taylor dried her hands on a red-striped terry dish towel, tossed it over her shoulder and faced him. "You don't mind if I put you to work, operating the grill...roasting the hot dogs?"

A cheerless smile slanted his mouth. "Nah. A guy likes to feel useful, y'know?"

As she crossed the room, Taylor made a mental note of the point. He'd just as much as admitted he was terrified that the operation would render him helpless, useless, dependent. She knew better. But how to convince him of it in his state of mind?

She slid her arms around him, pressed her cheek to his chest and closed her eyes. "I know you'll think I'm a silly, addle-brained twit, but I believe in miracles."

He gave a rough, ragged laugh. "I don't think any of those things. Fact is," he said, kissing the top of her head, "I think you're just about perfect."

"Nobody's perfect."

He held one finger aloft. "I did say *almost....*"

"Okay. I give up. Lemme have it. And don't sugarcoat it. I'm tough, remember?"

Chuckling softly, he tucked a bent forefinger under her chin and forced her to meet his eyes. "In my opinion, you have just one flaw. It's a biggie, but there's just the one."

Taylor thought she knew what he was going to say—that she'd had the bad judgment to fall in love with him. Taking half a step back, she rested both palms against his chest. "Okay, I admit it…I'm a sucker for wounded ex-flyboys." She looked into his eyes and willed him to read the love written there. "It's not against the law, far as I know."

He released a long, heavy sigh. "I wish I knew what on earth I've ever done in my miserable past to deserve a woman like you."

"Ever hear the old saying, 'Never look a gift horse in the mouth'?"

"Yeah, but—"

She whinnied, aimed a thumb over her shoulder. "Now hit the road, cowboy, 'cause I have places to go and people to—"

Alex silenced her with a lingering, hungry kiss that left her breathless and yearning for more. Standing in the open door, he said, "See you at one." He turned, started to pull it shut behind him, then stopped and faced her. "Do me a favor, will you?"

"Anything," she said, meaning it.

"While you're in church, say a little prayer for me…."

When Alex got home from Taylor's, his answering machine was blinking. He pressed the play button, and while the tape rewound, he tried to guess who the messages might be from. His mother, no doubt, and maybe Luke McKenzie. He hadn't spent much time getting reacquainted with hometown folks since his return, so that pretty much narrowed down the possibilities.

"Alex? It's your mother...."

As if she needed to identify herself, he thought, grinning.

"Rusty and I are having dinner with the Campbells after church. We should be home by five, in case you need anything."

Like a shoulder to cry on or a lap to cuddle up in? There was no mistaking the pity in her voice. Well, he didn't need pity just now; they hadn't chopped his leg off yet.

"Give us a call this evening, so we can discuss how you'll get to the hospital in the morning."

Hospital. In the morning. Each word felt like a punch to the gut.

Her "We love you!" was punctuated by a high-pitched beep. And following a brief pause, a man's voice said, "Alex, it's Luke.... Dr. Bricker has agreed to let me assist tomorrow. Now, don't get your neck hairs bristlin', I know I'm not a surgeon, but—"

Alex hung his head and braced himself for whatever might follow the "but."

"I just thought you'd feel more secure if you had a friend in there with you, keepin' an eye on things, so to speak."

Secure, my foot! Alex griped. Only way he'd feel secure again was if Taylor had been right, and a miracle happened.

"See you in the morning, seven sharp."

He glanced at the wall clock and did the math in his head. Twenty-one hours, give or take a couple minutes, and he'd have a whole new way of walking....

"Oh, and Alex?"

"What," he grumped at the machine.

"Don't bother to shave. Dr. Bricker's already married."

Comedian, he thought as the beep announced the end of McKenzie's call. And despite himself, he smiled.

"Hi, Alex."

Taylor...

He grabbed the answering machine with both hands, praying she wasn't calling to cancel this afternoon, praying she hadn't decided he was more trouble than he was worth....

"I'm standing here in the window with the portable phone to my ear, watching you back down the driveway. And you know how impulsive I am...."

Impulsive? Only impulsive thing she'd ever done that he knew of was to go and fall in love with a pathetic maimed creature. And that wasn't a hanging offense, far as he knew.

"So I decided to call and tell you what I'm thinking."

He closed his eyes, clenched his teeth and steadied himself in preparation for the painful blow to his heart.

"Did you know that your eyes are so big and brown that I can see them all the way from inside the house?" She giggled. "I'm one lucky woman to have a guy as handsome as you head over heels in love with me."

Relief made him release the breath he'd been holding.

Her voice, soft as white velvet, sighed into his ear. "Correction—I'm lucky to have a man as decent, as good, as bighearted as you in love with me."

Staring at the answering machine, he grinned.

"When I get to church in a few minutes, I'm going to pray that you'll never, ever change, because..."

In the middle of his wondering *Because what?,* Taylor began to sing.

"I love you just the way you are."

The beep seemed a totally inadequate way to end her message. His ears burned, his cheeks flamed and a breathless, swollen-hearted feeling overtook him as he stood there, beaming like a lovesick fool. Hand on the telephone, he considered calling her, but a glance at the clock told him she'd be in church by now...praying that he'd never change.

Well, he was going to change. A lot. Starting tomorrow. *How will you feel about me then,* he wanted to ask her.

He hit the repeat button instead, skipped the first two messages and went straight to Taylor's. Eyes closed, he listened to her brief, heartfelt song again, then listened to it again. "I love you just the way you are."

Would she feel that way tomorrow afternoon, when the lower half of his leg was in a Dumpster behind the hospital? Would she still love him "as is" while she rolled him around in a wheelchair, when he clumped about on rubber-tipped crutches?

If he had any sense, any sense at all, he'd hit Erase, get rid of her musical message permanently. If things changed tomorrow, or the week after that, or a year from now, he didn't think he could handle a recorded reminder of her devotion.

He made a fist. His thick forefinger popped free of it, trembling as it hovered over the small rectangular white button. But he couldn't do it, because if her loyalty waned—even a tad—he'd need this to remind him what he'd been, what he'd had, what life could have been like before...

Before nine o'clock tomorrow morning.

Tears smarted in his eyes, and he swiped angrily at them. If he knew what was good for him, he'd get a handle on his emotions, and get it quick. To do otherwise was slow suicide.

He depressed the replay button one last time, thinking as he half listened to the first two messages that, much as he hated the prospect of becoming a limping, lurching, one-legged leech, at least he'd be *alive*.

And as long as he lived and breathed, he had a chance to prove to Taylor that he was all the things she believed him to be. Slumping against the wall, he did something he hadn't done since childhood, and let the tears flow freely.

"I love you just the way you are..." sang her mellow, honeyed voice.

"Lord," he sobbed, "let her feel that way fifty years from now."

Fifty years from now...

Straightening his back, Alex cleared his throat, drew his shirtsleeves across his eyes. Maybe he'd lost his mind, and maybe not. Maybe the combination of grief and fear he'd been wrestling with for the past couple of days had combined to destroy what little remained of his sanity. And maybe, just maybe, the idea percolating in his head was the most rational, reasonable thing he'd ever thought of in his life....

"Pass the mustard, please." Their fingers touched when he handed her the bell-shaped jar, and she took her time relieving him of it. Silly as it seemed, she loved everything about this man, right down to a touch as slight as this. If only she could find the words that would make him see that nothing—not even an amputation—would ever change that.

"Potato salad's great," he said.

She knifed out a portion of the condiment. "Better than the stuff at the church luncheon?"

"Aw, that was strictly average stuff."

She made an "are you kidding?" face.

"But then," he continued, "it's really no surprise. Everything about you is better than average."

"Right back atcha, big guy." She leaned forward, puckered her mouth.

And he responded with a light peck to her lips.

Would it always be this way? she wondered. Would she feel this heady, heart-pounding way when he kissed her years from now? She laughed to herself, because a kiss wasn't even a prerequisite to her capriciousness; she only needed to see him walk into a room, or hear his voice on the phone, to set a whole series of giddy ideas in motion.

She hoped so. And to ensure it, Taylor had done exactly what she'd promised in the message she'd left on his answering machine, and prayed that he'd never change... except to grow closer to the Lord. When that happened—and it would, because she'd prayed for that, too—everything would fall into place.

He hadn't admitted fear, but of course he felt it. It was only human, after all, especially considering that the surgeon had made no secret of the probable outcome of the operation. It made Taylor wish that Alex had some kind of closeness with God right now. If he had, maybe his worries about what would happen the day *after* tomorrow would lessen somewhat.

Oh, he'd been wearing a brave face, right from the minute he stepped through the front door, cracking jokes, trying to be his usual cheery self. But tension had burrowed deep furrows between his eyes, had caused the tight set of his jaw, the slight edge in his otherwise resonant baritone. For that reason, Taylor had been careful not to make any references to his leg, to the surgery, to the difficult and painful days that would follow as he learned to deal with the world in a whole new way.

Sooner or later, though, the subject had to be broached. He had a right to know that she'd taken off work to be with him tomorrow. In fact, though Taylor had only barely returned from a two-week trip to Ireland, she'd requested and received a four-week block of time off that would enable her to be with him on a full-time professional basis after the surgery, too.

Truthfully, she didn't know how Alex might feel about that. Would male pride make him view her gesture as some sort of warped charity? Or would he read into it what she'd intended...proof that she loved him, that she'd continue to love him, no matter what, for the rest of her days?

"So how was church?"

"Fine. How was..." She grinned. "What *did* you do while I was getting holy?"

Chuckling, Alex helped himself to another spoonful of potato salad. "Ran a load of clothes through the washing machine. That's about it."

Preparing for the days to come, she realized.

"I wish I'd thought to offer...you could've brought your laundry here, so I could wash it while we ate."

He froze, midchew. "I'm not totally helpless, Taylor. I've been on my own for—"

"But Alex," she interrupted, "you're a *man*. What do you know about detergent and water temperature, when to use bleach, how many clothes to stuff into the machine?"

She watched his face relax as he realized that while she saw him as helpless, it was only because of his gender, and had nothing to do with his injury. "I think maybe after the operation, when you're feeling up to it, I'll give you a quick how-to lesson in the laundry room." She wiggled her eyebrows. "Might not be a bad idea to do a run-through on shopping, bed making, vacuu—"

Groaning, he rolled his eyes. "Stop. I'm getting tired just listening to you." One corner of his mouth turned up. "I haven't been doing half-bad, for a crusty old bachelor."

She bobbed her head. "Well, your house was neat enough, that's true. But..."

He looked genuinely surprised that she had no intention of babying him. Surprised, and somewhat disappointed.

"What's the matter, Alex? Did I deprive you of your 'I can do it all by myself' lecture?"

His brow furrowed. "What're you talkin' about?"

"Maybe I was wrong," she said, shrugging, "but I got the distinct impression you were fixin' to lay into me with a 'What do you think I am, a helpless cripple?' speech."

She scooted her chair back, got to her feet and walked around to his side of the table. With a wave of her hand, Taylor let him know she expected him to shove his chair away from the table, too. When he did, she gently slid onto his lap.

"Now then," she said, cupping his big face in her hands, "let's get something straight, right here and now." She watched his dark brows rise, watched his brown eyes crinkle at the corners in the hint of a smile. "Of all the things I feel toward you, about you, for you, *pity* isn't one of them. Oh, sure, I feel bad that you've gone through so much physical trauma in the past, feel badder still about what's to come."

Tenderly she kissed him. "But you can take this to the bank, big guy—I'm sorry for what you have to go through, not sorry *for* you. Got it?"

When he nodded, she kissed him again, longer, more meaningfully this time. When it ended, she snuggled close. "Remember a couple of days ago, when I asked you not to send me away?"

"Yeah."

"Well, I wasn't just whistlin' Dixie, dearie. I want to be there, right beside you, when they wheel you down the hall in that goofy-lookin' hairnet and those ridiculous ankle-high booties, when you wake up in recovery, even when you're bellowing at the pain. I can—"

"I know, I know," he interrupted. "You can take it, 'cause you're tough."

"Not as tough as you, but tough enough."

She felt him nod, heard him sigh. "I love you, Taylor."

Hands on his cheeks again, she said, "And I love you, too."

"I know that."

He sat there gawking at her, a crooked little grin on his face, for what seemed like a full minute. And then he cleared his throat. "I was planning to save this for after dessert, but this seems as good a time as any."

He stood her on her feet, pulled out the chair beside his and told her to sit down.

"Here?"

"There."

She did as he asked, but not without a puzzled "Whatever for?"

"Because I have something to say to you, and I want to say it right."

She pursed her lips. "But your hot dog is getting cold, and the beans—"

"I'm still full from that truck-driver's breakfast you made me this morning. Now be quiet, and let me get this off my chest, all right?"

Wincing, he got onto his good knee and sandwiched her hands between his. "I never thought the day would come when I'd be asking this question." He looked at the ceiling. "I especially didn't think I'd be asking it just a few weeks after—"

He met her eyes again, gave her hands a little squeeze. "You asked me earlier what I did while you were in church." Reaching into his pants pocket, Alex withdrew a tiny pink velvet box. "I lied. I didn't do any laundry," he confessed. "I went to the store, and I bought this."

The lid creaked when he opened it.

Blinking back tears, Taylor looked from the sparkling solitaire to his glittering eyes.

"Taylor Griffith," he whispered, taking her left hand in his, "will you marry me?"

A sob blocked her windpipe, keeping the *yes* she wanted to bellow trapped in her throat. So she nodded instead. Nodded until she thought her earrings would bobble from her earlobes.

He plucked the ring from its satiny bed and slipped it onto her finger. Just as he'd expected, it fit perfectly.

But she hadn't expected it, as evidenced by her wide-eyed, stammering question. "B-but...how...how did you know what—"

"When you were washing dishes the other day, I noticed you'd put your rings on the windowsill above the sink." He shrugged one shoulder. "I grabbed one of 'em, stuck it on my finger, just to see if something that tiny would fit."

He held up his pinky, wiggled it. "Slid to the first knuckle." He shrugged the other shoulder. "So in the jewelry store, I just—"

Taylor threw her arms around his neck, nearly knocking him off balance. And by the time she was finished dotting his face with kisses, he'd all but forgotten the throbbing discomfort in his leg, didn't know whose tears were on his cheeks...his, hers, or both.

She stood, held out her arm for support. "Get up," she said, voice trembling.

He looked up into her tear-streaked, lovely face and, grasping her forearm, let her help him up.

"That's the first and only time you'll ever be on your knees in this relationship," she told him. And flashing the ring in his face, she added, "We're partners now."

"Equal and inseparable."

Alex took her in his arms.

"United we stand...."

He drew her closer still and grinned. "Together we fall."

Taylor was laughing softly when she said, "Hip-hip-hooray!"

Helen and Rusty Martin, David Griffith and Taylor sat in the gray-and-chrome chairs lining the walls of the waiting room. Luke McKenzie, dressed in pale green scrubs, stepped through the double-wide door. "You guys can come back now."

"All of us?" Uncle Dave asked.

"Sure. But only for a couple minutes. They're about to prep him."

One by one, led by McKenzie, the group filed through the doors and into the pre-op room.

"Good grief," Alex said, grinning when they rounded the corner, single file, "I think you've forgotten someone."

"Who?" McKenzie asked.

"The Pied Piper."

Laughing, his mother hugged him while his stepdad shook his hand, and Taylor's uncle gave Alex's toe an affectionate pinch.

But Taylor hung back, letting them say their goodbyes.

When the doctor made a move as if to show them the door, Taylor raised her chin a notch. "I intend to be there when he goes to sleep, and I'll be there when he comes to." She showed him the glittering diamond on her finger. "It's official, so you can't make me leave."

"Actually," he said, "I can. Officially, only a wife can be in here once anesthesia is administered."

She'd never heard of a rule like that. Hadn't expected it, and so had prepared no argument to fight it.

"But it just so happens that Alex has made some arrangements, should this question arise."

Her pastor entered the room just then, carrying his battered old Bible, a bouquet of flowers and a small white pillow.

The smiles on everyone's faces made it obvious they'd all been in on the arrangements…whatever they were. Taylor looked at Alex, and waited for an explanation.

"I don't like leaving things to chance," he began, "so I made a few phone calls, pulled in a few favors."

The pastor withdrew an envelope from his Bible and handed it to Taylor.

She opened it. "A marriage license?"

Alex nodded and reached for her hand. "Just needs your signature."

She could hardly believe all the trouble he'd gone to to pull this off. But they'd been together practically every minute for the past few days. When had he had time?

Helen Martin slid a larger, thicker envelope from her purse. A proud, damp-eyed smile on her face, she said, "This is for you, too, dear." She wrapped Taylor in a motherly hug. "Welcome to the family!"

When his mother stepped back, Taylor met Alex's eyes. "What is this?"

"My will."

She gasped, but he held one hand in the air. "Not that I think I'll need it, mind you, but I've never liked leaving anything to chance."

The pastor stepped forward. "Alex has assured me that a few months from now we'll do this all again, in the church with—"

"With flowers and organ music, the whole nine yards," Uncle Dave said.

She met their eyes, each one in turn. "You all knew about this?"

And one at a time, her family nodded. *Her family!* She squeezed Alex's hand, too moved to trust her voice to thank him for everything he'd done.

Handing her a pen, the pastor said, "It's nothing but a

formality, really, but..." He glanced at Alex. "I've never liked leaving things to chance, either."

He gave the white satin pillow to Alex's mother, who passed it to Taylor's uncle. "I'm the best man," he said with a wink and a merry smile.

"That ring belonged to Alex's father," Helen explained, blotting tears with a lace-trimmed hankie. "I've been saving it for just this occasion."

Uncle Dave dug around in his shirt pocket and came up with a slimmer gold band. "This was your mom's," he said. "She told me to hold on to it for you."

With trembling hand Taylor signed the marriage license and handed it to the pastor, who traded it for the bouquet.

"Now then, are we ready to begin?"

While the rest of the family waited outside, Taylor stood beside Alex's bed, unwilling, unable to let go of his hand. The good-natured nurses worked around her, noting his pulse and blood pressure, hooking up IVs, sticking electrodes to his chest that would later be connected to monitors in the operating room.

The big round clock on the wall said 8:36. Any minute now, it would begin.

Luke McKenzie had explained earlier that the operation could take anywhere between three and twelve hours, depending on what Dr. Bricker found when she opened Alex up. Taylor wouldn't be able to talk to him for who knew how long. She had so much to say, but where to start?

"Sorry to drop things in your lap that way, Mrs. Van Buren," he said, interrupting her thoughts.

She leaned down, kissed his cheek. "Well, just don't make a habit of springing surprises on me, okay?"

"Thing is...I'm just worried doin' it that way didn't give you much time to think things through."

"What things?"

"Oh, I dunno…where we'll live, if we'll take a honeymoon, kids…."

"From what I hear, you're gonna be under the weather for quite a few months. I think maybe we'll have more than enough time to discuss all the details."

He squeezed her hand. "Yeah. I guess you're right." Alex took a deep breath. "Scared?"

She nodded. "A little, I guess. You?"

He nodded, too.

"But I've got everybody at church praying for you. This is gonna turn out great. You'll see."

"Okay. I'll see."

She grinned. "Honeymoon, huh?"

Chuckling, he said, "Well, sure. Every bride gets carried over the threshold." His smile faded. "Trouble is, don't know if I'll be able to do it."

"Aw, people make too much of stuff like that," she said, waving the idea away. "Why, you wouldn't believe how many accounts I've read of husbands who throw their backs out in the performance of that silly little tradition."

"Really… How many?"

Her cheeks reddened in response to the suspiciousness of his tone. "Well, I'm not sure, exactly. But there are lots."

He chuckled again, then looked toward the opening in the cubicle curtain. "Wish they'd come in here with that needle, already, get things rolling. This waiting is drivin' me nuts."

Combing her fingers through his hair, she kissed his forehead. "Let me share a piece of my daddy's advice with you. 'Don't wish your life away.'"

"Not the whole life," he corrected, "just this day. Sooner they get started, the sooner it'll be over, and the sooner it's over, the sooner I can get busy—"

"One day at a time, Alex, one day at a time." She got

onto the bed, lay on her side next to him. "You think the nurse will mind if I stay right here till you fall asleep?"

He wrapped his arms around her. "If she does, report her to McKenzie. He'll see that she's fired."

"You know...I've been thinking...."

"Uh-oh."

"No, seriously. When this is over, you're going to have a lot of time on your hands. Have you given any thought as to how you'll spend it?"

He shook his head. "Not really." Alex met her eyes. "But something tells me you have."

"Well," she said, "as a matter of fact..."

His laughter shook the bed and echoed throughout the pre-op room. "Now, why doesn't that surprise me?"

"Shh. There are other people in here, trying to sleep. Remember when you told me that when you were a boy you wanted to be a pastor when you grew up?"

"Yeah. So?"

"Well, I happen to know that your physical therapy will only take a few hours a day. The rest of the time you'll be required to take it easy, to rest and recuperate so you won't wear yourself out for the next session."

She levered herself up on one elbow. "So here's my idea. What do you say we buy a little house in the country, enroll you in...oh, I don't know what they call it...a seminary school or whatever. That way, you could use your R and R time to study, to become a pastor."

For a full minute he didn't say a word.

"Earth to Alex, earth to Alex..."

"Maybe," he said at last.

"Well, it isn't like you have to decide right this minute," she said, wiggling the fingers of her left hand to remind him of the hurried wedding that had just taken place.

"Touché." He hugged her tighter. "I'll think about it."

"Promise?"

"Promise."

The anesthesiologist burst into the cubicle, hypodermic in hand. "Well, my dearies," he announced, "it's countdown time."

"Can she stay?" Alex said, clinging tighter to Taylor.

"I don't see why not." He aimed a paternal digit at the new Mrs. Van Buren. "But the minute he's out, so are you. Got it?"

Taylor nodded obediently as he injected the anesthetic into the clear tubing attached to Alex's arm.

"Won't be long now," he told them. "If you have anything to say, better make it quick."

He left the cubicle and closed the curtain around them. Already she could see Alex's eyelids beginning to droop. "I love you," she said, pressing a kiss to his lips.

"Love you, too." He yawned. "Taylor?"

"Hmmm…"

"Do me a favor?"

"Anything."

"When I'm in the recovery room, and you see that I'm comin' to, will you sing to me?"

"Sing to you?" A nervous giggle escaped her. "But—"

"Tha' zong you lef' on my anzwering machine," he slurred.

She hugged him tight. "I'll be there, Alex. I promise."

"An' you'll be zinging?"

"And I'll be singing."

She could only presume by the silly smile on his face that he'd heard her before he konked out.

Lord Jesus, she prayed, *bring him back to me, whole and healthy and happy.*

The doctor stepped back into the cubicle, patted Taylor's hand. "He's gonna be fine, Mrs. Van Buren. I assure you, he's in good hands. Dr. Bricker is one of the best. And Dr. McKenzie and I will be there to keep a close watch on him, too, so don't you worry.''

"I'm not worried," she said, smiling. And in truth, she wasn't. She'd handed Alex over to her Lord and Savior for protection, and he couldn't be in better hands than that.

Chapter Twelve

She was on her knees at the altar in the hospital chapel when Luke McKenzie came to get her. The fact that the operation had lasted less than two hours worried her more than she cared to admit.

"We'll have the lab results in a few minutes," McKenzie promised as he escorted her to the recovery room. "I hafta tell you, everybody in there was amazed."

Amazed? At what? Had the procedure gone horribly, terribly wrong? Had the surgical team found something in Alex's leg so ghastly that they'd decided it was kinder, more humane, to simply close up shop rather than put him through the physical and emotional trauma of the amputation?

Her angst was so great that it prevented Taylor from formulating an intelligent question. And now, as she sat beside Alex's bed repeating questions that had no answers, she was paying the price for her doubts.

She supposed it was a blessing in disguise that she'd been given this time to think and pray, to shore up her courage. She had a feeling she would need it if, when Alex woke up, Dr. Bricker came to announce that his condition was hopeless.

Stop it, she scolded herself. *This kind of thinking won't get you anywhere!* Besides, it was a pointless waste of time. She'd lain her troubles, her worries at the foot of the Cross. God's promise to those who trusted in Him was answered prayer.

Alex was going to be fine.

It's what she had prayed for; it's what God would deliver.

Leaning over Alex's bed, she took his hand, held it to her cheek. He'd been out several hours already, and according to the anesthesiologist, there should be signs of revival any time now.

He looked so pale, so drawn, lying there against the white sheets. In a few days, when he'd recovered from the loss of blood, from the shock of surgery, his cheeks would glow with robust health. Unless...

The Lord is my shepherd, I shall not want....

Alex murmured, frowned, rolled his head from side to side as he struggled to open his eyes.

Taylor filled the plastic cup beside the bed with icy water, slid the flexible straw between his lips. "There y'go," she whispered. "Nice and cool and wet. Just the ticket for someone who hasn't been allowed to eat or drink since ten o'clock last night...."

Then she remembered the promise she'd made him.

Squinting, Taylor tried to conjure up the rest of the words. It hadn't been that long ago that, she'd perched on a stool behind a glossy black piano in one hotel lounge or another, leaned into a microphone and sung those very words. How could the lyrics have disappeared from her memory already?

Maybe he didn't need to hear *that* song as much as he needed the quiet reassurance of her presence. And maybe, as long as something musical came out of her mouth, he didn't care what. And maybe the best thing she could do for him now was to create a whole new song, something just for him.

She closed her eyes and, forgetting about the nurses, the doctors, the patients and their families, began to sing softly.

"In your eyes, love, I see my destiny.
When you smile, my whole world is at peace.
When that old world starts closin' in around me...
won't you wrap your lovin' arms 'round me,
just wrap your lovin' arms 'round me."

Alex's breaths came more quickly now. He licked his lips and murmured something unintelligible under his breath. The last thing he'd asked before they took him to the operating room was that she be singing when he came to. She'd given him her word, and Taylor intended to keep it. She continued to sing.

"Kiss me soft, love, and let me hear you sigh.
Touch me gentle, and set my soul afire.
In your arms, love, I'm woman and I'm free...
when you wrap your lovin' arms 'round me,
when you wrap your lovin' arms 'round me."

Though he hadn't opened his eyes yet, she could see the smile curving the corners of his mouth. Heart hammering with gratitude and joy, she felt the beginnings of tears pricking behind her eyelids.

"Taylor," he whispered. "You remembered."

"Course I remembered. What kind of woman would I be if I made a promise to my husband and didn't keep it?"

Opening his eyes, he turned his head. It took a few

blinks before he could focus. But when he did, there she was...his beautiful new bride.

She looked tired, a little rough around the edges. But then, he didn't suppose he looked too good, either. "How long..." He cleared his throat. "How long was I under?"

Patting his hand, she said, "Just a couple of hours."

He frowned. "What d'you mean, couple hours? Mc-Kenzie said..." Luke had said it could take a dozen hours, maybe more. A two-hour operation wasn't good news. Not good news at all.

"Thirsty?" Taylor asked, holding the plastic cup near his lips.

He took a sip. "Thanks." And rubbing his Adam's apple, he said, "Wonder how long I'll sound like this."

"Like you have laryngitis?" Taylor smiled. "A day, maybe two and you'll have your old voice back again, good as new."

Speaking of "new," Alex couldn't help but wonder what shape his leg was in. Lifting his head from the pillow, he chanced a peek at the foot of the bed.

He'd fully expected to see the outline of one leg...and the flat surface of the mattress where his other one used to be. It surprised him more than a little to see both stockinged feet poking out from under the white flannel sheet.

It could only mean one thing. Dr. Bricker and her team had found more cancer than they'd expected. He was so far gone, they'd decided it wasn't worth lopping off his leg after all.

Flopping his head back onto the pillow, Alex moaned softly. "Okay—" he sighed heavily "—lemme have it."

"Have what?"

"The facts." He waved a hand, inviting her to give them to him.

"I haven't heard anything yet, either. Honest."

He met her eyes, read the truth there. "So how long are

they gonna make me wait before they deliver the bad news?''

She kissed him. "It isn't going to be bad news.''

"If you haven't talked to anyone, how do you know that?''

Smiling, she said, "I haven't talked to the doctors...."

Alex stifled a groan, because he knew what that meant. She'd been praying, talking to God, beseeching Jesus. He would have laughed, except he couldn't conjure up energy. Maybe he ought to tell her how much praying he'd done after bouncing around the surface of the Caribbean. Maybe she should know that he'd begged God...pleaded with Him. *If You're gonna let me live, don't take flying away from me....*

But God had done exactly that, and Alex had been furious with Him ever since.

"Well, look who's finally awake," Luke McKenzie said. He opened Alex's chart, tapped the tip of his ballpoint against the top page. "You always were one to go for the record books, weren't you, Van Buren?''

Alex shook his head. The effects of the drugs must still be taking a toll on his reasoning skills, he thought, because McKenzie's comment made absolutely no sense.

"I guess you had something to do with this," the doctor said to Taylor.

Alex raised a hand. "Whoa, don't talk so fast. My head's spinning." He winked at Taylor. "Would you mind cranking me up so I can see what's goin' on?''

She gave his shoulder an affectionate squeeze, then pressed the button to help him sit up.

Alex aimed his next question at his old navy buddy. "Now, what exactly are you talkin' about?''

Shaking his head, the doctor lifted his shoulders. "We've run the tests three, four times, and they come out the same way every time.''

"What tests?" Taylor asked.

"Pathology. They've compared what we got in surgery to the biopsy results, and they don't compare."

"Don't compare? Why don't they compare?"

"Easy, Van Buren," McKenzie said. "This is good news. Real good news." Perching on the corner of Alex's mattress he said, "See, it's like this. Those samples we took from your leg last week, the ones we ran through our little test kits over and over again?"

Taylor and Alex nodded.

"Well, when we put 'em on slides beside what we got from you just now…" He exhaled. "They don't match. It's as though we got the tissue from two different people."

"Is it possible there was a mix-up?" Taylor wanted to know.

"I hand labeled and hand delivered the biopsies myself." He met Alex's eyes. "Look, I'm as confused as you two are. Things like this don't happen every day."

"Things like what?"

He turned to Taylor. "When Dr. Bricker opened Alex up just now, we expected to find…" He cleared his throat. "Let's just say we didn't expect to find normal, healthy tissue in that leg." He looked at Alex. "What we expected was that we'd have to amputate, with good reason."

Glancing from husband to wife, he added, "What we have here, Mr. and Mrs. Van Buren, can't be described any other way, except to say—"

"It's a miracle," Taylor whispered.

"Could be," McKenzie agreed.

Alex wiggled the toes of his bad foot, bent the leg at the knee. It smarted a bit at the surgery site, but other than that, nothing. No aches, no pains, no throbbing. "How soon can I get outta this bed?" he wanted to know.

McKenzie laughed. "What's your hurry?"

He tugged Taylor's hand, pulling her nearer. "No rush, but I would like to see how much weight the withered ol' thing will bear."

"Why? You planning to enter the Boston marathon?"

Alex shook his head. "No marathons for this old fly-boy."

He met Taylor's bright, tear-dampened eyes, returned her happy smile, because he could see that she knew exactly what he was about to say.

"Just feel like takin' a little trip over the threshold, that's all...."

Eighteen months later

Taylor stood behind him, rubbing his shoulders. "Enough, Alex, you've been at it all evening."

"Just a few more pages," he said, patting her hand, "then I'll quit. I promise."

She rested her chin atop his head. "And you call me stubborn."

"Only because you are stubborn," he said distractedly.

"Who insisted on buying a house way out in the country?"

He chuckled. "Well, okay. But who insisted it had to be a Victorian, with wraparound porches and gingerbread and tall skinny windows?"

"You were right, though...it's the perfect place to raise kids." She moved around to the side of him. "Happy?"

Alex rested his head on her well-rounded tummy. "Mmm-mmm. Very. How 'bout you?"

"There'd be something terribly wrong with me if I wasn't! I have everything I've ever wanted...a rose garden, a vegetable patch, even a tire swing out back."

"I've done pretty well, too." He hugged her. "Beautiful, devoted wife, twin boys on the way, great job in the wings...."

"Yeah. Great job."

He remembered how she'd talked him into enrolling in the seminary, saying dreams weren't only for children.

"A month from now, after you graduate and hire on as assistant pastor at Harvester Church, I'll probably never see you."

"Oh," he said, "you'll see me. You'll see me plenty, 'cause I talked the boss into hiring you, too."

Taylor laughed. "I have no training in the ministry."

"It isn't a ministry kind of job," he explained gently.

She narrowed her eyes and shook a finger under his nose, did an Oliver Hardy imitation. "What have you gone and gotten me into this time?"

"You're in charge of keeping the assistant pastor happy. It's full-time." He stood, wrapped her in his arms and kissed her passionately.

"With excellent benefits, I see," she said. "I don't know how you manage it, but you can still make me blush, even after nearly two years of marriage!"

He looked into her eyes, and saw the truth burning there, bright as ever.

"And to think I didn't want to settle down in Ellicott City after my mom died."

"I didn't want to come back either, after the crash."

"Why did you, then?"

He shrugged. "Don't rightly know. It was as if someone kept whispering—" he put a hand beside his mouth "'—Alex, come ho-o-o-ome.'" He kissed her forehead. "How 'bout you? Why did you come back?"

She took a breath. "Once I got back, I looked around and realized I was suddenly home."

He held her at arm's length. "That's it!"

"That's what?"

"Remember how you were talking about choosing a name for this place, painting it on a sign at the end of the drive?"

Taylor nodded and, smiling, said, "Suddenly Home. I like it. I like it a lot!"

*   *   *   *   *

Dear Reader,

What does the image of "home" conjure up for you? The sugary sweetness of toasted marshmallows, sagging from a gnarly, charred stick? Stargazing from a squeaky patio chair on a cloudless night? Listening to Mom laugh at Dad's timeworn jokes, or the feel of summertime raindrops pelting your cheeks?

Maybe "home" is the sight of multicolored blossoms lining the front walk, or the sky-lighting explosions of a patriotic fireworks display. It might be the crisp feel of line-dried sheets against your sunburned skin, or the feel-good sensation of a well-weeded garden. Do you rush "home" to share joyous news or hide there from the world...or both?

"Home" was all this and more for Alex Van Buren and Taylor Griffith. Though they'd left home...and returned...for completely different reasons, it was through one another's eyes that Alex and Taylor saw "home" as a haven. And it was in one another's loving arms that they realized the true meaning of the age-old cliché "Home is where the heart is."

If you enjoyed *Suddenly Home,* please drop me a note c/o Steeple Hill Books, 300 East 42nd Street, New York, NY 10017. I love hearing from my readers and try to answer every letter personally.

All my best,

Loree Lough

P.S. Be sure to look for the first installment of my new miniseries, available soon at bookstores near you.